TOUCHBACK

A Novel by Don Handfield

SKY VILLAGE

PRESS

Carlsbad, California

SKY VILLAGE

P R E S S

www.skyvillagepress.com

ISBN 978-0-9854552-8-6

Manufactured in the United States of America

First Edition, April 2012

Jacket design by Jeff Holmberg Design

Interior Design by Steven W. Booth, www.GeniusBookServices.com

To Robinson Dawn and Deacon Bragdon

May your lives be filled with miracles.

Chapter 1

EVERY CHILDHOOD HAS A moment that marks the end of wonder. Often it arrives in the form of a failure so profound, and so complete, that it signifies a fall from grace. An instant in time becomes the dividing point in a life, when the future goes from one of fairy tales, infinite possibilities, and the mantra of "I can do anything" to a cruel reality that strips those dreams from the heart.

Scott Murphy was seconds away from the end of his wonder.

It was deep into the waning minutes of the 1991 Ohio High School Football State Championship, and although his Coldwater Cavaliers were trailing the five-time defending champion Versailles Saints by four points, Murphy knew he could win.

He wasn't just a quarterback—he was a celebrity in Coldwater, and probably most anywhere else in Ohio or the Midwest that paid attention to high school sports. He had won forty-eight straight games, a national record. He'd won four District Championships, four Regional Championships, and had three top-five finishes in a division-less state tournament. He'd been unanimously voted Ohio High Schools' Mr. Football by every sportswriter in the state. This year, he had managed to lead his tiny farm town squad into the state finals against a big-city school from Cleveland that had twice as many students as his hometown's entire population of 1,614.

The only thing the Saints and the Cavaliers had in common was that no one else from Ohio could beat them. The Saints had pulled into town in an air-conditioned tour bus—the fancy kind with the upholstered seats and custom graphics on the side. Murphy's team rode to every away game in a rickety, dented yellow school bus with no heat or air conditioning. They'd broken down twice, and both times the team had to run a couple of miles down the freeway in school clothes in order to make kickoff.

Murphy resented that tour bus. He resented the Saints' whirlpool spas, strength coaches, private weight rooms, and brand-new uniforms. His squad—the sons of blue-collar workers and farmers—wore the same threadbare jerseys they'd had their entire high school careers. Murphy's battered helmet wasn't just a hand-me-down—it was a relic. The inside was sticky with layers of tape scrawled with the last names of all the other Coldwater kids who had worn it before him. O'Hora. McTeague. Johanssen. He knew every one of them. And they were all either in the stands or dead. No one ever really got out of Coldwater, not even in a box. And as far as Murphy was concerned, all that stood between him and a ticket out of this cowtown was eighty yards and eleven rich kids.

The stadium was filled. The folks who couldn't afford tickets parked outside the fence and, provided they kept their headlights on, it was a practice that the school condoned despite the loss of revenue. The field lights were crap and the car headlamps helped fill out the dark patches in the end zone. Even the old cemetery on the south side was packed with people camped out on blankets, careful not to block any headstones. In Coldwater, even the dead had the right to watch football.

The only reason the Saints had deigned to play the state championship game in this minuscule town was because they were forced to—they'd lost the coin toss. The game was supposed to take place at Ohio Stadium in Columbus—a temple of football known as the Horseshoe because of its U-shape. With a hundred thousand seats to fill, and an expensive new natural-grass playing field, the stadium had been ruled out when Coldwater couldn't sell enough tickets to cover the cost. Most of the town was heartbroken, but Coach Hand had called it a blessing: "Home field advantage."

When Murphy heard the Saints calling Coldwater "Backwater"

as they got off the bus and disparaging the shed his team used as a locker room, Murphy figured Coach was right. Let them underestimate his town. Let them ridicule his field with the peeling paint on the bleachers and the tent they used as a refreshment stand. It fired Murphy up. It made him want to break every privileged bone in their bodies and send them home in pieces.

Murphy played football like God was on his side. And he believed it. Because he believed it, it was true. The great paradox of faith. He only needed four measly points. One touchdown. And he had thirty-five seconds and a timeout to make it. He was sure he could. The eleven monsters the Saints called a defensive line stood ready to prove him wrong. They outweighed the Coldwater line by at least a double-cab pickup. And most of that was in the form of a linebacker named Alex Washington.

The game may have been a real-life battle between David and Goliath, but even on a team of Goliaths, one player stood out. When Coach Hand had prepared the Cavaliers for this championship, each player had been an X or an O—except Washington. He warranted his own number: 54. And it was in red chalk, so everyone could be clear on where he was going to be on every play. Fifty-four was the kind of player who was guaranteed to hurt you if he got near you, with a good chance of a maiming or crippling in the mix. He was twice Murphy's size, and genetically built to be a stronger and faster athlete. And not only did he want to win just as badly as Murphy did, he hated Murphy's guts. Washington thought the "Mr. Football" title should have been his. And that made it personal. And that made him even more dangerous.

No human being should be six foot six, 240, and run a 4.2 forty, Murphy thought as he caught the ball at a run from the twenty-yard line. It was a decent punt and hung in the air long enough for Murphy to understand he didn't have much time before Washington would be on top of him. He took off, and knowing he was a lot quicker than his line of blockers hustling ahead of him, he was careful not to get behind them. Instead, he cut outside and ran down the sidelines. Washington had the angle on him and was coming in hard for a tackle. He'd been punishing Murphy all night, but this was the first time they had met on the open field. Washington expected Murphy to do what every other quarterback he'd faced had done in this situation—slide, cower, and pray. Instead, Murphy ran *at* Washington, lowered his head, and butted it right into the center of his jersey—trucked him like he had watched Earl Campbell do countless times on *Monday Night Football*. Washington was caught off guard and flopped backward hard as Murphy ran over him and kept on going.

As good as Alex Washington was, Scott Murphy was better. He wasn't a superior athlete—on paper Washington could run circles around Murphy and bench-press double his top weight—but on the field anyone who saw them knew.

Washington was a phenomenon.

Scott Murphy was a freak of nature.

There would be no slow fade and burn for Scott Murphy. He would peak on a football field. For the next few seconds he would be, quite simply, the best football player the world had ever seen.

The crowd went crazy as Murphy crossed midfield, and it took the full body weight of three Saints defenders to bring him down just inside the thirty-yard line.

His oversized adversaries took their sweet time crawling off Murphy's battered body and he struggled to stand, head ringing. He called a timeout to get his team ready for what he was certain was the last play of both the game and his illustrious high school career. He pulled his helmet back to get air as Pierson, his lineman, waddled up behind him like a mud-stained two-hundred-pound mother hen to stuff Murphy's battered shoulder pads back into his bloodstained black-and-gold number 13 football jersey.

Flashbulbs sparkled as Murphy walked to the sidelines. With just seconds left on the clock, everyone in the stadium was agitated and restless, caught in a state of fear or faith. Murphy was neither, because he had a secret, something that kept him centered and focused, a ritual he had followed since he was a kid. Before every game, Murphy would kneel at the goal line and pretend to tie his cleats. Then he would line up his pennies right on the back chalk of the end zone.

The pennies were his magic pennies. He'd had them since he was a little boy, and it was the one part of his football game he'd never shared with anyone. Not even Coach. Four pennies: one for him, one for the girl he was going to marry, one for his mother, and one for the father he'd never met. The people he loved. So while everyone else was worried about the flailing crowd, the high stakes, the ticking clock, and the *Sports Illustrated* reporter on the sidelines…none of it fazed him. Scoring a touchdown was simple to him—he was just going to get his pennies.

He caught sight of Jenny Cleary on the sidelines. She was blonde, beautiful, smart, and the daughter of the wealthiest man in Coldwater. Murphy knew a corn farmer didn't get a woman like that. Winners did. If he wanted to hang on to her, he had to keep winning. Murphy understood that the world was a different place for winners, and if anyone ever tried to tell him any different, he knew they were lying.

Jenny was worth it, but the main reason Murphy fought upfield so hard was his mom, Thelma—the woman who came home every weeknight with bloody bite marks on her arms from wrestling mental patients. He wanted her to stop working fourteen-hour days. He wanted her to stop driving twenty-three miles each way to and from Mansfield Hospital—a state-run institution. She never came to the games. She always told her son she had to work late, but Murphy knew she found them too upsetting. She didn't like seeing him get hit. He also knew that when she could, she watched from afar, parked at the top of the radio tower hill two miles away. He could imagine her chewing the cuticles on her chapped hands as she listened to the game on the staticky push-button AM radio inside her rusted-out yellow Pinto.

The fourth penny was for a man who'd died in North Vietnam a few days before Murphy was born. His father had been killed in a battle Murphy couldn't pronounce in a country he had never been to, and because of it, Murphy had watched his mother struggle to make ends meet for as long as he could remember.

Coach Hand slapped Murphy's helmet and grabbed his face mask to pull him close, as if he was about to share a secret. "This is it, kid. Everything you've done. Everything you are. Everything you're ever gonna be. Comes down to this." To win, they needed a touchdown. They had less than ten seconds to move the ball almost forty yards.

Murphy nodded, but ignored the elaborate play Coach scribbled on the clipboard as he briefed the team. Murphy knew it by heart. He also knew it wouldn't work.

He would do what he always did: read the defense as he lined up and decide how to play in that moment. He'd invariably call his own number on an option—a play that gave him just that—the ability to keep the ball himself or throw it away if he got in trouble. He liked it not just because he was a scrambling quarterback, but because it gave him an out—a Plan B. No matter how far behind he might be on the scoreboard, Murphy always believed in his heart that there was a way to win.

"Fifty-four Right! Fifty-four Right!" Murphy shouted as he scanned the line to warn his lineman. Murphy knew there wasn't a Popsicle's chance in hell they'd be able to stop Washington, but he hoped they could at least slow him down for a half second.

"Don't worry where I am, fool! You'll feel me when I get there!" Washington yelled back at Murphy, grinning death out of his helmet. That grin was his trademark. It was more like baring fangs—and Murphy not only understood the gesture, he was probably the first quarterback in 54's life who'd smiled back.

It wasn't because he was cocky, or full of himself. It wasn't even because he'd already been offered a full scholarship to Ohio State, or because all the sportswriters were saying that he was going to win the NCAA championship and that he was a shoo-in for the NFL draft and that he'd get a signing bonus of a million dollars. For Murphy, it was a lot simpler. He was smiling because he loved playing football. He loved competing. And he loved winning.

Murphy could see the doubt creeping into the eyes of the

defensive linemen as they assembled across from the Cavaliers. They were wondering why these little farm boys hadn't given up yet. Coldwater didn't have a strength coach or a conditioning coach. They didn't need one. They had the kind of muscles you can't get from lifting weights—the unbending sinew built through a lifetime of hard work. They'd been bailing hay, milking cows, or raising hogs since they were knee-high to a bullfrog. It was a strength not just of muscle, but of will, forged from long, hard hours in a field and displayed by callouses on callouses. Murphy and his team might look like boys, but they had the hands of men…and the will. No matter how many times they got beat, no matter how many times they got pushed into the dirt, no matter how tired they were, they just kept getting up and hustling back to the line, ready for more. They were always the first team back to the line. Always.

Murphy ignored the glitter of flashbulbs as he knelt behind the center. Chris Hall, number 86, the Cavalier's receiver, leaned in and signaled to Murphy, ready to go.

Ten seconds.

Murphy scanned the stands, wishing his mom were there. He was about to win her a new life. From now on, it was going to be him taking care of her. In a few seconds, the Cavaliers would be state champions. In a few minutes, the Saints would get on their air-conditioned bus and drive back to the big city, knowing they'd been beaten by kids from a town smaller than their high school. Murphy was going down the field to get his pennies, and no one was going to stop him.

Murphy flexed his wrist and the center brought the ball up from the turf right into his hand. He did a seven-step drop and saw Hall break free of his coverage. He was open. Wide open. Murphy thought of throwing it for about a half second, but didn't want his future riding in anyone else's hands, not even someone as good as his best friend, the kid he'd been throwing passes to since he was seven years old. He pump-faked instead.

The ruse worked and the linebackers bit, backing up.

Murphy turned his body to the side, more like a dancer than a football player, more Mikhail Baryshnikov than Joe Montana, and slipped through them.

He could see daylight. He could see the end zone. He tucked the ball and sprinted.

Washington and the safety rushed to cut him off.

Murphy did a mental calculation as he ran—they would get to him around the two-yard line. They would be able to hit him, but wouldn't be able to stop him. His momentum would carry him through. A mere seven steps from the end zone, and Murphy knew that he was going to win the state championship—no matter what.

As he hit the goal line, the crowd was frozen—ready to holler in triumph or defeat. The universe hung there for a moment in that sudden quiet of hope.

The ball broke the plane of the end zone. Murphy had won the game.

He'd done the impossible. David had beaten eleven Goliaths.

"Touchdown, Coldwater! The new state champions of Ohio!" The announcer was ecstatic.

If Murphy had another second to enjoy it, he might have felt the same way.

But Goliath wasn't done yet.

Murphy, Washington, and the safety—three objects, airborne, all trying to occupy the same space at the same time—collided, and his ballet ended with an ugly pirouette. His leg snapped like a wishbone. The "POP!" reverberated through the Ohio Valley like a gunshot.

The cheers fell as fast as they'd risen. Silence echoed on the field as Washington stepped up off of Murphy, waving his hands wildly for someone to come help. The announcer turned somber: "Scott Murphy still down. Oh, my God…"

As Murphy lay on the grass, leg twisted to the side at an impossible angle, he screamed in anguish like a calf in a slaughterhouse—it was a sound that would haunt everyone who heard it for years to come. In that moment, Murphy caught a glimpse of his girlfriend Jenny staring in horror at him from the sidelines and realized something awful. He hadn't just ended his football career and any chance of taking care of his mother.

He'd just lost the love of his life.

Chapter 2

FAIRY TALES WEREN'T SUPPOSED to end this way. But here he was, stepping out of his battered truck on his fifty-cent leg, buckled from heel to hip in a metal brace so bulky it wouldn't fit under his pants. Murphy had gone from the eighteen-year-old town golden boy with a cocksure smile, a pretty girl on his arm, and a million-dollar throw, to a grumpy son of a bitch—a hollow man at thirty-eight.

He was doing what he did most Friday nights—delivering the drunks. Coldwater was a small town, and while he might be able to get out of watching the football games, there was no avoiding the off-season. The men he had grown up with wouldn't let him shirk his late-night drinking duties.

Murphy pulled his pickup into Gig's driveway first. Not because he was the birthday boy, but because he lived closest to the firehouse and it would give Murphy a chance to sober up some more before he took Winton and Pierson down Robinson Road to the state highway. That stretch of road had been nicknamed Suicide Hill for a reason. As a volunteer fireman—like most all of his friends and neighbors, since the town couldn't afford a real fire department—Murphy had pulled enough broken bodies out of mangled cars on that curve to be careful.

Murphy hitched to the back of his truck, the brace on his withered leg clanking on the sidewalk with every awkward step. He flipped open the gate and let it drop. A lifeless arm flopped over the side. Murphy pulled the body out and threw it over his shoulder—the fireman's carry was as good for drunks as it was for rescuing people from burning buildings.

As Murphy limped up the sidewalk, his load stirred, mumbling, "Home...No...Murph...I don't wanna...go...yet..."

"Too bad," Murphy said. "And stop moving before I drop your ass."

One of Gig's Rottweilers started to bark.

"Quiet, Rosie...Murph, I thought we were going to the firehouse. To play cards."

"We already did. You slept through it."

"Aw, man. Some birthday. Y'all shoulda woken me up!"

Murphy propped Gig against the wall like a roll of carpet and steadied him while he opened the screen, then pushed the inside door. He wasn't surprised when it opened. No one in Coldwater bothered with locks. They were a waste of time.

Murphy wedged the screen with his good leg and then picked Gig up by his belt, swinging him inside.

"You guys are lightweights. And I'm too damn crippled to be carrying you sons of bitches home every time you drink a couple of beers!"

"It was more than two, Murphy. It was the drinking games. Those did it. How come you didn't play with us? You never play drinking games with us."

"Because drinking's not a game, Gig."

Murphy had nothing against going a few rounds. He just didn't need an excuse. He was Irish, and as a result, could hold his liquor better than most of the guys, so he was usually in charge of getting everyone home safely.

Gig leaned on one of his big dogs as he made his way into the house.

"What? No tuck in? No kiss good night?" Gig joked.

"You're lucky I didn't drop you at the curb."

As he drove past the old mill to his next stop, Murphy wondered if it would have been better to go out like his father had.

He knew the way he walked—limping like a pirate with a peg leg, his brace clattering—was painful for people to watch. Still, most treated him like the town war hero—just like his dad would have been if he'd made it home. The comparison rankled Murphy. His father had died trying to save people that he loved. All he had done was wrecked his leg in a stupid game of football for no reason whatsoever. The only thing he had in common with his dad was a last name and a run of genetic bad luck.

Murphy honked the horn as he pulled up to Winton's house.

The porch light flashed on and Winton's wife, Betty, came out in a flannel housecoat, hair in curlers, face bunched up in a witchy scowl that made her much older than she was.

She didn't offer to give Murphy a hand as he struggled to drag the unconscious Winton across the gravel driveway.

"Where do you want him?" Murphy asked, a little annoyed.

"Right there is just fine," she replied as she pointed at the ground.

Murphy set him down as gently as he could and hitched back to his truck without lingering to chat. He was never one to get involved in domestic issues.

"Thanks, Murphy," she shouted, relief seeping into her voice.

Murphy started the car, smiling to himself as he saw her unwind the garden hose. He even chuckled for a minute at the sight of her spraying Winton down in his rear-view—Winton flopping around like a fish.

By the time he'd turned the corner, he was deep in his fantasies again. Though Murphy avoided the football field at all costs, and never discussed it with anyone, not even his wife, when he was plowing his soybeans or driving his pickup to get seed, he imagined he was back in high school. He had vivid, Technicolor daydreams in which he was still golden. He could run. He could throw. He was alive.

Even when he was with his wife, he couldn't help but think of Jenny, the pretty blonde he had lost along with his football scholarship. He hated himself for it.

And when he was with his two young daughters, his mind was usually out in the field with his crops. The Murphy family was struggling. And seeing the holes in the soles of his girls' shoes or their hand-me-down clothes reminded him of his own childhood and made him hate himself for not doing better. He wanted to give his girls the kind of life a star quarterback—not a half-crippled soybean farmer—could provide.

He could deal with being lame. He couldn't deal with being a loser. And in Murphy's mind, any man who couldn't provide well for his family was just that—a loser.

Pierson's house was the farthest away, so Murphy had saved it for last, hoping his fat ass would be sober by the time they got there. No such luck. He could lift Gig okay, Winton was a struggle yet he managed, but Pierson weighed over three hundred pounds.

Murphy couldn't haul Pierson. And no way was he gonna let him sleep it off in the truck. Murphy had a wife and kids to get home to. And a field to work in the rapidly approaching morning.

Murphy yanked the passenger door open and a half-empty bottle of whiskey fell out of the cab. He snatched the bottle mid-air by reflex before it hit the pavement. He thought about stuffing it into the big man's overall pockets, they were roomy enough for it to fit, but figured he needed it more than Pierson did, so he screwed the cap tight and set the bottle on the floor of his pickup.

"Come on, Chubb Rock. Time for bed."

"I thought I wasn't your type, Murphy," Pierson said as he made himself more comfortable on the bench seat.

Murphy knew there was only one way to get Pierson into his house under his own power. He had to piss him off. "Get the hell out of my truck, you one-balled bastard."

It worked. Pierson cocked an eye at him. He didn't like anyone referring to the getting-out-of-bed-accident that had sent him to the hospital shortly after high school. He'd gotten a bad case of blue balls making out with Leslie Dickerson in a motel hot tub, then collapsed getting out of bed the next day with a torsion of the left testicle, basically a Gordian knot in his balls that the doctors had to cut to fix. Pierson never quite recovered. "What did I tell you about calling me One Nut?"

"I can't remember, Uni-ball. What was it?"

Pierson opened both eyes. *Good, he was mad.*

"Murphy…I'm warning you. It's not funny."

"Is the chopped nut still floating in there or did they replace it with a plastic one?"

Pierson sat up, reaching his hammy hands for Murphy's throat.

Murphy stepped back as Pierson stood. That did it.

"Stop talking about my nuts!"

"Is it nuts? Or nut? I thought you just had one. Singular."

"You one-legged prick! I'm gonna—"

He dodged and weaved as Pierson lumbered at him like a drunken elephant, trying to smack him. Murphy was surprisingly nimble for a cripple.

And this son of a bitch is surprisingly aggressive for a man with one ball.

Murphy finally reached the lawn and Pierson was next to him, eyes red with rage.

"Nowhere to run to, Murphy. Nowhere to hide."

"Come and get me, you one-balled bastard."

Murphy let him come, then ducked to the side like a bullfighter while Pierson kept going, stumbled, and landed with a thud on the grass.

"Ow! Wait a second, Murph. Hang on," Pierson said, his rage forgotten as he pressed into his lower left belly with his hands. "What side is your appendix on?"

"Right side. Now come on. Get up!" Murphy said, straining to lift the big guy to his feet.

"That's the side that hurts. Aw, hell. Appendicitis. I knew it. Ouch. Man. It hurts, Murphy. I'm dying. Call it in! Get me to Celina before it bursts!"

Pierson crumpled, pulling Murphy down with him.

"Dammit, Pierson!" he said, extricating himself from the tangle of meaty drunken limbs. Now Murphy was pissed, too.

14

"It's gonna burst…I'm dying." Pierson reached up and grabbed Murphy's shoulders, bringing him closer. "I made you my beneficiary. You know that, right?"

He was drunker than Murphy had thought.

"You gotta take care of my mom…for me, Murphy. Promise me. If I die. Promise."

"No. I got enough people to worry about. And you're not dying! Your stomach hurts because you ate three dozen damn wings! Now get up or I'm gonna leave your ass out here."

"I'm dying…Murph."

"We're all dying, Pierson. But I can guarantee you it ain't happening tonight."

"My brother will put her in a home, Murphy. You'll make sure my money goes to her, right? Make sure my brother doesn't put her in a home?"

"What money? What are you talking about, you drunken idiot?"

"My Fireman's Fund. Our life insurance. It's a boatload of money, Murphy. We're worth a lot dead! When I go, you're my beneficiary…after you take care of my mom, you can have whatever's left!"

Murphy pulled the big oaf up and felt woozy for a moment, like he might fall straight back onto the lawn. He threw all of his weight forward and the two men managed to career up the rickety porch steps, their momentum propelling them through Pierson's screen door hard enough to smack it shut behind them.

Pierson hung on to Murphy. "Spinning…things are all… spinning…not long now…I think it might have already burst."

"It didn't burst. You're not dying. Get inside."

"Murph, I know the bank's been hassling you. So if I buy the farm, you can buy the farm, you know what I'm saying?"

After he dropped Pierson on the floor, Murphy limped out of the house without saying another word.

Pierson kept yelling as Murphy retreated down the driveway. "I'm just saying, don't let those rich pricks push you around! You were Mr. Football in '91 and you sent them packing! Don't you ever forget that! You were the best there ever was!"

Murphy got in his truck and slammed the door. He made a mental note to speak to his wife about broadcasting their personal business.

Chapter 3

IF A BIG PIECE of yourself lives in the past, then you can never be completely present. Murphy left more than his good leg on that football field and inhabited his memories more often than not lately. That golden time of trophies and winning became his fortress of solitude. Not many people can look back on their lives and pinpoint the exact instant it went wrong, but Murphy could. His decision, under fire, to ignore Coach and change the play at the line of scrimmage—that choice, that moment, had sentenced him to life as a cripple. And ended his dreams. He was leading a ghost life. But he was hoping his soybean field would change that—be his second chance for success.

Murphy sat in his truck, staring up at his bedroom window. He knew Macy was awake. Waiting for him. He just wanted to rest for a minute. He wasn't ready to face her yet. He was Irish sober, which meant he was functional, but he'd broken a promise he'd made her and she'd smell the liquor on his breath.

He stared at the worn medal hanging on a tattered ribbon from the rear-view mirror. It spun slowly back and forth. On the front was an engraving of a quarterback frozen in motion. On the back:

Scott Murphy—Mr. Football 1991

Next to the medal hung a cheesy drugstore keychain, and printed in an optimistic font was:

Murphy's Law...
I never had a slice of bread,

Particularly large and wide,
That did not fall upon the floor,
And always on the buttered side.

Murphy used to think the family law didn't apply to him and that he could outrun that string of Irish bad luck that befell his forefathers. He used to think he could make his own destiny.

Now he knew that was just wishful thinking.

Murphy picked up Pierson's fifth from under the passenger seat. He thought long and hard about finishing it. In fact, he did more than think. He put his hand on the cap. He could hear it calling to him. The promises whisky whispers in exchange for one sip.

He'd already knocked back half a fifth and it hadn't done anything. Besides he had a new prescription for pain pills so he might as well take advantage of them.

Murphy was sure the girls would be up soon, and he had a heap of work to do on the beans, so he got the better of himself and got out of the truck. He hefted the bottle, cocked his arm back—his stance awkward because of the brace on his unbending left leg—and launched it toward the metal trash barrel. The first twenty feet of its trajectory were beautiful—an aerodynamic miracle, since Jack Daniels bottles weren't built for flight. It soared through the air in a perfect spiral. Then, the drag coefficient and sloshing liquid took effect and the bottle wobbled, finally flopping end over end and shattering in the rocks behind the barn.

Dammit.

Murphy cursed himself, his arm, Jack Daniels, the state of Kentucky, the inventor of glass, and his bum leg as he limped over to pick up the shards.

You're a dumbass, Murphy.

He wondered if Macy had seen it from the bedroom window. He could hear her voice in his head: "When you break something or spill something, it is just God telling you to be on the lookout. He's giving you a sign that something special is going to happen."

Macy was always breaking things. And he didn't see too much special going on in her life. She was stuck—married to him—and

18

he certainly wasn't magical. Murphy thought it was hokum, but his wife believed it and he wasn't going to argue. If she wanted to believe in Santa Claus, he'd play along. After all, he did have that bank meeting this afternoon. Maybe the loan would go through and he could stop worrying.

He doubted it, though. Nothing much had gone right for him since his injury. It was like he'd avoided Murphy's Law for the first eighteen years of his life, but once it caught up with him it was making up for lost time.

Chapter 4

MURPHY MADE IT INSIDE without his family noticing. Now he stared at his shirtless torso in the bathroom mirror. Flabby. Pale. He glared at himself. *You're a hairy marshmallow. A flabby, pale, balding old joke...*

Once Murphy was done despising himself, he propped his bad leg up on the toilet seat and undid the brace. He couldn't shower in the brace, so he had to bathe. And every time he bathed, he had to stare at his pale, twisted, skinny remnant of a leg beneath the water like some kind of malformed albino fish.

Murphy's crippled body traveled forward in time at exactly one second per second, giving him no choice in the matter. His mind, however, could move through time in any direction, any time he chose. He would often close his eyes and imagine the pleasures of playing high school football as well as the fleshly fringe benefits he enjoyed as a result.

But inevitably the time trip would take a wrong turn and he would end up reliving the nightmarish years of rehab, the failed operations, the painful rebreaking of his leg after it set wrong the first time, the doctors telling him he would never walk again, the crushing disappointment and depression that had set in from the moment his life as he knew it had ended.

The time travel of our memories is supposed to allow us to pay for an experience once and then enjoy it repeatedly at no additional charge, learning new lessons with each repetition. For Murphy it had become a prison for his soul.

He popped open the medicine cabinet and stared at his own personal pharmacy. Vicodin. Percocet. Oxycontin. All to kill the pain. He had Ambien for sleep. This must be what Elvis felt like, but Murphy was no Elvis. Not even close. He wasn't even a Backseat Boy or whatever the hell the name of that band was that Macy used to listen to that drove him crazy.

He tapped a couple Vicodin into his palm.

Tap. Tap. Tap. Someone was at the door.

"Dada?" he heard Krista intone. He scolded her for not calling him Dad or Daddy; she was old enough to say it right now.

"One second, baby," he said. She tried to open the unlocked door and he reached over to hold it shut. "I'll be out in a second." He didn't like anyone seeing him naked in the light of day. Not even his wife. It wasn't his privates or his balding pate. It wasn't even his twisted leg as much as it was the spare tire he carried around his waist.

If it weren't for my leg, I'd be a stereotype. The balding, overweight former high school quarterback.

The leg made him more than a stereotype.

It made him a damn cripple.

Murphy stuffed the pills in his mouth and stuck his head under the running faucet to wash them down.

When he'd put the clothes and the brace back on, he limped out of the bathroom and his daughters ran at him, wrapping their arms around his legs and hips. Krista wore one of his old football jerseys and he shook her arm, the sweetness of the moment gone.

"Where did you get that?" he asked his daughter.

Macy answered, as she shuffled up the stairs. "I found it in the attic. She wanted to wear it to the game tomorrow if you didn't go."

"I don't want them wearing that stuff. I told you that a million times," Murphy said as he pulled it off over her head and balled it up. His anger wasn't driven by protectiveness toward an old relic of his football glory days; it was motivated by fear and superstition.

What Murphy couldn't tell Macy and could barely admit

to himself was that he was superstitious. He was afraid of that jersey, the number 13. The scientific term was triskaidekaphobia but all Murphy knew was that the number filled him with dread. Particularly that jersey. The last time Krista had gotten it out was for Halloween—and the next day the plant had shut down as the auto industry collapsed, putting Murphy and half of Coldwater out of work. If his mom hadn't saved the jersey and passed it on to Macy for the girls, he would have burned it a long time ago.

Thirteen used to be his lucky number. He had been given the jersey by default at his first football camp—he had said he was a quarterback and the coaches had taken one look at his dinky body and chicken-skinny prepubescent legs and proceeded to let every other quarterback at the camp pick their jerseys first. By the time the head coach reached into the box, 13 was all that was left. By the time the camp ended, 13 was something of a legend—Murphy scored more touchdowns than all the other young quarterbacks combined. The next year at camp the kids fought over the number 13, but it belonged to Murphy—whether he liked it or not.

"Honey, she wears it at night so she feels safe. And if you were home to tuck her in more often, she wouldn't need it."

"It was Gig's birthday, Macy. It's not like I wanted to go. If I don't drive those idiots, they'll put their cars in a ditch or worse…"

"I'm all for you seeing your friends, I encourage it, but can you arrange it so you have them home at a decent hour?"

Murphy hitched into the girls' room and dug through the drawers for another shirt for Krista. His frustration grew as he had trouble locating one that fit.

"Where are her normal shirts?"

Macy sighed, walked to the closet, and took one down off a shelf.

"What are they doing up so early, anyway?"

"They heard you pull up," Macy said, refolding the clothes Murphy had rifled through and gently pushing them back in the drawers. "They missed you last night."

"Well, I can't be in two places at once," Murphy grumbled back as they walked into the kitchen.

"You know you've got the bank today?"

"Yeah, Macy. I do. And so does the whole town. Stop telling people our business."

"I only told Sasha because I need her to babysit…"

"We live in Backwater, Macy. You tell one person something, you might as well put up a billboard. It's bad enough we're broke without the whole world knowing it…"

The girls grew quiet, picking at their breakfast as they sensed the fight about to escalate. The tension was broken by a familiar melody of tones beeping across the scanner. An instant later they echoed on the fire pager on Murphy's belt. The whole family froze in anticipation. Each township had its own scanner tone, but this one was unmistakable. This was a call for the Coldwater Volunteer Fire Department. It was such a small community that every call meant something was most likely going wrong for someone they knew. There were no strangers in Coldwater.

"Celina to Coldwater Fire, Coldwater Ambulance. Signal fifty at Twenty-Seven Robinson Road."

Murphy knew what "signal fifty" meant, and worse yet, he was more than familiar with the address.

Gig's house was on fire.

"Son of a bitch."

"Swearing isn't gonna help." Macy said as he grabbed his coat and hitched toward the door. "You're not ten forty-six, are you?"

Murphy glared at her. That was the fire code for drunk.

"No. You wanna ten fifty-five?" Murphy replied, the fire code for fight. He let the screen door slap shut behind him.

Chapter 5

MURPHY SPED BY THE old metal clock on Main Street toward the state road. The signal light at the intersection wasn't exactly a light. Murphy called it an idiot's stop sign, because the town had paid twelve thousand dollars for some workers to string it up. It was a box, with stop-sign graphics on each side and a light that went on at night. The town wasn't even big enough for a blinking light, just an illuminated four-way stop sign.

Murphy blew through it in his truck, racing toward the station. He saw the doors open and activity already going on inside.

Son of a bitch.

The faded Smokey Bear sign outside the station proclaimed "Fire Danger Low Today!"

So much for that.

Murphy parked his truck and headed into the already buzzing fire station. He hitch-hopped to his gear locker, grabbed the pull-up bar above it, and hefted himself up and into his boots, pulling up his pants and buckling on his jacket. As he tugged on his oxygen tank and took down his helmet, he noticed he was the fire chief this month.

"What is this? Why am I chief?" he asked no one in particular.

"'Cause it's your turn, Murphy," Rodriguez shouted across the room as he loaded the oxygen tanks into the back of the truck.

"Don't I get a say in it?" Murphy replied.

"No," Coach Hand yelled from the passenger seat of the red

pumper engine, "Now get your ass in here and let's get going!"

It wasn't that big of a deal, certainly not to Murphy. The town was so small they took turns being chief, and it didn't matter, because the buck stopped with Coach anyway.

"You see where we're going?" the old man barked as he turned on the siren.

"Yeah," Murphy said, clambering up into the driver's seat, knowing he was in for it.

"Any idea why?" Coach asked, eyes boring into his face through the wide rear-view mirror.

"Because he's an idiot?" Murphy offered as the big old diesel engine rumbled to life.

"Yeah, well. You were supposed to get all the idiots home!"

"I did," Murphy replied. "Didn't know I was supposed to babysit them, too."

"Come on, Rodriguez!" Coach barked as Rodriguez jumped on the back. "Let's go, get the wheels turning!"

Murphy drove faster than usual. As much as he hated to admit it, he was worried. Gig was one of Murphy's closest friends. Gig's claim to fame was being on the same high school football team as the best quarterback in the country and never once catching a pass. Murphy didn't have much use for a receiver who couldn't catch back then, but they had much more in common now. Gig was one of the few African Americans in a mostly white town, and Murphy was a cripple. So they both knew what it was like to draw stares and have people whispering when they walked into Friendly's for an ice cream.

Gig was a goof, but he had a big heart and when a redneck of a particular flavor would glare over at Gig, Murphy would glare right back, wishing, wanting them to speak up so he could break something over their heads.

As Coldwater Engine No. 3 pulled up in front of 27 Robinson Road, Gig was standing outside in a bathrobe and cowboy boots, waving a spatula in the air like a distress flag. His back porch was in flames and threatening to take the entire house with it.

"Little early for a cookout, Gig!" Coach yelled as Greenway and Rodriguez jumped off the truck and grabbed a length of hose.

"I was just making a birthday burger, minding my own business, when I saw Bernadette walking down the street. Man, she looked good. And we started talking and then next thing I knew—Whoosh! It went up on me!"

Rodriguez tied the hose around the tire of Gig's truck and slapped the side of the fire engine, signaling Murphy to go. He drove the truck away from the house, watching the hose unravel behind them in the large side mirror. Ducks scattered as he turned down a dirt road, bouncing over the potholes toward Butler Pond.

The old brick Mill House was still here, and it hadn't functioned since 1927 when a bigger one opened in the city, but it was as close to a fire hydrant as you got in these parts.

Murphy set the brake and jumped off the fire truck, grabbing a floater pump from the back as Coach made the hose connections.

Murphy revved up the floater and kicked it into the pond as Coach flipped a switch on the side of the pumper engine. Water from the pond rolled into the truck then out the hose, causing it to dance and wriggle as it filled with water flowing back to Gig's house.

"Charge the line," Coach intoned into his walkie-talkie. Rodriguez and Greenway opened the valve and started hosing down Gig's porch.

Murphy stared out at the pond, distracted, as the pump whirred in his ear. He hadn't been here since he was in high school. It was a late-night spot his gang came to when they wanted to get away to drink beer or have a quiet place to make out.

"So. You gonna grace us with your presence tomorrow, or what?" Coach asked.

"I'm covering the station," Murphy said, not meeting his gaze. The Homecoming game was tomorrow and some genius had decided to turn it into a twenty-year anniversary celebration of the big state championship win. Murphy didn't think that game was anything to celebrate.

"We have mutual aid. Rosalia knows what a big deal this is. They already said they can cover us."

"Rosalia is forty minutes away. But hey, if you don't need me at the station, I got plenty of work to take care of at home."

"What work? Babysit those beans? If you'd planted corn like everyone else, you wouldn't have to worry so much. You could just sit back and watch it grow."

"Sit back and watch it grow, huh? That how it works? Didn't know you were coaching farmers now, too. How many acres you plant this season?"

"Zero. But I got a yard of common sense and it's all I need. Coldwater is called corn country for a reason."

"Yeah. It used to be football country, too. But, you guys are... what? Four and seven?"

"Four and six," Coach responded, rankled. "And if you think you can do any better, bring your ass down to the field after school and coach my quarterbacks."

"Sure," Murphy scoffed. "Soon as you come help me work my back forty."

"I'd help you plant some corn," Coach shot back.

The radio squawked, signaling the fire was out and everything was clear—at least as far as the fire was concerned. Tension hung in the air between Coach and Murphy. Nothing they weren't used to.

Murphy slammed the pump switch off. Started reeling in the floater. "I didn't plant corn. I planted beans. So how 'bout you worry about your field and let me worry about mine."

Chapter 6

"MAKING A VICTIM FILL out his own paperwork. That's cold," Gig said as he sat in the station house's common room putting pen to a stack of forms. He was wearing his tattered bathrobe and cowboy boots, but was still too caught between drunk and hungover to care.

"The only victim here is us, Gig," Coach said. "It's bad enough the whole town has to listen to you drunk fools all night. They don't need to wake up to a siren and your sorry ass burning your porch down."

Rodriguez chimed in, fully awake now, and ready to rib. "Look at the bright side, Gig. You finally caught something—on fire."

Laughter rippled through the room—everyone except Coach.

"I caught a few in practice. Didn't I, Murphy?" Gig pleaded.

"You probably caught a few in your dreams," Murphy offered, setting off a few more guffaws.

Coach, a man who valued every player equally, whether they rode the bench or led the conference, didn't think it was funny. "Rodriguez. Go help Murphy roll hose."

"Me? It was Gig's mess!" Rodriguez protested.

Coach glared and Rodriguez shuffled off, penitent. The old man could still make all these grown men feel like juvenile delinquents with a single glance.

"Hey! That's us on the news! Turn it up!" Rodriguez said, pointing at the old tube TV on the counter.

Gig grabbed the remote and raised the volume.

The crew stared into the tiny time machine—watching grainy footage of Murphy running through, around, and over the best defense high school football had to offer the world in 1991.

"Damn. Look at him go," Gig said, nostalgia glowing on his face.

"Murphy! Come check it out, man. You're on TV!" Rodriguez added.

Murphy put the last bit of hose up on the truck, craning his head so he could hear the anchor. *"It's homecoming in Coldwater and the twenty-year anniversary of the little team that could...NFL All-Star receiver Chris Hall is expected to make an appearance..."*

Murphy caught a piece of the TV reflected in the plexiglass-covered county map on the wall—edited clips of Chris Hall making catches in the NFL were interspersed with shots of Murphy as he connected with Hall on the field. *"That team was led by Mr. Football, Scott Murphy. He and Chris Hall connected for a record five thousand three hundred and twenty yards, a number that still stands as the most yardage in a single season for any quarterback-receiver combination..."*

Great. Mr. Big Time is coming back to Coldwater.

"Come on, Murph. You're missing it!" Gig shouted.

"I've seen it plenty before," Murphy lied as he hitched out to his truck.

The truth was, Murphy had never watched the replay of that game or of his leg breaking. Coach kept every Coldwater game tape from every game Coldwater ever played on the shelves of his cluttered fire station office. Except that one. That one was locked in a drawer. Murphy knew where the key was, and he knew everyone else liked to watch the victory, but he had never once watched it.

It wasn't just a game tape to Murphy. It was a snuff film. It captured on video the death of the football star Scott Murphy. And although some people would say he was still alive, Murphy knew better. A bigger part of him than his leg died on that battlefield. Neither his body nor his soul had ever been complete since that day. He lost both of his great loves that night: football and Jenny.

Murphy felt the bile of bitterness well up from his stomach and tightness pull at his chest. There aren't many people in the world who have the worst moment of their existence captured on videotape.

The truth was, Murphy couldn't remember anything from the second half of that game. He remembered the field had been covered in fog the first quarter, but it had burned off by halftime. After that, it was a blur—from halftime to when he woke up in the hospital didn't exist in his mind.

"Selective memory," the doctors called it. They said it must have been such a horrible experience that Murphy's mind erased it. That, or because the injury was of such an intensity that the moment after it happened, his brain had been flooded with so many painkilling chemicals, they had wiped his memory out.

"I'm still expecting you at the halftime ceremony!" Coach yelled after Murphy.

Murphy didn't care. He already had plans. He was going to drive into the Indian liquor store in Chickasaw and buy a fifth of Jack Daniels, get wasted, and open that top drawer. He was gonna sit back on the firehouse couch. Dim the lights. And relive that game.

He was gonna man-up and finally face his fear.

Chapter 7

THERE WERE HOLES IN the kitchen wall. He could still see the horsehair inside the hundred-year-old plaster that covered the old lathe. The wallpaper was torn back in spots, revealing different patterns from different decades, depending on the depth. It was a time capsule of sorts, exposing the varying tastes of a century of occupants. When Murphy surveyed the decaying walls, or the sawhorses holding up a door that needed hinges, or the plastic that covered the dining room window—he saw failure. Macy saw the mess as a necessary and beautiful step toward creating something new—a work in progress. Kind of the same way she saw her husband. A grump in a cocoon, who would one day spread his wings and become a butterfly. She hadn't lost hope.

Murphy had. Every section of peeling wallpaper, every stack of unopened bills, was a monument to his shortcomings. The only thing that gave him hope was the Fireman's Fund calendar tacked up on the side of the kitchen cabinet. Other than the fact that the flyswatter hung on the same hook, or that last year's calendar was off kilter beneath it, there was nothing particularly special about the calendar. In fact, every member of the Coldwater Volunteer Fire Department got the same one every year at Christmas. Murphy took pride and solace in the red circle near the end of this month— harvest. It was just a few weeks away. Salvation day. It was the date when the soybeans would fully mature and he could pick them and for once in his life, be able to pay his damn bills.

The fire scanner on the top of the fridge squawked periodically as it rolled through the fire and police bands. There had been one in every home Murphy had ever lived in and he'd learned long ago only to hear the specific melody of tones that signaled Coldwater.

Murphy turned on the faucet and waited for the water to get hot. When it was as warm as it was gonna get, he stuck his battered John Deere coffee mug under the tap and watched it fill with cloudy water. Macy always pre-loaded the cheap little coffee maker for him, even changed the filter, but Murphy preferred to stir his coffee rather than hassle with brewing it. He took down the half-empty jar of instant and shook some onto the water. He watched it dissolve, moving the cup in a small circle to mix the crystals in. He was already drinking before they hit the bottom.

His reverie was broken by a little hand smacking the side of his hip. He looked down and saw Jamie, their youngest daughter, smiling up at him.

"What do you want, little one?" he asked as he set down his cup and delighted her by scooping her up and onto his good hip. "Huh?" Murphy pressed his face up as close to hers as it would go. She pressed hers right back, giving him a playful growl.

"So you never told me—how was the party?" Macy asked, her slippers sliding on the wood floor as she trudged into the kitchen.

"It wasn't a party. Just eight guys getting drunk," Murphy grumbled. She was just asking an innocent question, but with their financial affairs such a wreck, any recreational efforts made Murphy feel inadequate—if not downright useless.

"Well, if that's not a party, what is?" Macy said playfully.

"What shapes do you want?" Murphy asked as he started mixing up a batch of pancake batter. Pancakes were a meal that worked for breakfast or lunch.

"A football!" his oldest, Krista yelled without hesitation.

"How about a flower? Or Mickey Mouse or something?" Murphy asked.

Krista rolled her eyes. "I want a football, Dad. With laces."

Murphy had indulged her love of football when she was very

young, but now he wanted it to go away. Her mom had read her a newspaper story about a female quarterback in another township and ever since then, she was set on being a quarterback like her Dad. Over Murphy's dead and crippled body.

He plopped a flower-shaped pancake down on Krista's plate.

Krista's disappointed glower was about to turn into a gripe, when Macy interrupted.

"Honey! Where's the detergent?"

She walked back in, her face concealed behind two unfamiliar clothesbaskets. The bottle of generic detergent was on the counter and she was on a collision course with it.

"It's right—"

Macy spun her baskets and knocked the detergent bottle off the table. Murphy's hand whipped out and caught it before it hit the ground.

"—here."

She peeked out from behind the baskets, curling her lower lip to send a blast of air up toward her forehead and blow her wispy brown bangs out of her eyes.

"Oh. Thanks, honey. Set it in my arm, will you?"

Murphy nestled the bottle in the crook of her elbow and she smiled and continued on, knocking the glass bottle of fake maple syrup off the table as she squeezed by.

The girls giggled as Murphy caught it and set it back on the table. This was routine and one of the ways Murphy and Macy seemed made for each other. Macy knocked over vases, ketchup bottles, coffee cans, and milk cartons. Anything and everything taller than it was wide was susceptible to Macy's errant elbows or hips. She wasn't clumsy. She was just exuberant. Like a Golden Retriever, she had a hard time containing her love and excitement and she bumped into things.

As Macy set the baskets on the nearby washing machine, Murphy tilted his head toward them. They didn't have a purple laundry basket. Or a green one…

"What is all that stuff?" Murphy asked.

"Just some wash," Macy replied cheerfully as she unloaded the burden and started separating it into piles on the dryer.

"*Whose* wash?" Murphy asked, darkening.

"The Kagans just had another baby. They could use the help and we could use the cash," Macy explained. "That worked out well, huh?"

Irked, Murphy took a bite of Jamie's abandoned pancakes and stared at the red circle on the calendar. H-Day. Harvest day. Less than three weeks away.

"The beans are coming in soon. You don't need to be doing other people's laundry," Murphy said.

"There's no shame in workin', Scotty. Beans or no beans." Macy handed him a plastic hanger sagging under the weight of his old corduroy blazer. It smelled like mothballs.

"I steamed your coat in the shower. And there's a raspberry rhubarb pie on the windowsill for Frank."

Murphy's stomach perked up. "Raspberry rhubarb? How come Frank gets a raspberry rhubarb pie and we don't?" he asked, mock offended.

Krista and Jamie parroted Murphy's complaint. "Yeah, *Mom...*"

Murphy cracked a devilish smile and Macy gave him her wide-eyed mock how-dare-you scowl and scrunched her nose up like a witch. Even when she tried, she couldn't look angry.

"Frank gets a pie because he's been good enough to help us out with our loan. And if you weren't so busy complaining, you might have noticed there's an extra pie on the stove."

Murphy looked at the girls. They smiled. The race was on. He grabbed a fork and dove for the pie for all he was worth.

The back door opened a few minutes later and Sasha entered without knocking. Everyone except Murphy greeted her with enthusiasm. She was Jamie and Krista's godmother—or *ninang*, in her mother's native language. Sasha was half Filipino. Her father was one of the few Coldwater men of his generation to come back from Vietnam alive and intact, and he had brought two things home with him—Sasha and a new wife.

Sasha smiled tightly at Murphy. There was no love lost between them. "Scotty."

"Saw-sha," Murphy said, mispronouncing her name just to bug her. She insisted it be pronounced Saah-sha, which annoyed Murphy to no end. Anyone who wanted people to say their name the hard way just to be different was putting on airs.

Sasha flicked her hand out and whipped an ugly, scratchy blue polyester tie at Murphy. He was barely looking but he caught it in mid-air. He stared at it in his hand like it was a dead snake.

"What the hell is this?" he intoned.

"It's a tie, Scotty. T-I-E. Tie. Respectable men wear them around their necks every now and then," Sasha said, annoyed at his ingratitude.

Murphy snorted and tossed it back like a hot potato. "No, thanks."

It landed on Sasha's head and she stared at him as if wanting to claw his eyes out.

Macy lifted it off Sasha's head and put it on the hanger with the sports coat.

"I'm not wearing a monkey suit, Macy," Murphy protested.

"You look good dressed up, Scotty. And Frank's going out on a limb for us with this loan reissue, so at least look respectable for him."

Murphy kissed her forehead to calm her down. "Mace. I'm gonna walk in, we'll talk about football for a while, and then he'll sign off. It's no big deal."

Chapter 8

MURPHY WALKED OUT THE back door. It was a warm day for November. Indian summer. St. Martin's summer, named after the Roman soldier who cut his cloak in two and gave half to a beggar to keep him warm. He hitched toward the field, happy to be free of the talk of banks and ties. He was happy to focus on something he could control—work.

His mom's yellow Pinto sat rusting on blocks at the edge of his soybean field. The car wasn't worth a damn thing, and he wasn't planning on restoring it—ever—but he couldn't bear to part with it. Now it was an eyesore; overgrown with weeds. He stared in at the immaculate interior, still shining from how his mother kept it. Every time he looked at it, the crippled car reminded Murphy of his greatest failure. He'd never been able to take care of his mom. Never been able to get her a nice house. Never made enough money to have her retire early. It reminded him of how she'd worked herself into her grave to support his failed dreams and how he'd never been able to make it up to her. He knew he should haul it off to the scrap heap, but he couldn't. Because despite all that, it also reminded him of what an amazing woman his mother was. So Murphy kept it right on rusting right where it was.

As he crested the hill, Murphy saw a familiar sight, one of the few things that brought him comfort these days—three hundred eighty-seven acres of linear perfection—his soybeans. A sense of calm swept over him.

Murphy gazed out like a crippled general surveying his troops, optimistic about the battle ahead. Irrigation sprinklers on wheels stretched across the rows like giant insects.

It was time to water his babies.

Murphy stepped into his soybean field, careful that his bum leg didn't crush any of his precious beans. The bushes had lost most of their leaves and had gone from green to a golden yellow. It was almost time to harvest. Another few weeks and everything would be okay. Financially, anyway. He'd get them through another winter. That was all that mattered. Make it over the next hump. Make a few more payments on the farm and the equipment and be one step closer to owning his life again.

Three more weeks. Three more weeks and we're in the clear.

Murphy would die before he asked for help. And he would rather be raked over hot coals than accept charity. He was an American workingman and had always been defined by what he did—his vocation was who he was. When he played football, he was a football player. When he worked at the car plant, he was a line supervisor.

When the plant had shut down, he had been unemployed. After a few months, he had become unemployable. And then his mother had passed away and left him a small fortune—almost one hundred thousand dollars. She had scrimped and saved and gone without her entire life to leave him that kind of money. The realization had overwhelmed Murphy. It was too much love and sacrifice for a man who felt like a failure.

He had vowed to make good on his mom's legacy. When he'd bought the Kelly farm, it was in pretty bad shape and a lot of the old equipment had given out right away. Murphy had to take out a loan to get seed and a used harvester. It wasn't a big loan, but it was something called an ARM, an adjustable-rate mortgage, which had been sold to him as a cheap alternative. After a couple of shots of Jack, Murphy would say his farm had cost him an "ARM and a leg." The payments had ballooned and now money was tighter than ever.

People had said he was crazy to buy the farm.

And when he planted soybeans, they were convinced he was certifiable.

No one grew soybeans in Mercer County. No farmer worth his salt, at least, because they all knew what their daddies knew and what their daddies' daddies knew: this valley was too cold and the soil was too hard. Caliche soil in most parts. Sand, mixed with clay, which made it tricky to farm and to water.

But Murphy was a stubborn son of a bitch and knew most farmers want to plant it and forget it. Murphy was willing to babysit the damn beans if he had to—and he knew if he was careful, and spent time measuring the soil and making sure it didn't get too wet or too cold, he could pull it off. Delicate or not, a field of soybeans was worth three times a field of corn. And growing one year of soybeans would replenish the nitrogen in the soil and yield a better crop of corn in the years to come.

Murphy was never much good at math, but it didn't take a genius to look in the newspaper and see corn futures trading at $3.49 per bushel and soybeans at $9.54 and 6/8 per bushel, and know which crop made more sense from a profit standpoint. It was one big three-hundred-acre lottery ticket as far as he was concerned, except this time, if he worked hard, the odds were in his favor. Murphy and his family would be done with struggling. No more of his wife doing laundry for other people. No more of the shame of driving around with a pickup truck that had two different-colored doors, and an inside window handle made out of an old pair of locking pliers.

The risk was there. It was a long pass on third down, but Murphy knew the payoff was victory. His family would be out from under the creditors and own their farm. He would leave a piece of something for his daughters when he passed on.

If it all went right—he might be able to send them to college.

Murphy cursed under his breath as the girls' mutt, Clutch, ran so close to his feet he almost tripped him up. He wasn't swearing at the dog so much as himself. He'd only petted the damn thing once and it had followed him around ever since. He swore he'd never make that mistake again. A few people around town assumed that the dog was named for Murphy's renowned ability to come through in a pinch during his glory days of high school football. The reality was much simpler and far less glorious. A few winters back, the little station wagon Macy was driving at the time needed a new clutch. The girls wanted a dog for Christmas. Murphy wanted to do the practical thing, but lost out. The girls asked him to name the dog and his little inside joke stuck.

Murphy turned on the center pivot and watched the water cascade out across his soybeans. He was counting the money and imagining the new clothes he'd buy for the girls, the new roof he could put on the barn, when the day's dose of humility brought him back down to Earth. One of the wheels on the center pivot tower had a flat tire. Murphy found a piece of metal wedged in the tread and had to hitch all the way back to his toolshed for some needle-nose pliers. When he yanked it out, he saw it was an old rusted three-sided nail. It was a forged nail, at least two hundred years old. Whoever owned this farm in the 1700s had probably made it. He'd probably been out plowing this field and his horse had thrown a shoe. A regular Joe would have found the shoe and hung it up for good luck. Murphy's Law dictated that he got the nail and had to change the tire on his sprinkler.

Murphy rolled the new tire out into the field. It was an awkward affair because of his uneven gait and the eighty-pound hydraulic jack he had slung over his shoulders like a battle-ax. When Murphy had gone shopping for a new jack to use on the farm, he spared no expense. He might need it to hoist up a thirty-ton combine. And anything capable of holding up thirty tons had to be made out of heavy, tempered steel.

Whenever Murphy got some momentum, the tire would outpace him, then veer off to the side and flop over. He remembered running down the road behind tires as a little kid and keeping them upright with a stick. *The playthings of poor people.* Murphy wondered what it would be like to run again, to feel the wind moving across his ears, getting louder and louder as his feet pumped in a staccato rhythm. He wished he could experience that feeling again—that natural rush of the wind against his face—then squashed the thought. He needed to save his wishes for more important things. Like survival.

"Need a hand?" someone called from above like the disembodied voice of some nerdy God.

Murphy was on his back, covered in sweat and axle grease, the sun bright in his eyes.

A shadow fell over him. He saw a pair of pale twigs their owner called legs stuck out from under a government-issue postal uniform. Murphy recognized the legs and the voice. It was Todd White, the mailman.

"No," Murphy answered, wondering what Todd possibly thought he could do to help him. The guy weighed a buck-thirty tops, and that was soaking wet. Murphy followed up with a "What's going on?" He was a little irked that Todd didn't just stuff the mail in the box and move on. "Kind of got my hands full here. Can you just leave it on the porch?"

Murphy pulled himself up on the sprinkler, then turned the jack handle and listened to the satisfying hiss as it dropped the replacement wheel to the ground.

"No. I actually need an autograph. Certified Mail," Todd said, thrusting a clipboard in his direction.

Murphy ignored it, tightening the lug nuts on the new wheel. Todd waited, taking in the field. "No rush. You know, people said you were crazy for growing soybeans out here. But they look good to me!"

Lugs tightened, Murphy stood up and wiped his sweaty brow on the back of his sleeve. He held out his greasy hands for the clipboard. Todd made a face at the dirt Murphy was getting on his pen and clean paperwork, but satisfied with the greasy signature, he handed Murphy an ominous-looking envelope. Murphy stared at the *Final Notice* stamped on it in red ink and then stuffed it in his back pocket. He didn't need to open it. He knew what was inside.

"Everything all right?" Todd asked.

"Fine," Murphy snapped in a mind-your-own-business tone of voice. "Just put the rest on the porch."

Todd hesitated, staring back at the Murphy house, nervous. "Is, uh, Sasha around?"

Murphy stared at him. Sasha might be his daughters' babysitter and godmother, but Murphy would be damned if he was her keeper. "She took the girls to the park. Why?"

"I just. I, you know. I got her mail, too. I figured. You know, I could kill two birds with one stone…"

"Christ, Todd. The door's not locked, just put it inside on the table for her," Murphy said as he grunted and moved the newly mobile sprinkler to the next row of plants.

"No, that's okay. I have to loop back around on my route anyway. I'll just pop by later on…"

Murphy stared up at the sun, then down at the lengthening shadows all around him. It had taken him longer to change the tire than he anticipated. Pangs of fear stabbed at his belly as he grabbed Todd's skinny arm and pulled it toward him so he could check the time on Todd's calculator watch.

"Dammit. I'm gonna be late," Murphy said, dropping Todd's arm.

Todd followed Murphy as he lurched back toward the house to clean up, carrying the flat tire over his shoulder. Murphy kicked the lever and turned the irrigation system back on. It sputtered to life, showering the soybeans. As water settled on the plants, it pooled in places, then beaded off. Rivulets dripped off the sprinkler down onto the heavy- gauge steel of Murphy's hydraulic jack. It lay between the rows, glazed with rain. Forgotten.

Chapter 9

IT WAS EIGHTY-SEVEN miles to Celina, but Murphy made it in an hour. He'd cheated, using the red light on his truck dash to ignore a few speed limits on the way there. It was one of the advantages of being a volunteer fireman.

Downtown Dayton traffic was mercifully light and Murphy was a mere five minutes late. As he drove his rusted-out 1977 Chevy Silverado into the parking lot full of shiny newer Hondas, Nissans, and Toyotas, he felt out of place. A smattering of BMWs and Mercedes added insult to injury.

He hefted his withered leg out of the truck and sensed a few furtive stares from the line of people waiting at the ATM.

Don't worry. It's not contagious.

A guy coming out of the bank nearly fell over himself trying to open the door for Murphy. The pity turned his stomach. It was why his "Handicapped" sign for the rear-view mirror was at the bottom of his glove compartment, still in the envelope it was mailed to him in over a decade ago. Another wary stare of sympathy greeted him in the vestibule.

Murphy couldn't blame them. Old Lefty Simms was the only cripple in Coldwater before Murphy came along, and he remembered pestering his mom with questions. "What happened to his arm?"

"Farming accident," Ma had said, and left it at that, though the truth was much more grisly. He'd gotten a log caught in his combine blade and had reached in to pull it out without shutting off the machine. When he moved the log, the machine lurched and took his arm in with it.

"Was he right- or left-handed before his accident?" young Murphy had pressed her after passing Lefty on the street, mystified.

"Doesn't much matter what he was before," Ma replied, matter of fact.

It mattered to young Murphy. He had climbed up the Tessier's silo as a boy and fallen off the barn roof. Broke his right hand. Had to relearn everything with his left while it healed—a series of trials that had made him ambidextrous. He couldn't throw the long bomb with his weaker hand, but he could pull off a good screen or pitch with left or right, which meant he could roll out comfortably in either direction.

Still can't stop thinking about football.

As he limped into the bank lobby, he regretted wearing the mothballed coat and Sasha's grandfather's polyester tie. No one else had a tie on. Most of the customers were in jeans and T-shirts. He felt like he was trying too hard and it showed. He hated banks. He hated suits. He hated money. And he certainly hated looking like a hayseed in a worn-out corduroy blazer carrying a leaky rhubarb pie.

Murphy smiled at the pretty blonde desk clerk who greeted him.

She didn't return the courtesy.

"Here to see Frank," Murphy said, trying to remain upbeat. "Sorry I'm late."

"Have a seat," she mumbled as she stood and disappeared into a back office.

Murphy remained standing. He didn't like to sit in public, because he couldn't bend his leg and it stuck out in front of him like a three-and-a-half-foot sore thumb. As he scanned the bank, embarrassed to be alive, he saw a cardboard cutout by the tellers' windows that made him feel even worse. It was Mr. Big Time himself—Chris Hall, number 86, in a Chicago Bears uniform.

A cartoon bubble sprouting from his mouth announced *Fidelity Bank: Whether you're small town, big time, or both!*

Murphy choked back a laugh. Chris Hall had gotten his millions and disappeared from Ohio so fast that people speculated he must have left a body buried somewhere. He'd been back a couple of times for photo ops, or with reporters delving into his roots. He'd shown up on Murphy's porch with some Tom Slick type from *Sports Illustrated* who was doing a roots piece on the old team. Murphy had sneaked out the back door.

As the door slammed again in Murphy's mind, a skinny man in a shiny suit smoothed his gelled hair and approached Murphy. This guy was tan in November, had a hawk face, and wore a thinly veiled look of disdain. At least he was wearing a tie.

"Mr. Murphy? I'm Phil Pepper."

Murphy shook his hand. It was soft, like a woman's. This guy had never done a real day of work in his life. "Where's Frank?"

"Frank's not with the bank anymore."

"Oh?"

"I've taken over your account, Mr. Murphy. Follow me."

Murphy hitched into his office—what was supposed to be Frank's office—and his stomach sank. The room was bare, with the ghostly outlines of the family photos Frank had on the wall the only remnant of him ever having existed.

"Where's Frank?" Murphy asked again, unable to contain his apprehension.

"I'm afraid Frank isn't with Fidelity anymore. Have a seat."

Murphy knew that people only used "I'm afraid…" when the response was something unhelpful. In other words, he was screwed. He sat down to find the chair too close to the desk to accommodate his leg, so he turned at an angle to give himself more room. It made the confrontation uncomfortable. Football and life were all about angles. It could mean the difference between being tackled and making a touchdown. And in this situation, Pepper had the angle on Murphy.

Murphy realized he was still holding Macy's pie in his hand. He had to explain it or it would be too awkward. "My wife. My wife baked a pie for Frank. It's good. If you want it…" Pepper subtly recoiled. "Thank you. But I don't eat pie."

Who the hell doesn't eat pie?

"Are you able to make a payment today, Mr. Murphy?"

"Payment? No. Frank said we could work out a forbearance or do a fixed-rate mortgage. We filled out all the paperwork." Murphy juggled the pie as he reached for the folder Macy had given him. It was sticky with rhubarb juice.

Pepper took the folder with the tips of his fingers and opened it. He glanced over the contents and clearly found them inadequate. He looked up at Murphy. "So you can't pay anything today?"

"No, sir. I'm a farmer. I can't pay anything until my crops come in."

Pepper sighed, and then his spidery fingers began to click across his computer's keyboard at an escalating pace.

"My wife and I bought the place in pretty bad shape. It came with a lot of old equipment that kept giving out. You've heard of Murphy's Law? Whatever can go wrong, will? Well, my last name's Murphy, so you can imagine…" Murphy said, pasting on a fake smile at the end.

Damn, he hated this. He felt like there was always a path to victory—and that finding it rested on his own shoulders. Win or lose, it would be on him. So the thought that his life actually depended on a skinny twenty-something punk just out of some fancy college, or some credit report, or some bozos on Wall Street, sickened Murphy.

"We can't do a mortgage adjustment in your case, Mr. Murphy. The property isn't worth enough. If you can't make a payment today, we're going to have to call in your loan."

"What do you mean, 'call in my loan'?" Murphy asked. The room seemed to get quieter as adrenaline filled his ears with the beating of his frightened heart.

"Your loan had an acceleration clause. If you miss three payments, the entire amount of the loan comes due. I'm sorry, Mr.

Murphy, but we'll have to foreclose."

Murphy wanted to reach across the table, grab Pepper's tie, and pull it until his eyes popped out of his head.

"Foreclose? But I just need a little time until my crops come in. A few weeks at the most and I'll be able to pay everything I owe you and then some," Murphy pleaded.

"You're already over a hundred and twenty days late on your payments, Mr. Murphy. I can't do anything. And to tell you the truth, based on your credit history, this loan should never have been approved in the first place."

"If you shut me down, my crops are gonna spoil and you're going to *lose* money. If you give me a few weeks to bring in my beans, you'll get *all* your money, plus interest!"

"I'm sorry, Mr. Murphy. There's nothing I can do."

"Then let me talk to someone who can do something!" Murphy said as he stood up, slamming his rock of a fist onto the desk so hard that Pepper's pencils rattled.

Fear crept into the weasel's face as he pushed a button on his phone. Murphy saw the security guard making his way toward them from across the lobby.

"Listen, I work for a living. I'm not asking for a goddamn bailout like the one your company got when you spent all your money! I'm just asking for three more weeks!"

Pepper stood up, stepping back from his desk. "I'm sorry, Mr. Murphy," he said, still flustered, as the door opened and the bank security guard, a stocky black man about Murphy's age, with graying temples, stepped in.

"You got to go, man," the guard said, almost apologetically.

"If you can raise a significant sum before we get any offers, we might be able to take another look," Pepper added, like a consolation prize, as Murphy was led away.

Murphy started for the door and then doubled back without warning. Pepper flinched and the security guard nearly drew his gun, both assuming Murphy was going to take a swing. He didn't. But he'd be damned if he was going to leave his wife's rhubarb pie behind with this butt clown. He slam-dunked it into the trashcan on his way out the door.

The people lined up at the tellers' windows all stared at Murphy as he stormed toward the exit, his brace creaking and clacking, the security guard in his wake.

"Eight hundred billion we gave these idiots! They can't give me three weeks!" Murphy yelled as he hitched across the lobby, wanting to spit in Hall's cardboard face.

As they got outside, out of earshot of the other employees, the security guard spoke up. "Don't sweat that prick, Murphy. He has no idea who he's dealing with. "

Murphy was surprised anyone would so cavalierly disparage his employer, especially in this economy. "Excuse me?" Murphy said.

"Earl Morris. I was strong safety for Mater Dei in '89. You smoked us in the playoffs."

Murphy stared at him and imagined fewer wrinkles and a face mask. "Number seventy-seven," Murphy nodded.

A broad smile broke out across the guard's face. Murphy had just made his year.

"How the hell'd you remember that?"

"They switched you to cornerback. You intercepted me in the first quarter."

"That's right. Damn. That's right!"

"I never forget a screw-up," Murphy said, then paused, afraid he'd have to clarify that he meant his own mistake, not the man standing in front of him. There was no need—Morris was still basking in the best football player of his generation recalling not only his number but also the greatest moment of his own sports career.

"I was proud to pull that ball down. You didn't throw many picks."

"I threw a strike. Hall ran the wrong pattern," Murphy said, businesslike.

Morris broke into laughter. Even crippled, twenty years later, Murphy was still as competitive as ever.

"Must be hard seeing your old buddy as a piece of cardboard making millions. He wasn't half as good as you," Morris added.

"Yeah, well he's better than me now," Murphy said as he struggled to start his old truck. The engine finally kicked over.

The shock of the whole situation was settling into his bones. Not only did he not get the loan, he'd barked in the face of the one man who might be able to help him.

"Don't sweat it, Murphy! You'll find a way to win! You always did!" Morris yelled as Murphy backed out of the parking lot.

That was football, buddy. This is life.

Murphy was about to lose everything. And there wasn't a damn thing he could do about it.

Chapter 10

MURPHY CARRIED KRISTA, AND Jamie took his hand as they climbed the stairs to the second floor. He opened the door to the attic and a garden of dusty football trophies emerged from the shadows. Murphy didn't say anything but he saw both girls stare in fascination. To them, these were solid-gold treasures and more desirable because they were off-limits. Murphy redirected their attention to the stacks of old board games on a shelf right inside the door. The games were classics—most had belonged to Murphy as a kid, and all were in pristine condition. He had grown up an only child of a hard-working mother and had learned to care for the few things he had.

"Okay, ladies," Murphy said as he pointed to the games. "Pick your poison."

"Monopoly!" Jamie said without hesitation.

"Life!" Krista shot back and they started to bicker.

Murphy scanned the row of old games. Life. Operation. Monopoly. He decided he'd had enough of all three for a lifetime. He grabbed an old deck of playing cards from next to the Yahtzee box.

"How about Go Fish?" he asked, and that seemed to settle it.

Chapter 11

MACY WAS ALREADY OUTSIDE when Murphy pulled up to the motel. Her shift had ended a while ago, and she was still in her maid's uniform, hugging herself to keep warm. Despite being left out in the November weather for twenty minutes, she still had a smile for Murphy.

"Sorry I'm late. I fell asleep with the girls."

"Everything all right?"

They'd been married for almost twenty years and he knew there wasn't much she couldn't tell about him with a single look.

"Yeah. It's fine," Murphy said, hitching out of the truck to grab the trash bags at her feet. They'd drop them by the dump on the way home, getting what they could back for the effort from the bottles and cans that Macy had already separated out from the rest.

"How'd the bank meeting go?" she asked, searching his face.

"Fine," Murphy lied. "Gave him the paperwork. He didn't think there would be a problem."

Murphy lurched back to the truck, and held the door open for her. It was an old habit.

Macy smiled, bobbed in a mock curtsy, and stepped in. He gave her a playful pinch on the butt, making her blush. "Scotty!"

"Best part of opening your door," he said.

Macy slid over and buckled in the middle of the seat, putting her head on Murphy's shoulder when he got in. He hated lying to her, and rarely did it on account of how terrible he was at it, but the bank was his problem, his mess, and he was going to clean it up. No sense in worrying her about it. Nothing she could do, anyway.

Murphy slowed down at the illuminated stop sign at the center of town and hit the brakes as he heard what sounded like thunder coming up on his right. It was the finest motorcar ever to grace the streets of Coldwater—a fire-engine red Porsche 911 GT3.

That particular color and model of automotive perfection was his dream car, and had been since he was a boy. He'd had the poster tacked up on his wall, right between Joe Montana and Cheryl Tiegs, and went to sleep dreaming about it every night.

Someone stole my damn car. Murphy knew exactly who it was.

"Oh, my God," Macy exclaimed, bouncing a little in her seat. "Look who it is!"

The Porsche slowed, and then ran the light, stopping right in front of Murphy's truck. The door glided open like the wing of an expensive, German-made metal bird.

God wasn't happy with a wink. Now he wants to rub my nose in it.

Murphy watched Chris Hall get out of the car, slide down his eight-hundred-dollar sunglasses, and hold out his arms wide, like he wanted to hug Murphy's whole truck. He was wearing his old Coldwater High School letter jacket. It clung to his body tightly, he had filled out since high school. *Steroids?* Regardless, he looked like a movie star. A few million dollars a year will do that to you.

"Scotty! Get out here, bro! Now!" The saw-toothed grin that Murphy had been so familiar with growing up had been replaced by perfect, pearl-white teeth.

As much as Murphy wanted to throw the truck in reverse and peel away, he couldn't. *Might as well get it over with.*

"Hey, Hall," Murphy said as he climbed out, embarrassed. People at the gas station across the street were staring. This was the last thing he needed.

"'Hey, Hall? What the hell is that, man? How the hell are you?" Hall pulled Murphy into a rough man hug.

"Hi, Scotty."

He knew that voice. Murphy looked over Hall's shoulder

and saw the old love of his life, his little high school cheerleader sweetheart, all grown up. Jenny was even more beautiful than he remembered, and carried herself like someone who spent a lot of time in front of a camera. Her good side was always facing you. *Did she even have a bad side?* She was lithe, blonde, and when she was eighteen, she used to bang his brains out. She was always, even then, the kind of woman with a shrewd business sense. Murphy knew she was at least half the reason why Hall was more than just a football player—he was a commodity.

Murphy's mother hadn't liked football; had known nothing about colleges, recruiting, or scholarships. Jenny had provided Murphy with all kinds of advice and counsel during that difficult decision period, finally settling on Ohio State.

"Hey, Scotty," Jenny said again as she walked over.

Murphy nodded to her. He could tell that it pained her to see him almost as much as it pained him to see her, but for different reasons.

"Jenny." Murphy wanted to leave it at that.

"You guys are back for the big game, aren't you?" Macy asked. "That is so great! I don't watch a lot of football, Chris…but Jenny, I see your newscasts on Jack Greenway's satellite TV every Wednesday night at bingo. If you guys are in town for a while, you could come by the house…"

Jenny tossed Macy a condescending glance hidden behind a megawatt smile. "Thanks, Marcie. That's sweet."

"Macy," Murphy jumped in. "Her name is Macy."

"Right, Macy! Sorry. We meet so many people, you'd think I'd be better with names…"

Murphy knew Jenny well enough to know she called her Marcie on purpose. She was too calculated to make a mistake like that. And it pissed him off.

Murphy and Jenny stared at each other for a long beat, and then she smiled at him, like a cat, amused by his ire. Tension hung in the air, the same kind of tension that caused them to fight so much and screw so hard in high school. He hoped it made Hall uncomfortable. Even crippled, Murphy was still a lion.

Hall cut in. "I send you tickets, man. Fifty-yard line. You never come up!"

"Yeah, unfortunately, I work for a living," Murphy replied.

"What? You still down at the plant? I'll talk to your boss, sign a jersey or a football or something…"

"I don't have a boss. I'm farming now," Murphy said, rankled by the fact that Hall seemed to have forgotten the plant had closed down three years ago.

"You're a farmer?" Jenny was incredulous.

"Really?" Hall chimed in.

"He's a great farmer," Macy said, all sincerity and pride. "Soybeans!"

"Nothing to brag about. But we get by," Murphy added, remembering his family was days, if not hours, away from losing everything.

"Listen, man. I rented a tour bus! After this halftime thing on Saturday, I was going to load it up with anyone from the old team wants to come up to Cincinnati. Take a day off, man. Come watch us play the Bengals. Got a block of fifty-yard-line seats, hotel rooms, all of it, so you guys had better come!" Hall said.

"Wow, that sounds fun," Macy said.

The casual mention of a taking a day off rung in Murphy's ears.

I'll take "Things a Millionaire Would Say" for two hundred, please, Alex.

"Yeah, it's too bad we won't be able to make it." Murphy hitched over to open Macy's door. "Come on, Mace. The girls are waiting."

Hall wouldn't quit. "That's right, we heard you had some little ones. We might go there someday."

Jenny shot Hall a glare.

Murphy knew Jenny had never been interested in kids. They pulled focus. He closed Macy's door and hitched back to his side.

"Nice seeing you," Murphy said, getting in. *Good riddance.*

"We're gonna see you at the game tomorrow, right?" Hall added, confused.

"Not me. I'm on call at the station."

"Come on, Murphy! Coach said it was covered. The whole team's gonna be there."

Murphy backed up his truck and pulled around the Porsche.

Macy waved apologetically.

"We're meeting at the DQ after the game if you change your mind!" Hall yelled.

When Hell freezes over.

Murphy accelerated away from the intersection, hoping those two were out of his life for at least another twenty years.

Chapter 12

TWO DAYS AGO, MURPHY hadn't been sure if the ache in his chest he felt whenever he thought of Jenny was actually gone, or he had just gotten used to it in the same way he'd grown numb to the constant dull ache coming from the tattered remnants of his left leg.

Now, he was quite sure it was neither. It was more like a scab. And seeing Jenny downtown had just peeled the damn thing off. He hated himself for still being so caught up in her. He hated thinking about her when he was with the mother of his children. It wasn't fair to Macy.

Murphy didn't even understand *why* he still thought about Jenny. She didn't deserve his consideration. She'd left him when he was *crippled*. Right when he needed her most. She'd made a good show of it, dropping by the hospital for the first few weeks. But he could see it in her face every time she came to visit and he was still bedridden. The visits became phone calls, the phone calls became letters, and the letters became holiday cards. And then there was that final late-night telephone conversation when she'd called him Chris instead of Scotty. When you learn the love of your life is cheating on you at the same moment you learn your best friend has betrayed you, it's like losing two loves at once. Murphy had sworn a long time ago that he would never forgive either of them.

Macy was used to his brooding but she wasn't going to let him do it the whole way home. When they turned down the old state highway, she broke the silence. "I thought you'd be excited to see them. You all were so close in high school."

"High school was twenty years ago, Mace." Murphy tried to tune something in on the radio that might shut her up. Thinking about it was one thing. He was damned if he was gonna talk about it or be psychoanalyzed.

"I just think it would be good for you to catch up," she pressed on.

"Good for what? To talk about me getting laid off when the plant closed? Or good so they can come by and see the holes in the kitchen walls and the plastic tarp we're using for a window?" Murphy shot back angrily. Their house was the worst kind of construction zone, the kind where the contractor had run out of money and all that was left were half-things done and half-done things. Skeletons of lost optimism.

"Scotty. If they want to see holes in the wall or plastic on the windows, they don't need to be in the kitchen. We have that right on the porch." Macy smiled at him.

Murphy couldn't help but laugh. Macy had no shame. In a good way. Where Murphy looked at their house and saw failure, she saw hope.

"She called you Marcie, Macy. Twice. I got nothing to say to them," Murphy added, hoping that would be the end of it.

"It's nothing personal. She's just jealous."

"Jealous?" Murphy snorted, incredulous. *God, I love you, Macy.*

"I took her boyfriend. The best man in Coldwater," Macy said, squeezing his bicep.

Murphy shrugged his shoulder to push her off. Macy was just trying to make him feel better. Jenny had dumped him like a hot rock the second it was clear he'd never throw another touchdown. She wasn't jealous; she was condescending. And that made the fact that he couldn't stop thinking about her even worse.

"It's okay to talk about this stuff, honey," Macy added.

"Talk about what? There's nothing to talk about."

"What? Aren't you a little mad they're together?" Macy inquired.

Murphy shifted his shoulders in discomfort. Macy wasn't book smart, but her emotional intelligence was off the charts. It was one of the things Murphy loved about her, although it freaked him out sometimes. She wasn't exactly psychic, but he always felt like his heart was an open book. He just didn't want her to read too much. She might get hurt.

"No. I could care less." Murphy lied, doing his best to look disinterested.

"Well, if I saw my high school flame with my best friend, I'd feel a little weird."

"You would?" Murphy asked, taking note of the glimmer in her eye.

"Yeah, you know. Wonder about what might have been," she added.

"Who the hell was your high school flame?" he demanded, instantly jealous.

Macy smiled at his ire. It was genuine.

"What are you gonna do? Meet him at the bike racks after school?"

"Maybe. He still live in town?" Murphy fished, failing in his attempt to be nonchalant.

"Wouldn't you like to know?" Macy teased, giving him what he called her "secret smile." It was as close to a mischievous grin someone as sweet as Macy could get and Murphy loved it. It reminded him of the poker faces their little girls tried to put on when he played Go Fish with them. Murphy was sure of one thing in the universe, and that was that his wife loved him. This knowledge had kept his demons at bay for almost twenty years and it was precious to him and worth protecting.

"So who the hell is this chump?" Murphy said, spirits lifted, as his hand crept across the seat to give Macy's knee a horse bite. Her laughter was high and lilting.

"Hey. We weren't Class Couple like you and Jenny were or anything, but if I hadn't fallen for you when you were laid up at the hospital, who knows?"

Murphy stared off into the distance, slowing the truck as they passed an Amish horse and buggy. He wondered if she thought about this guy as much as he did about Jenny.

Chapter 13

MURPHY SLEPT ON TOP of the covers in his clothes, as usual. If a fire call came in, it took him too long to deal with his brace to get dressed. At least that was the excuse he'd been using; Murphy and Macy hadn't made love for almost eight months.

Women seem to have a crazy notion that coital droughts have something to do with them. They don't. But those thoughts make a woman feel less sexy, which in turn makes her less sexy, which only compounds the issue.

Murphy and Macy's lack of physical intimacy had nothing to do with her, of course, but he'd never bring that up, because she'd never believe it and the mere fact that he'd brought it up would, in her mind, instantly make it true. So he just avoided the subject altogether.

Murphy wasn't a scientist, and didn't understand emotion very well, but he was, at age eighteen, the alpha male of an entire town. He was familiar with the dynamic of men and their role in a pack. Sex led to children, children led to responsibility. Mouths to feed. Which was a good thing if you were the alpha male. You wanted sex. You wanted mouths to feed. You wanted to conquer the world. The alpha male was the rainmaker, the breadwinner, and the playmaker. He was the winner. He won, therefore he could provide. He could provide, therefore he deserved to make love to his wife. If men were hard-wired to believe sex was free to any loser, and not just the gift for the hunter who has returned from the long hunt able to feed his family, then the human race would have ceased to exist a long time ago. Mankind would have just hung out in caves and had sex and babies without being able to feed them and that would have been the end of it.

That was Murphy's theory, anyway.

And right now, Murphy found himself squarely on the other side of that equation—he was not a provider. He was squeaking by. And as he lay there, staring at the ceiling, worrying about bills, his stress was compounded by knowing he wasn't making love to his wife, and that wasn't making her feel good, which meant he was being even more of a failure at taking care of his family.

He heard Macy's rhythmic breathing as she snuggled up against him in the comforter, content. He had almost drifted to sleep when the bedroom door creaked open.

"Daddy," Krista pleaded.

Murphy's eyes snapped open; he was fully alert. The tones on his pager hadn't gone off, but he was already sitting up. Something wasn't right.

He wiped the sleep fog from his face and turned on the light. His little girls stood in the doorway. Krista was wearing that damn football jersey again, and Jamie had on one of his old T-shirts, hanging down to her knees. They were shivering.

"Can we come sleep with you? It's c-c-cold," Krista finished, teeth chattering. Murphy could almost see their breath.

He craned his head over toward the windows, as terror filled his gut.

Tiny crystals of frost covered the lower third of the panes. Last night's soft rain had turned into ice.

"No! NO!"

Murphy ignored Macy. He leapt out of bed and hitched past the girls, taking the stairs three and four at a time. He burst out of the back door and stared at his 387 acres of hope. His heart broke.

Icicles hung from the sprinklers and a glassy sheen covered his entire soybean crop as far as he could see. Every plant was encased in ice. It was the agricultural equivalent of a horror movie.

The entire field...

Murphy ran to a bush and grabbed a branch. He yanked it off. The ice crackled and he felt the bean.

...frozen.

"What? Scotty? What's wrong?" Macy called from the porch.

"They're frozen. The whole goddamned field is frozen!"

Murphy threw the plant in frustration. He imagined all the farmers who had clucked their tongues and sucked their teeth when he answered their question of "What you planting?" with "Soybeans." He remembered the blank stare Red Robinson at Robinson Tractor gave him when he asked him to have a new blade put on the combine—a blade for cutting and threshing soybean plants. Coach Hand's words rang in his head. "Coldwater is corn country, son. Beans don't grow worth piss in this valley."

Macy's voice and her hand on his elbow brought him back to the present.

"It's okay, honey. Look! The sun is coming up. They'll thaw."

"It's too late, Macy. They already froze. If we don't harvest them in the next twenty-four hours, they'll rot on the bush."

"Okay. So we harvest them now. What's so bad about that?"

"We'll get twenty, thirty percent less..." Murphy trailed off. *Thirty percent less...a month early...* Murphy realized this little act of God could save them. He could harvest now. Suffer a significant loss, but get the crop in, in time to pay off the bank and keep the farm.

Murphy's Law might save his ass, for once.

"I'm gonna call Red. See if the combine is ready. If it's not, we're done."

"If it's not ready, he can get it ready. How long can it take to put a blade on?"

"It takes a crew of three men two or three days, Macy. " Murphy had worked for Robinson Tractor during the summers to pay for football camp, he knew first hand.

"Let me get the girls dressed, I'll come with you."

Murphy started to protest, but realized if the combine was

ready, he didn't want to waste any time figuring out what to do with the truck. He just wanted to jump in the combine, start up the engine, and drive it to the farm.

He stalked into the house and Macy followed him into the kitchen. He rifled through the junk on the counter, looking for his cell phone like he was robbing the place and angry about it.

"Scotty, you need to calm down, honey. Have some faith."

"I don't need faith right now, Macy. I need a goddamn soy combine."

Chapter 14

"YOU ARE ONE LUCKY son of a bitch, Murphy," Red Robinson said as he shuffled into his shop. "That there is the only soy combine in this part of the state. Freeze hit everybody—I already had three calls for it. Some poor son of a bitch offered me twenty grand for it for a half day."

Red talked as he watched his coffee cup spinning inside the little microwave at the back of his cluttered shop. He was a burly man, a lot older than Murphy, but the stocky son of a bitch could crush a beer can in his hand like he was crumpling a piece of paper. An old Model T, halfway through restoration, and tons of old junk—antiques, or "mantiques," as Red liked to call them: old gas pumps, farm tools, and the like—littered the shop. Red had never set foot on a train, let alone conducted one, but he always wore a blue-and-white-striped engineer's cap, covered with grease.

"Me and my guys just finished putting that damn thing on last night, for Chrissakes. We put it on early so we could hit Cincinnati for the Bengals game. You hear? Hall rented a damn tour bus! With air conditioning. The S-O-B has more money than he knows what to do with, huh?"

"Yeah, Red. We gonna sit and B.S., or are you gonna give me the keys?" Murphy said impatiently.

Red ignored him. "Come on, it's a twenty-six-foot header. I'll have Chard park the off-loader right on your property and you'll be done before the sun goes down. Hell, you can probably make the game." Red looked at him, arching an eyebrow.

"I'm watching the station," Murphy said.

Red snorted and let out his trademarked five-second "bullshit." "Bu-ull shi-it, come on. Get your ass down to the football field or I'm gonna toss these combine keys out into Potter's field!"

"Red. This is my life here. The last thing on my mind right now is a stupid football game."

"Hey. If it weren't for that football game, this combine wouldn't be ready. Remember that."

The microwave beeped and Red swung the door open, nodding for Murphy to look inside. "See that?"

"You heated your coffee. Congratulations."

"Not the coffee. The handle. Look. It's perfectly facing me. Fifty-seven seconds. Perfect temperature, and the little tray turns around just enough times that I don't have to mess around reaching back for the handle—it's always facing me."

Red grabbed the cup, savoring his coffee, and dropped the keys in Murphy's hand.

"That's great, Red. You should write a book on microwaving coffee."

"I should!" Red shot back. "Get to that football game, you crusty old bastard!"

Murphy turned and hitched to the combine sitting out back. He waved at Macy and the girls as they pulled away in the truck, his mood lifting as he climbed up into the cab. He almost smiled as the engine purred to life. Almost.

Chapter 15

MURPHY SAT IN THE cockpit of the John Deere 9550, looking out at the uniformly spaced thirty-eight-inch rows of soybeans. Even rotting and covered with ice, they were beautiful. He spun the wheel and lined the combine's 220 head up with the plants, feeling better than he had in months. Even sixty percent of his field would make them enough money to keep the bank at bay.

The combine is so named because it combines the tasks of harvesting, threshing, and cleaning crops. What used to take three passes and three different machines was now done in one pass of one machine. The only waste left behind on the field was the chopped remains of the stems and leaves.

The cockpit was temperature-controlled and as comfortable as a first-class airplane seat. Or so Murphy had been told. He'd never flown first class in his life, and didn't plan to.

The spinning combine blades tore into his crop. They plucked, chopped, cut, and separated the soybeans with ruthless efficiency. The beans went into the storage bay at the back of the truck, and then the waste was spit out behind the combine and laid flat.

Fertilizer for next year. His spirits lifted. He was going to be on this farm for a while.

He couldn't wait to waltz into Pepper's office with that big fat check. See the look on his lizard lips. *Hell, maybe I should wait and buy my own farm back at a discount!* That would show those sons of bitches.

Murphy didn't like to gamble. But he was happy to take risks. He saw them as two entirely different things. A gamble was something you had no control over—putting money down on the flip of a coin, or the turn of a playing card. That was downright idiotic and he would have no part in it. But a risk, a risk was going for it on fourth and eighteen. It's what made him great on the football field. And in this case, he felt like he had real control.

The sun was behind him, or he might have noticed the glint of metal between the rows sooner. When he did see it, he reacted as quickly as he could—but it was too late.

The thresher blade spun down and caught the upturned hydraulic jack handle, picked it up, and spun it backward into the cutting blades.

Sparks flew and the whole combine shuddered. The blades snapped and shards of metal flew up toward Murphy inside the cockpit, spider-webbing the glass. The handle spun into the auger and was sucked up and dragged along the length of the entire blade. He hadn't just destroyed the header. The entire combine was destroyed.

Murphy sat in the cockpit, staring at a sharp piece of metal half embedded in the glass. Another few inches and it would have pierced his abdomen, ending his money problems forever.

Chapter 16

MURPHY PULLED INTO ROBINSON'S, a piece of the mangled blade in the back of his pickup truck. The place was, as he expected, deserted. A poster announcing *Go Cavaliers!* hung in the window, the Coldwater equivalent of a "closed" sign.

Murphy ignored it and walked in the door. It wasn't locked, and even if it was, he'd worked there enough summers to know the key was under the seat of a rusted-out International Harvester tractor near the door.

Pinned on the bulletin board was a list of every combine dealership in the state. Murphy called each one and confirmed that he had just trashed the only available soybean combine in Ohio, Indiana, and western Kentucky. Anyone who had a soy combine didn't have it anymore, and a quick glance at the newspaper headline told him why: "Early Freeze Threatens U.S. Soybean Crop."

The newspapers knew about it before he did! The fact that some pencil-necked geek in a cubicle had time to write an article about Murphy's life being ruined before he even realized it made him want to throw up.

He cursed Red and his crew for going to a stupid football game when his entire life was falling apart, but it was an empty curse. Even if the whole staff had been here, ready with a brand-new blade, it would still take days to put it on.

He drove home. Numb. For the second time in his life, Murphy was about to lose everything.

Back at the farm, he threw his keys on the kitchen counter and leaned against the fridge, nauseated. He stared out the window at his beans. He could see the water bleeding off them. His life, their future, was rotting away right before his eyes.

He stared over at the calendar. Three weeks from harvest. He'd gotten within three weeks of winning at something after all these years of losing and it had been taken from him.

Murphy punched the wall. Failure rose up from inside his stomach and pooled inside his chest cavity, aching like a future heart attack.

His mind raced. He was on the field. Five seconds left. Three hundred eighty-seven acres to go and down by a few hundred thousand—what the hell was he going to do? How was he going to come up with that kind of money?

The date circled in red on the calendar mocked him. "The best-laid plans," or whatever that book he'd had to read in high school said. Mocked by the cosmos. Once again, God had cursed his very existence and refused to give him one goddamn break.

He'd been in plenty of these situations and won. Hell, he'd scored three touchdowns in forty-five seconds against Defiance. He'd scored from his own fifteen-yard line on a bootleg option in the last three seconds of a game against Lima Central. He'd thrown a sixty-five-yard pass against New Bremen that was so improbable that a local sportswriter blasphemed an entire religion and the sport of football by wanting to rechristen the famous Hail Mary pass the "Hail Murphy."

But that was football.

Murphy scanned his kitchen like the quarterback he'd once been—the little red lights racing across the police scanner, the kids' drawings, the yellowing ultrasounds that had given his oldest daughter her nickname, "The Bean," because of what she looked like in those first few weeks of her existence. He was looking for an out. Anything that might give him a small piece of hope right now.

His eyes raked to his usual source of joy, the red circle for the harvest marked on the calendar. It now provoked only feelings of failure. As his eyes bored a hole in the calendar, the advertisement running across the bottom of each page caught his eye.

Fireman's Fund Life Insurance

Life insurance. It was the one perk of doing a dangerous job for no pay. At the very least, they wanted to make sure if you kicked the bucket while you were doing it, your family would be taken care of.

Pierson's voice echoed in his head: *We're worth a lot dead, Murphy.*

They called it "buying the farm" for a reason. The life insurance was more than enough to pay for the farm and save his family.

Now all he had to do was die.

Chapter 17

MURPHY'S DARK REVERIE WAS broken by the timpani of stocking feet racing down the stairs and the voices of his daughters, caught in mid-argument.

"I get it!"

"Mom gave it to me!"

"Get off!"

"You already got in trouble for it!"

"It's my turn!"

Macy's weary voice followed after them, "Krista. Jamie. Settle down."

But the ruckus continued until his two little girls ran into the kitchen, and stopped cold, surprised to see him and afraid they were about to get yelled at.

The prize they were fighting over was the last football jersey Scott Murphy had ever worn. They wouldn't know from looking at it, but the brown stains along the bottom weren't mud; they were Murphy's blood. It had never washed out.

"She took your jersey out! She asked Mom for it!" Jamie tattled. Fearing Murphy's wrath, they both now wanted nothing to do with the old shirt.

"They want to wear it to the game today. For the halftime ceremony," Macy said defensively, walking in behind them.

"That one's a little big. Why don't you wear it?" Murphy suggested.

Macy did a double take. "Me?"

"Yeah. My mom kept some peewee ones that the girls can wear. They're packed up in my football junk in the attic." Murphy knelt down to tie his daughter's Barbie shoe and caught sight of her pink heart sock peeking through the purple rubber soles. He wondered how a little girl could wear out a pair of shoes, and then remembered that they had belonged to Krista first. Murphy's face flushed in shame that his youngest daughter had never had a new piece of clothing. They'd never been able to afford it. It pained him to think about his kids going without. Murphy had been poor his whole life. He wasn't embarrassed about being poor. He could wear the same clothes, drive the same truck, and kiss the same wife the rest of his life and he'd be satisfied. What killed him about being broke was not being able to take care of the people he loved. It made him understand why people robbed banks.

Macy followed—stunned, but happy. "You found another harvester!"

"Yep…in Huber Heights. They got it on a flatbed headed this way. It's all taken care of, honey. You and the girls got nothing to worry about. You just go to the game and have fun," Murphy said, only half lying.

Next week, his wife could buy both girls new shoes.

Chapter 18

MURPHY HEFTED HIS DAUGHTERS, one on each heap, even though the extra weight shot a shiver of pain through his leg at every step.

This is it. This is goodbye.

When he got to the end of the driveway, he drew his wife in for a family hug.

Each of his women wore one of his old number 13 football jerseys. It was something that would have made him squeamish before, like sending a triple shot of bad luck out into the world, but in this instance, he knew his luck had turned. He had one final play he could run that guaranteed a victory.

Murphy kissed Macy's forehead, drinking in the smell of her sun-freckled skin. He did the same to Krista and Jamie's towheaded curls and then handed them off to their mother as Sasha pulled up in her minivan.

"You sure you don't want us to stay here and help with the harvest?" Macy inquired, in a manner that made Murphy suspect her intuition might be kicking in.

"It's a one-man job, Mace. And someone has to go represent me at the game. Right?"

She didn't seem convinced.

"Besides, I have to watch the scanner. At least until the guys from Huber Heights get here with the combine," Murphy added.

Sasha honked the horn, and that seemed to seal it for Macy.

"Okay. But you're gonna meet us after the game?" Macy questioned, hopeful.

"Yeah. I'll meet you guys at the diner after for the party." Murphy hadn't lied this much since high school. And he'd never told this many tall ones to his wife.

Whatever he'd said had worked, because in a few moments he was kissing her goodbye on the cheek and waving to his little girls as they drove away.

Murphy wasn't sure whether he had convinced Macy he was telling the truth about the harvester, or she was just so happy he was gonna come to the party afterwards that she wanted to leave before he changed his mind.

Either way, he didn't have to worry about being found out.

Chapter 19

THERE WAS SOMETHING HOLY about the Coldwater High football field. The stands were unimpressive and too small to accommodate even half the town's population, but they didn't need to, because the field itself was nestled in a small valley that formed a natural grass cathedral, surrounded by oaks and poplars, lush and green in the summer. In the early fall, it seemed as if the trees changed their colors to gold and red for the same reason everyone else in Coldwater did—to show their support for the gold-and-black Cavaliers.

The walk to the field from the high school was a bit like a caroler's journey to grandmother's house—over the river and through the woods. And then it came upon you. It was a meadow in a bowl, as if God had sculpted the very plains around this spot for the sole purpose of playing the game of football.

The McCann paving company had a rock quarry on one side of one hill, just beyond the graveyard. Murphy drove his truck through their lot and parked on the bluff overlooking the football field so he could watch the action from a distance. He had seen enough dead bodies as a volunteer fireman to know what people looked like after asphyxiation, so he'd chosen this spot because he knew the first person to find him would be one of the workers at the gravel pit, not his wife or any woman or kid.

It didn't take Murphy long to figure out how he would off himself. He breathed his answer every day he drove his battered old

Chevy pickup. His mother had bought it for him, fully restored, during his senior year of high school. The thought rankled Murphy now. She couldn't afford that truck. Murphy felt the sting of shame that he had let her buy it and his cheeks flushed. There she was, driving that piece-of-crap yellow Pinto to and from the mental hospital, working extra shifts so he could drive a fancy new truck to and from a high school that was within walking distance of their house. And it wasn't like his mother bought into the football-star-who-was-gonna-be-making-millions hype, either. She was always like that. Giving him more than she could afford for as long as he could remember. Sacrificing until the day she died so he could have nice things. It wasn't until years later that he had the self-insight to realize that he was cut from the same cloth. Here he was, preparing to kill himself to provide for his own family. Maybe it was genetic.

You were right, Ma. This truck is going to take care of me.

A fallow cornfield stretched over the horizon, with the lights and uprights of the football field visible just over it. Murphy could hear the echo of the drums and the crowd. He squinted to see the scoreboard as his mind wandered back to his own days of glory, when his mom would park her battered Pinto up by the radio tower so she could hear the game on the radio and see the lights, but not have to deal with the violence or watch boys slam into her only son.

It won't be long now.

Murphy backed his pickup into the steep embankment so it would clog his old tailpipe and send the carbon monoxide in through the rusted floorboards of the cab. It was probably overkill, since the exhaust system already leaked so much, even without a clogged tailpipe. Murphy had been driving around in the winter with the windows down for the last three years because the exhaust kicked such heavy fumes into the cab and he knew how bad the stuff was to breathe. Blue smoke wafted up and grew thicker as he rolled up the windows. The passenger-side window was no big deal; it still had a handle. He struggled a little with the driver's side since the handle was long gone. The Vice-Grips that had replaced it were a pain to turn, despite having worn a circle in the vinyl door upholstery a long time ago.

Murphy tapped the Mr. Football medal on his rear-view mirror and watched it move like a pendulum, slowly twirling so he could see both sides.

The medal had been shiny once. Just like Murphy.

He remembered how proud he had been to receive it. Every sportswriter in Ohio had voted him the "Most Outstanding Football Player" in the state his senior year. From that day on, for the next decade, he'd been called "Mr. Football" as often as, if not more than, he'd been called by the name on his birth certificate. Hall and some other outsiders still used the moniker, mostly out of pity or cluelessness, but most everyone in Coldwater had quit ten years ago after Murphy almost knocked Mitch Jacobson out for yelling it in his ear a little too loud at the Moose Lodge social.

Murphy had scrawled a little goodbye note for Macy and the girls and tucked it under the windshield wiper. It was just three words long, but they were significant to Murphy and he knew they would be to his wife, as well. In all the years they'd been married, Murphy had never uttered them. In fact, he'd never uttered those three words to anyone—not his mom, not Coach, not Jenny, not anyone he really cared about. His mom was a Yankee, born in the woods of Maine, raised on a farm in Connecticut, and married to an Irish farm boy. They didn't say, "I love you." They just did it. But because he wasn't going to be able to do it much longer, Murphy reckoned he should write it down once in case Macy hadn't gotten the message in the almost twenty years they'd been together. He also couldn't think of what the hell else to write—goodbye seemed redundant.

As the gas clouded in around him, he felt his eyelids flutter. He let his gaze follow the medal as it swayed. Dots of rain were still hitting the windshield, but it had let up a bit. Not enough to matter for him, but it was just something Murphy noticed as he sat there, waiting to die.

People think suicide nullifies a life insurance policy. It doesn't.

But most policies have a two-year suicide clause. You have to have had the coverage for a certain amount of time for it to be valid. That way people can't just take out insurance on Wednesday and off themselves on Thursday. After two years and a day, you can kill away.

The blue smoke roiled up from the floor, filling the cab. Murphy had shoddy valve seals on his truck, which meant oil was leaking into his engine and burning, which was the reason he could actually see his exhaust. It smelled bad, it was nasty to breathe, but burning oil wouldn't kill him. That was the job of the carbon monoxide—invisible, odorless, and colorless. And it was somewhere inside that blue smoke, seeping into Murphy's body, slowing squeezing out all the oxygen. Brain cells were dying and he was starting to get a headache.

Murphy's eyelids grew heavy. His body started to slump in the seat. The drums of the marching band and cadence of the cheerleaders echoed across the valley. *There she was, still in his head after all these years. Jenny.* Murphy had often wondered if he would ever get over her, and here he was, mere minutes from death, and he feared the answer was no. She was the one relationship in his life where he hadn't been quite prepared when the end came.

Murphy hadn't loved many people in his life, and when he did, he did it all out. He tried to examine what he felt, though he was no psychiatrist. He likened a relationship to two trees intertwining their roots. If you had some time to untangle them, a breakup would be a lot easier. But hell, Jenny just chopped off the roots and went and replanted herself somewhere else—with his best friend, Chris Hall. It had ripped him apart.

The rest of his life started to blur now. The candy striper with the cute smile who came by his room every day of rehab, long after all the other well-wishers stopped. Murphy had never met a more compassionate woman in all his life and he loved her for it. Hell, he'd married her for it. He was just never fully able to let go of Jenny. That haunted him even now. The mother of his children deserved a hell of a lot better than that.

"Coldwater six-five, this is Celina. We have an eleven-eighty at the school. Do you read me? An eleven-eighty at the high school, back parking lot."

Murphy's eyes snapped open. A fire call.

Killing himself was one thing, but the thought of someone needing help and not getting it on account of Murphy being dead was inexcusable. Even sitting forward in the seat was a Herculean task, and Murphy barely managed it. He fumbled for the CB, but had been without oxygen long enough now that the world was muddled and his brain wasn't quite connecting with the rest of his body. His hands overshot and knocked the CB off its cradle and onto the floor—lost in the blue fog.

The call came through again: *"Coldwater six-five, this is an emergency."*

Murphy lunged for the door, pawing desperately for the makeshift window handle. He got a hold of it, but when he yanked, the pliers popped off instead of turning.

God... no.

As the world closed in toward death, a final rush of chemicals to his brain provided Murphy with some clarity. It was in this moment of *not* wanting to die that he realized it was all a big mistake. *I want to live.* Just before he passed out for good, Murphy knew that killing himself was hands-down the stupidest thing he'd ever done.

Chapter 20

IT WAS ODD. MURPHY could feel his body, but couldn't tell where he was. It was like he'd been buried in a snow bank and had no idea which way was up. When he tried to open his eyes, they squinted shut in protest. He realized he was on his back, and a soft, bright light was shining on his face.

His sense of smell kicked in first. It wasn't exhaust. Or the oil and manure odor he associated with his truck. It was different— slightly chemical but sweet. It was something he hadn't encountered in a long time, something vaguely medicinal. A pang flashed through his chest as he thought about the long months and the many operations he had endured in the hospital after he had been crippled.

No. This smell wasn't antiseptic.

But it was very familiar and hard to place at first: it was new car smell.

What else would Heaven smell like?

You killed yourself, you idiot. Why would you make the cut for the Pearly Gates?

If he wasn't in his truck, he was either at the hospital or dead. He forced his eyes open and sat up, fully awake. He was inside a truck...but it wasn't his truck. For one thing, it didn't have Vice-Grips for a window handle. For another, it was brand-new. The odometer only had 216 miles on it. The seats, the chrome, everything gleamed.

But it looked so familiar.

Then he realized that the eternal dull ache that he called a leg wasn't there. He reached down. His brace was gone. And the withered and twisted length of scarred bone and sinew had been replaced with a real leg. Muscular. With a working knee.

Holy crap! I am in Heaven.

He tried to look outside, but the windows were fogged up.

Maybe I did make the cut.

Tap. Tap. Tap. A shadow bounced on the window and Murphy jumped, frightened. "Scotty!" a young voice shouted.

Scotty? Hardly anyone called him that anymore. God has a sense of humor.

Murphy wiped a patch in the sheen of condensation that covered the windows and peered out—he recognized that face.

Chris Hall.

What the hell was he doing here?

Chapter 21

"WHAT'S GOING ON?" MURPHY asked as he got out of the truck. The door glided shut behind him; none of the usual creaks or groans in protest like his old crap-heap. Murphy stared back at the truck. It was gleaming. Pristine. It was brand damn new.

Murphy didn't linger to admire because his blood started to boil. "I don't know what's going on, but if you bought me this, I don't want it. My old truck was fine, I don't need any charity from you."

"Dude. Are you drunk?" Hall asked. He sounded genuinely concerned.

As Murphy's eyes adjusted to the brightness, he got a good look at Hall. He was still wearing his letter jacket, just as Murphy remembered from their encounter downtown a few hours ago, but something was...different. He seemed agitated and...younger. As Murphy took a closer look at Hall, he realized what it was. There was not a wrinkle on his entire face. And almost as striking—he had a damn mullet haircut.

What the hell is going on?

Murphy peered into the side-view mirror of his truck and was awestruck. His own face was as smooth as Hall's. The day's worth of stubble he usually wore between shaves was gone, the gray hair with it. The teardrop scar on his right cheek he'd gotten in a bar fight in Dayton had vanished, as well. As if it never happened. Just like his leg.

Please don't let Hall be Saint Peter. Make Saint Peter be somebody I don't hate.

"Come on, man. Hurry up or we're gonna be late!"

Murphy didn't get it. What the hell was there to be late for in the afterlife?

"Late? Late for what?"

Just then, a bell rang. Murphy looked up to see the red doors of Coldwater High School burst open. Kids streamed out. Hall dragged Murphy by his coat sleeve toward the school and Murphy almost stumbled as he followed, unused to two fully operational legs.

"Hey, Scotty!" a pretty girl chirped as she walked by him. She looked familiar. Wendy something. Couldn't remember her first name. From high school. But Murphy had an odd feeling he had seen her somewhere more recently.

The bank.

She was the receptionist at the bank. When he went for his meeting, she had acted like she wouldn't spit on him if he were on fire, but now she looked like she'd do anything he wanted with him under the bleachers right now.

"Hey, Murphy!" a freshman in braces called out.

Wherever the hell he was, everyone was sure happy to see him.

Though he had lived in Coldwater his whole life, he hadn't been back inside the high school or anywhere near the football field in almost twenty years. There was something strange about returning to a place you hadn't visited since your youth. The hallways seemed narrower, the ceilings lower. He hadn't grown, but it was as if his awareness had expanded to such a degree that his body would never fit into this space the same way again.

"Scott Murphy. Where have you been?"

Murphy looked up and saw Jenny Cleary, curly blonde hair bouncing in the sunlight as she sauntered down the steps to greet him. She had a scowl on her face, but still looked beautiful.

Even pissed off, she is effing gorgeous.

"If you are going to skip sixth period, at least tell me. I was waiting for you outside Mr. Donahue's room like an idiot!"

Murphy stared at her, a big goofy grin spreading across his face. She was angry, sure, but underneath it he saw something else entirely. She returned his smile and reached around him, shoving her hips into his.

"Grrr. Why can't I stay mad at you?" A devilish smile illuminated her face, revealing two rows of perfect white teeth. She kissed him flat on the lips.

Murphy blinked, stunned. Something about it felt right, but Hall…she was married to Hall. Murphy felt a jealous tug on his sleeve. It was Hall—pulling him away into the school.

"You guys make me sick! Come on."

Murphy tripped up the steps and followed Hall. Before the door shut behind him, he turned to give Jenny one last look and saw her hair glowing in the sunlight. She was, by every definition, a vision. And she was looking right at Scotty with love in her eyes.

"Am I dead or what?" Murphy asked.

"We're both dead if you don't hurry up!" Hall shot back.

Murphy crept down the empty hallway after him, tentative, as if every door Hall opened might be the one leading to the mouth of Hell. He had, after all, committed suicide, and although he had stopped going to services at St. Sebastian's with his mother after the accident, he was Irish enough to know that killing yourself would land you downstairs instead of up.

Murphy stared at the dust particles riding the sunlight across the hallway and onto the trophy case. Inside was a shrine to his youthful achievements.

Murphy followed Hall across the Coldwater High School gym floor, under the basketball hoop, and down a narrow cinderblock corridor. Murphy's steps faltered as he realized where they were going. Hall reached up to touch a hand-carved wooden sign above the door: *Attitude Is Everything*. The sign was worn down from two decades of hands repeating this gesture.

Murphy couldn't help but do the same as he crossed the threshold. It was tradition. And it was the only way you were allowed to walk into the Coldwater High School football locker room.

As Murphy entered, the oily-sweet smell of the training room liniment and the permanent bouquet of sweat and mustiness from the old lockers assaulted his senses. He saw Pierson, buck-naked, a six-pack where his beer belly used to be, taping up his hands like a boxer getting ready for a fight. Pierson glared at Murphy as he walked into the locker room. Murphy stared at Pierson in awe. He was so skinny. So young. And a glance down told him more than he wanted to know.

"What? What the hell are you looking at, Murphy?"

"You're *skinny*. And you have both balls…" Murphy was too stunned to be tactful.

The veins on Pierson's temples pulsed and he blushed red, pulling up his jock.

"Yeah, Murphy. We'll see how skinny I am when I smash your dick in practice! I don't care what color your jersey is, I'm gonna put you on your ass!"

Winton and Gig grabbed Pierson to hold him back.

Murphy blinked. He'd never seen Pierson so mean. Or so angry. At least not that he could remember. Hall tugged on Murphy's shirt, dragging him across the locker room.

"Dude. Come on. Stop starting trouble and let's get dressed."

Murphy turned toward Hall's tug and found himself face to face with a familiar battered locker, the number thirteen and his name scrawled on a piece of masking tape at the top of it.

As he opened the locker door, a cloud shifted, and sunlight came in through the low windows of the basement room and bounced off the shell of his battle-scarred football helmet. He lifted it off the hook, not believing it could be real, and held it out in front of him, staring at it like Hamlet surveying Yorick's skull—as if contemplating the very nature of his existence. Murphy had never been much of a thinker, and this experience was beyond anything he could wrap his mind around. He had never been much of a spiritual man, either, so he couldn't even wrap his heart around this one.

Maybe this is Heaven.

He smiled. As much as he'd avoided football during the last twenty years, it wasn't for the reasons everyone thought. It wasn't because he hated it on account of his injury; it was because football had been the first love of his life and he couldn't bear to just sit and watch it without participating. Murphy knew for sure that if he went to Heaven, there would be football involved.

A clipboard smacked the bench behind him. He looked back and caught Coach Hand glaring at him, shaking his head. "You gonna stand there all day or put your damn pads on?"

Murphy wasn't sure if Heaven allowed cussing or not, but figured it probably wouldn't feel the same without Coach around.

"Sure thing, Coach," Murphy said as he pulled out his number 13 jersey and turned it over in his hands. He immediately felt a twinge of loss. The last time he had seen this jersey, Macy had been wearing it as he said goodbye to her. He wondered what she was doing right now. *Probably at my funeral.*

"Mr. Greenway said you weren't in math class today," Coach continued, as Murphy pulled off his shirt, still so confused.

"No," Murphy snorted with a smile. "I wasn't anywhere near class today."

"Is this funny to you, Scott? Because it's not funny to me!"

The room fell silent. The players gave them a wide berth as Coach laid into Murphy. "I know you've got one foot out of this town, and I know most people around here only care about what you do on Friday nights, but I'm not one of them! I want you to leave here a man who's good more than one day a week. So if you miss another class, I'll bench you. I don't care if I have to play a freshman quarterback in the state championship, I'll do it!"

State championship?

Murphy stared at Coach. He could barely cope with where he was. He lost his breath as he understood *when* he was.

"We play Versailles this week?"

Coach Hand set his jaw and for a moment Murphy thought he

might reach out and hit him. He settled for slamming his clipboard into the corner of the locker door. The metal part flew off and clattered against the tile floor, making a few kids jump out of the way. Coach got in Murphy's face. "Is this a joke to you? You might not care about this town because you think you've got it made, but this place is important to me. Do you understand? This game is important to me!"

Murphy blinked, sobered by the old man's passion. He remembered it now. But that was twenty years ago.

Coach stared at him. Seeing Murphy's confusion, he crumpled, suddenly looking every one of his fifty-six years. When he spoke again, his voice was hoarse. Raspy. "Do you have a problem with the fact that I expect more from you than you expect from yourself? And dammit, son, this is your game. Your team. Your hometown. It should mean something to you, too."

He turned and walked out of the locker room and Murphy felt the eyes of every player on him. And not one of them was happy. Even Hall just stared and shook his head. "Come on, Murph. Chill out. We've only got four more practices. Don't give him a heart attack before the big game."

Murphy pulled his pads over his head, calculating. Four more practices and a game on Friday. That meant this was Monday: less than a week before the biggest day of his life; less than a week before the worst moment of his life.

The other players recovered, dressed in a rush, and then hustled out to the field. As Pierson, now a hulk in heavy pads, passed by, he slammed his fist on the locker next to Murphy. *Wham!*

"Come on! If you're late, Coach is gonna make us run suicides!" Pierson said, pissed.

Suicides. Murphy had no trouble remembering Coach's version of the act. Run to the twenty-five yard line, then back, then turn around and run to the fifty, then back to the other twenty-five, then back, then end zone to end zone. It amounted to a five-hundred-yard sprint and usually ended ugly. Puking. Passing out. Or even worse: another round.

Murphy sped up the pace with which he got dressed. He'd had enough suicide for one day. And if this wasn't heaven...and wasn't hell...then maybe it was another chance. A chance to play the game and do it right. Not get injured. Go to college. Play in the NFL. Have the life he was *supposed* to live before he got injured.

How many times had he wished for this? More than he could count.

Maybe that's what Heaven is. Getting your wish.

Chapter 22

MURPHY HEARD THE SATISFYING crunch of his cleats in the crushed rock beneath his feet. Here he was, walking down the narrow gravel road that led from the parking lot, past the concession stand, and into a little clearing in the surrounding woods—the Coldwater High School football field. Just past the graveyard, he could see the spot where he thought he'd last parked his old truck. It was nowhere to be seen.

"This is crazy," he muttered under his breath. Dreams didn't last this long. He never remembered smelling fresh-cut grass in a dream. Or feeling gnats flying around his neck.

Murphy watched, amazed, as the team ran suicides back and forth across the field. Coach Hand finally noticed him and blew his whistle. "Wonderful. Our quarterback has decided to join us. Let's go, ladies. Line it up!"

The team glared at Murphy as they stopped running, hands hitting knees as they tried to catch their breath.

"I didn't say rest. I said line it up!" Coach yelled and the team hustled into three distinct groups. The second-stringers and the bench-warmers, led by Gig, went toward the sidelines as the defense and offense paired up, facing each other at the line of scrimmage.

"Red Twenty-four, let's run it," Coach said to Murphy as he walked by.

Murphy put his helmet on, and fumbled to fasten his chinstrap. It had been a while.

"Red Twenty-four?" Murphy asked, scanning through his memory bank.

"Red Twenty-four!" Coach yelled back, giving him a hard smack on the helmet. "Let's go!"

"Is that Rodriguez in the slot?" Murphy whispered to Hall.

"That's not funny man," Hall said, pushing him away.

As Murphy moved behind Winton, the center, he put in his mouthpiece and tested his bum leg. He was half afraid it would give out on him and he would wake up crippled again.

The team was ready and itching to play. Like racehorses held in the starting gate for too long, they kept shifting, restless. Murphy was hesitant, his mind racing. It all felt so goddamn real.

Winton put his head down and looked back up at Murphy from between his own legs, his hand resting heavily on the ball. "Come on, Murphy. Geez."

Murphy stepped behind him and knelt in an awkward, lopsided squat. He had almost all his weight on his right leg, still favoring his once-crippled left, although it seemed okay so far.

"Twenty-four…" his voice cracked and trailed off in a high-pitched squeak. He had a frog in his throat. Murphy's hands felt clammy. Pierson and a few of the other defensemen tittered.

"Funny you should talk about missing balls, Squeaky!" Pierson yelled from across the line of scrimmage. Murphy noticed Pierson wasn't in his usual spot—and wasn't wearing his usual jersey, either. He had on number 54. Murphy realized he was playing Washington. The guy who broke Murphy's leg. Versailles' Goliath.

Murphy understood why his voice had cracked. This had been his dream for twenty years. And now that it was about to come true—he was scared out of his mind. His face turned red from embarrassment. Pierson gave a satisfied smile, probably thinking it was because of his taunt, but in fact it was Murphy cursing himself for being afraid. He cleared his throat and began again, getting his rhythm back. "Twenty-four! Red! Red! Red! Hut!"

Murphy moved his hands as Winton jacked the ball up from the grass into them. He started back into his five-step drop and found himself immediately off balance because all of his weight was on his right leg. It cost him.

Pierson flew across the line like a charging bull, coming to clean Murphy's clock. *Wham!*

He barreled into Murphy, hammered him hard, and brought him down. His helmet flew off and rolled across the grass.

Pierson jumped up, elated. He started to do a victory dance. He'd just accomplished something he'd never done before. He'd sacked Scott Murphy. In the thousands of times he'd tried since they started high school, he'd never been able to do it. This was cause for celebration. "I got him! I got him! I told you, man! I told you I'd get you one of these days, Murphy! Yes! Suck on *those* balls, Murphy. *Both of them.*" Pierson leapt over him and looked down.

Murphy struggled to breathe. Pierson's shoulder pad had gone right up into his sternum and—like a three-hundred-pound Heimlich maneuver—forced every bit of air out of his lungs. And now Murphy was gasping like a fish, trying to draw air into the vacuum left behind by the force of the blow.

He rolled over onto his back and yanked off his helmet.

Damn, that hurt.

"You okay, son?" Coach Hand looked down on him, face flushed with fatherly solicitude. Pierson and some of the other players leaned into his field of vision.

"Oh no, no, no. Oh no…dude. *Dude.* Are you okay?" Pierson said, ghost white. Though in high school there was no love lost between him and Murphy, the team didn't stand a chance on Friday without him.

"Nice job, Pierson. Dumb ass," Rodriguez said, looking down on Murphy.

Hall leaned over him, blocking out the sun. "You all right, man?"

"Wind…knocked…" was all Murphy could choke out.

Coach Hand pushed his way into the scrum. "He's in a red jersey for a reason, Pierson."

"He didn't move. He usually moves." Pierson was scared now.

Murphy lifted his head up, and then dropped it back to the grass, woozy.

"What the hell is wrong with you? You do remember how to play football, don't you?" Coach asked Murphy as he helped haul him to his feet.

"It's been a while, Coach," Murphy said as he struggled to stand, still wobbly.

Moments later, Murphy was back behind the center, yelling out his cadence again. His head was still ringing, but he had real pain to worry about this time, and he tried not to favor his left leg so much. "Set! Hut! Go!"

Winton snapped it. Murphy started his seven-step drop a moment too early, and bobbled the ball. He had to stop to get his hands around the pigskin and saw the large shape of the number 54 jersey coming at him like a freight train. A memory or a thought—some kind of recollection of his final game—flashed through his mind and like a shell-shocked soldier, Murphy froze.

Pierson pulled up short and grabbed Murphy's jersey, thrusting him back six yards. Murphy didn't go down, he just stared at the number on Pierson's chest.

He remembered his leg snapping.

"Dude. What is *wrong* with you?" Pierson asked, genuinely concerned now.

Coach Hand blew his whistle and came over in a rage.

"What the hell was that, Pierson? You gonna pull up like that against Versailles?" Coach Hand pushed past Pierson toward Murphy.

"And you! What the hell are you doing, son? You're a rushing quarterback! If he comes in, you run! You move back from the line like a crippled goat and you won't last two downs on Friday night!"

Murphy felt anger flare up at the word "crippled."

Coach Hand grabbed Murphy's face mask and held it in place so Murphy had to meet his gaze. "Look at me, son. I don't know where your head's at right now. But you'd better get it here, on the field, or you're in for a world of hurt."

Coach Hand reached for the thin red mesh tank top that was over Murphy's practice jersey. The red shirt was a signal to the defense to use kid gloves and not tackle the quarterback so he wouldn't get injured before a big game.

But Coach Hand was from the old school. And he'd practically raised Scott Murphy and knew he was the second-most pigheaded man in Mercer County—Coach being the first. By removing the red jersey that was meant to spare Murphy tackles, it meant, essentially, that it was open season on Scott Murphy.

"He does that again, Pierson, you put him on his ass. Hard. Anybody gets to Scott Murphy on this play. Put him on his ass, you understand me?" Coach yelled to the entire defense. They all yelled "Yes, sir" back.

Murphy stepped behind Winton, sinking the nerves fluttering up in his chest down into his stomach. It was something he'd learned to do as a kid to help him focus. The world got quiet as he let his mind still and his senses take over.

"Set! Hut! Go!"

Murphy's seven-step drop was fluid, his footwork immaculate. Pierson charged across the line and Murphy danced to the right— he barely seemed to move, but it was so quick and so graceful that he sent Pierson grabbing air and then eating grass as he sprawled onto the turf.

Murphy read the coverage and saw Hall had Rodriguez beat deep. He rolled right and let it go.

The ball soared out of his hand in a perfect spiral and dropped right into Hall's fingers. He didn't even have to break a sweat as he stepped into the end zone.

Touchdown.

A smile broke across Murphy's face. He'd forgotten how good that felt.

"Let's do it again!" Murphy shouted to no one in particular.

The next few hours were a blur for Murphy. He was a kid on a playground. Running, juking, and jumping. He was alive for the first time in twenty years.

Mom was right. Youth is wasted on the young.

When Coach blew the whistle to end practice, Murphy's disappointment at it being over was tempered by the happiest thought he had had in some time. *I am in heaven.*

After practice, Murphy hung back with Coach Hand to help him collect the equipment. As he watched Coach gather the extra balls into a net, Murphy couldn't help thinking he looked like a fisherman on a sea of grass. He was so much younger than Murphy was used to, but somehow that made Murphy feel the old man's mortality more than ever.

"Hey, Coach. Can I ask you something?" Murphy handed him the last game ball.

"No, I don't know if the damn game is gonna be on TV. Stop bugging me," Coach replied tiredly as he cinched up the net of balls and slung it over his shoulder.

"No, it's not that." Murphy already knew it was going to be on TV. He'd be haunted by the game highlights for twenty years to come. "I was wondering if you ever had a dream that you were young again."

Coach Hand laughed, surprised at such a philosophical question from a kid who only cared about money, girls, and football.

"Almost every night."

"What if it wasn't a dream? What if it was real?" Murphy asked.

"That would be something…" Coach Hand replied, still not taking him seriously.

Murphy stepped in front of his coach, forcing him to stop. He saw for the first time that Murphy was dead serious—he wanted an answer.

"This is real, right?" Murphy went on, "You're here. I'm here. We're both standing here?" Murphy searched Coach's eyes and then reached up to squeeze the man's shoulder like it was a four-pack of

Charmin.

Coach stared at him, incredulous.

"Son. Don't make me start testing for drugs. Not before the biggest game this town has ever played." Coach clucked his tongue in concerned disgust and walked off.

A grin broke across Murphy's face. That was exactly what the real Coach Hand would say.

Maybe I'm not in Heaven. Maybe this is real.

Maybe it's a second chance.

Chapter 23

MURPHY CROSSED THE PARKING lot back toward the locker room, walking alone, helmet off, his mind abuzz. He had a strange feeling as he did so, kind of like the bad feelings his mom used to get sometimes. Hers were usually right, but she didn't like to call them premonitions or psychic intuitions. She was too practical for that nonsense. In her mind, memory kind of worked both ways, but it was just a hell of a lot easier to remember the past than it was the future. She thought the feelings usually came just before something that was really gonna change your life forever. Something so strong, you couldn't forget it, even if it hadn't happened yet.

Murphy knew the exact moment in time that his life had changed for the worse. It was less than a week away. And he wasn't sure he could do anything about it. He didn't think that was what he was feeling right now, but he was troubled by one aspect of all this. He still didn't know if what he was experiencing was a road trip or a roller-coaster ride. You can steer a car wherever you want on a road trip, you can decide to go to the Grand Canyon or Niagara Falls if you want. A roller coaster is different. All you can do is hang on tight.

Murphy hated roller coasters. They didn't let you choose your destiny. And besides that, he'd already done the "crippled guy who can't pay his bills" ride once, and he for damn sure didn't want to do it again.

The marching band was spread out in the parking lot, gearing up, tuning their instruments, and getting ready to take the field.

Murphy had so much on his mind—and so little interest in the band—that he would not have given any of them a second glance if it weren't for the loud clatter of a stack of instruments falling over like dominos.

He caught the last of the instrument cases as it skidded across the pavement and couldn't help but notice something familiar about this symphony of klutz. There, at the center of it, was a rosy-cheeked cherub, all smiles.

Murphy stopped in his tracks.

That band geek in braces and overalls was his future wife. She was just seventeen, but he'd recognize those green eyes anywhere. She had none of the wear in her face he was accustomed to, but her smile seemed to come just as easily as ever.

"Sorry!" she exclaimed.

Those dimples.

She began restacking the instrument cases. "I've got it. Don't worry!" she assured him as she backed away from the stack. It held.

"See…" she said as she backpedaled into a tuba case. It crashed down onto a trumpet case, and then sent a flute case skidding across the parking lot into a stack of drums. They thumped to the ground in a heap and the bass drum rolled in a circle like the runaway wheel of an old metal tractor.

"Sorry!" she said again as she fumbled to pick it all up.

Murphy smiled at her goofiness. Her spark. Her internal joy. He had never known her in high school—well, actually, that wasn't true. Everyone knew everyone in Coldwater. He'd never *noticed* her in high school. Not really. But now, standing on two good legs in the band parking lot, sweaty in his football uniform from two hours of doing what he loved most, he couldn't help but fall in love with Macy all over again. For the first time. She was so innocent and so awkward, so cute and so kind. Captivating.

"Macy!" Murphy's shout cut through the air and everyone stopped what they were doing. The tuning stopped. The cleanup stopped. Time stopped.

Everyone else drifted out of existence for a moment as Murphy and Macy locked eyes across the parking lot and something hovered in the space between them. A timeless recognition. For a brief instant, she wasn't looking at Scott Murphy, the disagreeable cocky quarterback—she was staring into the eyes, heart, and soul of her husband of twenty years.

As quickly as the connection was made, it disappeared again into the ether. Anything that had passed between them, any memory of past or future, withered away, replaced by the hard reality of high school. He was the most popular kid in Coldwater. She was a nerd who did 4-H and played clarinet in the band. The Scott Murphy she knew would never shout her name to proclaim timeless love. The kid she knew would only shout her name to make fun of her for being a klutz, or in anger at her for disturbing his walk to the locker room. Macy's face flushed with embarrassment as the world started to turn again and she knelt down to collect the instruments.

Murphy never took his eyes off her.

"Come on, man! Let's get inside while there's still hot water," Hall said, tugging on Murphy's jersey, wondering why the hell he was staring at some dorky band geek when he could be in the parking lot, putting his hand up the shirt of the prettiest girl in five counties.

Murphy stole one more glance back just before Hall pulled him into the locker room. Macy was talking intimately with some guy wearing a tuba.

Murphy felt a stab of jealousy hit him in the midsection. *Was that her high school flame?* He was surprised at how much he cared about Macy. The thought of her with another man made him crazy. And the thought that the thought of her with another man made him crazy, made him even *crazier*.

But that wasn't the most troubling thing. He couldn't get the way she had looked at him out of his mind. She wasn't like every other girl in the school. They all seemed to cast adoring stares in his direction, just like he remembered. But Macy was different. He had known his wife long enough to catalog all of her moods—he could decipher all of her expressions. And though this was one he hadn't seen very often, he was dead sure of what it meant. And he was flabbergasted.

Macy Edwards, his future wife, hated his guts.

Chapter 24

MURPHY STOOD, TEETH CHATTERING, under the ice-cold water.

"What the hell are you doing, man?" Hall asked through the steam coming from his shower across the room. "We still got hot water!"

"I thought it might wake me up," Murphy responded, turning the handle to hot and smiling like a Cheshire cat as the water turned warm.

It's real. I'm really here.

Murphy ran his hands down his chiseled midsection, admiring his youth.

Nothing hairy or marshmallow about this body.

"You okay, man? You've been acting weird all day," Hall said as he stared at Murphy.

"Yeah. I just forgot how good it felt."

"What? Touching yourself?"

"No. Being young. Playing football," Murphy clarified, soaping up.

"Yeah, well, you got your scholarship. You're on your way to getting millions of dollars to do it," Hall said, still clearly worried about his own prospects.

"I'd do it for free," Murphy said, matter of fact.

"Free? Come on, Murphy. The papers are calling you the six-million-dollar kid with the bionic arm. You're gonna be doing sneaker commercials. I'm just hoping to have a few scouts see me catch a few balls Friday night so I can get a scholarship somewhere."

"You'll get a good scholarship. Don't worry," Murphy added, knowing that Hall would get an offer from Ohio State and become a standout player there.

"I hope so," Hall said darkly as he shut off the water. "Because if I had to stay here in Coldwater the rest of my life, I'd freaking kill myself."

Murphy was haunted by the truth of this statement. He *had* been stuck in Coldwater the rest of his life. And he'd done that very thing.

Chapter 25

MURPHY GOT INTO HIS new truck and marveled as he turned the key and the V8 roared to life. The engine purred as he pulled it out of the school parking lot. He saw a familiar figure walking down the sidewalk, wearing a giant gray Jansport backpack. If he had any doubts as to the identity of said figure, they were dispelled by the name written in big marker on the back of the pack: TODD.

"Todd!" Murphy called out as he slowed to pull alongside him. "Hey!"

Todd White looked over, frightened, and pushed up his tinted tortoiseshell glasses as he sped up to avoid talking to Murphy.

"Hey man, slow down! You want a ride?" Murphy asked, sincere.

"The last time you offered me a ride, I ended up hanging in the girls' locker room by my underwear," Todd said, lisping slightly from the tiny rubber bands twisted into his braces.

Murphy vaguely remembered something about that. It had seemed like harmless fun at the time. And regardless, he didn't really know Todd well then. In the future, they would be fairly close. Almost friends, even.

"Come on, Todd. That was a long time ago."

"That was last Tuesday!" Todd scoffed, peeling off toward the school.

Murphy watched him, puzzling. His reverie was broken by a silky voice.

"Scott Murphy. Stop torturing dorks!" Jenny said with a smile as she climbed in the driver's side door. Murphy shifted uncomfortably as she climbed over him in a tangle of tight cheerleader shorts and tanned limbs. She was, just as he remembered, a dream.

"And why don't we talk about how great next year is going to be instead?"

Murphy smiled and started driving. He wondered again if he might be dead because here it was the middle of winter, but the sun was shining. He even swore he saw some wildflowers in the church field as he passed by it. He fidgeted as he drove, keeping one eye on the road and the other on Jenny, half afraid she might disappear.

Why was he so damn nervous? He realized this woman *intoxicated* him. He watched her manicured hand as it flew up and down while she talked, like a bejeweled bird fluttering out of his truck window. "My dad said Coach Cooper told the head of the Alumni Association that he was probably going to start you next year!" she said, ecstatic.

Murphy looked at her with a dumb smile. She was, quite possibly, the most beautiful woman he had ever seen. And she smelled *perfect*.

Maybe the injury was just a nightmare, and now I'm awake.

"That means no red-shirt year, Scotty. You can go pro early. I already worked out my schedule so I can graduate early with you. I'll get a TV job in whatever market you end up playing in. It's going to be so amazing." she spoke dreamily, excited about their future.

Murphy knew enough about what happened to Jenny to know she made good on all of it. The only difference: it wasn't with him. It was with his best friend. She sidled over to him, running her hand up the inside of his leg suggestively. The leg she chose to fondle happened to be the same leg he injured. It brought him back to reality, or as close to it as he could be in this surreal situation.

"What if something changes? What if I get hurt?" Murphy asked, eyeing her face sidelong like a cop interrogating a witness and waiting for the lie.

Jenny blew him off. "Don't talk like that. You're not going to get hurt. You're the best. No one can touch you." She ran her hand up to the center of his crotch. "Except me." Murphy jumped, blushing.

Jesus. She's eighteen and I'm pushing forty. And married. I can't do this.

Murphy cursed himself for being moral in this situation.

Either I'm dead or this is a dream. Either way, no reason I shouldn't enjoy myself.

"Scotty! You just passed my house!"

Murphy slammed on the brakes and his tires barked as he skidded to a halt. It had been a while. He backed down the street and angled his truck into the driveway of the large white Victorian. It was somewhere between a manor and a mansion. The ornate wooden porch and immaculately landscaped lawn were very different from Murphy's trailer in the weeds on the far side of town.

Murphy threw the truck into park as Jenny rubbed up against him like a cat.

"My parents aren't home right now," she said as she moved her hand back to his button fly. "And I know how tense you get before big games…" She smiled at him as she slithered beneath the seat, hands fumbling to undo his belt.

"No. Wait! Jenny. I can't…" Murphy said, cursing himself before the words were even out of his mouth. *Why the hell not?*

"Just relax…" she purred, digging deeper.

"Jenny…" Murphy's last protest was cut short by the honk of a horn. He looked over to see a long black Cadillac pull into the driveway next to him and stop. It was Jenny's dad, the big-city lawyer. Home early.

"Mr. Football!" he exclaimed, making Murphy almost jump out of his seat.

Murphy was speechless. Sputtering. Cold busted.

"Uh…hey. Um. Hey. Mr. Cleary," Murphy stuttered, wondering why the man seemed so cheerful, given the circumstances. He realized that Mr. Cleary couldn't see Jenny from his point of view—

just the blushing red face of Scott Murphy.

I'd shoot me if I were him.

"Where's my little girl?" he asked.

"Um. She just went inside," Murphy lied as Jenny stifled a giggle at his feet.

"Don't let her distract you, young man! Keep your mind on what's important! Football!" Mr. Cleary added, opening his garage with a clicker.

"I'll try," Murphy responded, doing his best not to flinch as Jenny buttoned his pants.

The car disappeared into the garage and as the door closed, Jenny popped back up, smiling like the devil.

"Wow. That was close. We'd better try something else, we don't have much time." She started digging down below again and Murphy stopped her.

"No. Jenny. I can't," Murphy said. "It's just..."

Just what, you moron? Just that you're twenty years older than her? Just that you're married? None of it makes sense.

"I get it," Jenny said. "You're right."

"I am?" Murphy replied.

"I know how superstitious you get before a big game. Save your energy. I can take care of myself." She leaned in suggestively, adding: "But after the game, you are mine!"

Murphy watched her back end strain against her tight cheerleading shorts as she walked away. He wasn't sure what troubled him more—Jenny's advances or his own refusals. Probably the latter, because he had a feeling they had nothing to do with him or Jenny. Here he was, staring at the finest piece of tail in Mercer County, and he couldn't get the band girl in the parking lot out of his head.

Son of a gun. I love my wife.

Murphy realized that if this wasn't a dream, things had just gotten very complicated.

"Hey," Jenny turned to yell as she reached her front door. "Don't forget to tell your mom about the recruiter dinner Thursday night!"

My mom?

His mother had been dead for almost four years.

Chapter 26

WHEN THELMA MURPHY DIED, she left her only son her entire life savings, which was modest by most standards, but for a woman making her salary, it was a small fortune and more than enough for a nice down payment on the Kelly farm. Murphy knew his mom had scrimped and saved and put up with horrors at the state hospital for every penny of that money, and her sacrifice made the prospect of losing the farm that much more devastating.

If he could talk to his mother again, maybe it would help Murphy settle one thing—he could be pretty sure he wasn't in Hell.

Murphy's truck wheels crunched down the gravel driveway toward the double-wide trailer that was his boyhood home. Fall leaves were piled up around the plywood football helmet sign with his number thirteen painted on it that was planted in the lawn. It was exactly as he remembered it.

The yellow Pinto was there, parked in the driveway. The car looked twenty years younger, with all four tires and a body that wasn't punctuated with rust.

Murphy exited his truck to the sound of a chain clinking and a plaintive bark. He looked over to see Biscuit, the old mutt he'd grown up with. The dog had a gray snout and was too old to move very fast, but he was happy to see Murphy. The graying tail wouldn't stop wagging as Murphy stepped out of the truck.

"Biscuit!" he exclaimed as he knelt down and pulled the big dog on top of him as he had done thousands of times when he was a boy. The old dog's scratchy tongue scraped across his smooth face and Murphy broke into laughter. This wasn't just a dog; it was his first best friend.

The screen door squeaked open.

"Stop messing with the damn dog and get your dinner. It's getting cold!" Thelma said as she stepped out of the trailer to scrape leftovers into the dog bowl.

Murphy and Biscuit untangled and the dog hobbled toward the steaming pile of scraps. Murphy stood up and stared at his mom as she disappeared back into the trailer.

She's alive.

Murphy's eyes grew wet and he was afraid to speak. Afraid he'd wake up before he got to talk to her. Before he got to look at her. Before he got to smell her and hug her tight.

He was a few steps closer to the door when it snapped open again and Thelma walked out, carrying her lunch pail and work boots. She was dressed as she always was for work, in her Dickies. She wouldn't change into her nurse's uniform until she got to the hospital. She wasn't fastidious, they were just poor, and she didn't want to risk tearing it or getting it dirty if she didn't need to.

"Mom?" Murphy said, drinking her in. The waning sunlight crowned her face and hair, giving her an ethereal quality.

"Always late. Just like your father," she said, putting on her coat.

"Mom. You look beautiful."

Thelma had been called a lot of things in her life but beautiful wasn't very high on the list. She smiled wide and a guffaw burst from her lips, followed by her trademark cackle. Thelma spoke and laughed loudly, and loved her son at the same volume.

"Get outta here!" she said.

Murphy threw his arms around her and held her tight. She was so surprised that she almost dropped her lunch. They hadn't hugged since he was a little boy. She tolerated it for a moment, and then gently pushed him away.

"Come on, you're gonna make me late," she said, heading for

her little yellow chariot.

Murphy ran after her and blocked her path.

"Why don't you call in sick? We can order pizza and cook some popcorn and watch some old movies or something…" Murphy remembered doing that with her—exactly once, on a Christmas. The thought of doing it on a weekday or a work night was high comedy to Thelma and her laugh let him know as much.

"You're crazy," she said, pushing past him with a patiently furrowed brow, dealing with him the same way she did with the mentally challenged adults she had to wrangle every night at work.

"Mom, I'm serious. Come on, just this one night. Let's just hang out together. Talk or something," Murphy pleaded.

Thelma looked up at him, sadness pulling at the edge of her eyes.

"Not until my numbers hit, kid," she said, starting up her little car. She gave him a wave as she backed down the driveway. Murphy watched her drive away, cursing himself for not making her stay, but resigned to the fact that no one made his mom do anything she didn't want to do.

There was no quit in Thelma. No nonsense, either. Her ancestors had come across Ohio when it was just a territory; she was descended from that special stock of women who went out West with the frontiersmen in the 1800s—women who survived. Thelma was a modern pioneer woman, the kind who could sew and cook, laugh and love—and when trouble came and you had to circle the wagons, she'd be happy to pick up a musket to protect her loved ones.

That's partly why she wasn't too keen on football. Watching two or three people twice the size of her boy trying to smash his brains in wasn't her idea of a fun way to spend a Friday night.

His mom was hard to define in words, but her actions—and the actions of those who knew her—spoke volumes. After Murphy's injury, all the nurses in her district—half the state—had pooled their vacation time together and donated it to Thelma so she could care for her crippled son at home and still put food on the table.

She hadn't asked for it, they had done so unsolicited when word got out that she couldn't go back to work and would have to quit her job.

The State Administrator had driven out to Coldwater all the way from Columbus just to meet her before he signed the order, because in the fifty years he had worked for the government, no one had ever given vacation time away. Not one person, not one day, ever. And he wanted to meet the woman who had changed that.

Sure, a few of them might have been football fans. But the majority were just Thelma fans. They stood in admiration of how hard she worked and how hard she loved the person she valued most on this earth—her only son.

Murphy knew about that love, and for the last twenty years of his adult life, it only compounded his sense of failure.

Chapter 27

MURPHY STEPPED INTO HIS boyhood home cautiously, half worried he might find the dead father he'd never met sitting at the dinner table. He didn't. His old man was still the only place Murphy had ever seen him—in a faded snapshot of two Marines under glass with a set of worn dog tags, the only things that came back from Vietnam in one piece.

If his mother resented losing her only love, the father of her only son, in a war she didn't understand, she never showed it. Those kinds of thoughts were impractical and she was resilient.

As the almost forty-year-old Murphy stared at the photo pressed under glass against a folded American flag, he realized something his young self never did. They were boys. Not much older than the body he was in now. And he also understood that, in an odd way, that war was why he played football.

Murphy's dad, Patrick, had played football in high school, but was never a standout and had never far with it. His best friend, Bobby, however, was good enough to have gone to college and played, but when Patrick got drafted, Bobby enlisted to keep him out of trouble. They ended up in the Marines together, but Patrick didn't come back.

Murphy had never heard the details, but he did know that Bobby Hand never forgave himself for his best friend's death. Bobby probably figured taking care of his friend's son was one step on a never-ending road to redemption, and Thelma probably figured Murphy needed some kind of a father figure. So Bobby came in as a surrogate father for his best friend. And since Bobby Hand coached football and was a volunteer fireman, Scotty played football and was a volunteer fireman. Murphy certainly never made it easy on the old man he only knew as Coach, but he loved him as deeply as any son could.

As Murphy crept down the hallway toward his boyhood room, he caught his youthful reflection off the glass fronts of the framed family photos that covered the narrow hallway from floor to ceiling. Thelma didn't believe in albums and didn't think pictures of her loved ones should be hidden away.

He noticed all the photographs of himself in football uniforms. He'd been playing forever. While his mom had no love for the game, she had thought it would be something to give him a little confidence, and keep him out of trouble after school. She had no idea he would take it so seriously or get so good at it. She had come to watch him play once in the seventh grade. Scotty had tried to explain the rules to her. Four tries to go ten yards. Go ten yards and get a first down. Get the ball into the end zone. Score seven points. Kick the ball through the uprights. Score three points. It was all a wash to her.

All she saw when she looked down at that field was eleven very big boys in plastic armor doing all they could to pulverize her only begotten son.

She tolerated it because he loved it so much. The fact that colleges and coaches were offering him scholarships to play football was nice, too. She had been saving for years to send him to college, but the thought that she could give him that money and he could use it for something else made her think it was almost worth it.

Murphy remembered overhearing his mom and Coach Hand almost arguing about it late one night through the thin walls of the trailer. Her main concern was what happened after football. It was so much a part of who he was that she was worried about how he would react if it was taken away from him. And though she didn't know much about football, there was one thing that was pretty clear in her mind—no one could play forever.

Murphy stepped into his childhood room, and felt a pang of spoiled guilt. He was in the master bedroom. His mom was tucked away in a tiny space behind the living room. The kid Murphy hadn't given it two brain cells of thought, but it rankled the adult inside him.

The guilt was slowly pushed aside by wonder. His boyhood walls were covered with posters and sports memorabilia. An Ohio State banner. The framed picture of the red Porsche, *his* red Porsche, the one Chris Hall had stolen. The blonde beer models in skimpy bikinis that all resembled Jenny, though she was prettier than most of them. And an entire wall covered with sports clippings. His own. But he had only kept the negative ones. The *Columbus Dispatch* predicting a loss. The *Cleveland Plain Dealer* calling him too slow and too small to be a great quarterback.

Murphy went to bed every night, and woke up every day, surrounded by missives of doubt—how he was overrated, not agile enough, and not physical enough. He read them every night as he did push-ups and revisited them every day as he dressed for school. He didn't bask in the believers; he was determined to prove all the doubters wrong, hoping that if he vanquished them, he might eliminate the doubt within himself.

Murphy took off his letter jacket and hung it carefully in the little closet. The jacket was real leather and had cost a couple hundred dollars, and his mom had raised him to take care of things, particularly the ones that they couldn't afford to replace. High school football success only paid in popularity and opportunity. There was no money in it. Yet. Scott Murphy, the best quarterback in the state of Ohio, arguably the best in the entire country, had exactly two pairs of jeans, a couple of T-shirts, dozens of football jerseys, and one suit to his name—and Thelma had bought the suit from Goodwill.

As he walked to the small desk in the corner, a flash of sunlight blinded him for a moment. He turned and found the culprit hanging from a tack. It was the Mr. Football medal. Gleaming golden and new, with a red ribbon and bas-relief of a football player untarnished by time.

This is crazy.

Chapter 28

MURPHY DECIDED TO TRY to cope with his time travel—or possibly being dead, insane, or caught in a dream predicament—the way any self-respecting Irish-American washed-up athlete nearing forty in an eighteen-year-old body would. With libation.

The fridge door creaked open and Murphy tugged on the bottom drawer and fished out a green bottle of Rolling Rock. There were only a couple down there and his mom didn't drink. Murphy remembered the beers were strictly off limits and meant for guests—particularly the gaggle of good-old-boy recruiters and assistant coaches that had been making the rounds to the Murphy double-wide to try to get him to commit to throwing a football for their various schools. Most refused the beer offer—which left four cold ones for Murphy.

I'm more than old enough. Inside at least, he thought as he flipped off the cap with a satisfying *pop*. He reflected only briefly on his non-drinking pledge to his wife. He was pretty sure this would qualify as a special circumstance.

Murphy tilted the beer and chugged half of it. The bitter familiarity of the hops made him hopeful he was actually alive and this whole thing wasn't a dream. He sat on the couch and went through the stacks of recruiting letters he'd found on the tiny desk in his room. Most were unopened because he'd always had his heart set on Ohio State, but this time Murphy wanted to weigh all of his options. He unchained Biscuit and let the old boy come in and sit with him on the couch. It was a pretty big no-no, but a small sin compared to the beer.

Murphy felt an even bigger twinge of guilt as he thought about the kiss Jennifer Cleary had planted on his lips. It still tingled. No matter how Murphy tried to justify it—he couldn't. In his mind, he was still married and had been for ten years.

But he'd never chosen to be with Macy. It had just happened. She'd been a candy striper at the hospital to be near her ailing mother, and the hospital had been his second home for eight months of surgeries and rehab. Murphy had helped her through the death of her mom, and in return Macy had helped him through the death of his football career. They had bonded over grief and formed a love that he feared was a product of default happenstance, rather than the unquenchable fire that comes from the union of true soulmates.

Murphy had often wondered why his wife was with him. He figured maybe it was just Nurse Nightingale syndrome, or whatever they called it. He'd always suspected her admiration for him was built on a foundation of pity and that haunted him. Maybe she didn't even really love him. Maybe she just felt sorry for him. He certainly loved Macy. He just wasn't sure. What was it people always said? He just wasn't sure he was *in* love with her.

But he'd seen her today after practice. And she'd looked so young. So happy. And he couldn't get her smooth apple-round and dimpled cheeks out of his mind. Her easy smile. The way her brown eyes sparkled when she spoke. To anyone.

No. I had that life. I'm not doing it again. What good is a second chance if you don't use it? Besides. Macy hates me. And I've got enough to worry about trying not to get busted up again in that football game.

Murphy had to learn how to be great at football again. And he only had four days to do it. He needed to focus. The irony of chugging a beer as he thought this was not lost on him, and he almost jumped out of his skin when the screen door squeaked open.

He barely managed to get the beer between the seat cushions

before someone barged in. For a moment he figured his mom had forgotten something, and then he saw Chris Hall step in, unannounced. It irked Murphy.

"Don't you knock?" Murphy said.

Hall looked at him like he was crazy. "Why would I do that?" he asked as he opened Murphy's refrigerator and helped himself to a can of Squirt. Murphy had forgotten how close they had been. Like brothers.

"My dad is on my ass again. Said I should go run. He saw me drop that pass in practice and said Coach didn't get on my ass hard enough," Hall said tiredly as he sat down on the ottoman, turning on the crappy little TV in the corner.

Murphy softened as the memories flooded back. Hall and his father lived in a trailer the next lot over. Sometimes Hall's dad and mom fought so loudly over money even Murphy couldn't sleep. He'd heard Hall get chewed out and hit with a belt enough times to make him sick. It got so bad one time when they were twelve, Thelma had gone over with a shotgun and told the old man that if he hit that boy one more time, she was gonna blow him open. Hall came around a lot more often after that. Thelma wasn't very big, but she meant what she said and said what she meant and didn't bring much else to the conversation. Except a twelve gauge, when she needed it.

Still struggling to secure a suitable TV signal, Hall turned back to Murphy, noticing for the first time the green bottle clutched in his throwing hand.

"What the hell are you doing, Murphy?" Hall asked, aghast. "Are you crazy, man? We got the State Championships on Friday! I know we aren't gonna win, but I'd at least like to score!"

Murphy put down the beer, his ire rising. "You don't think we can win?"

"Hell, Murphy, read the papers. No one does. Versailles has six guys as good as you and they're ten times our size. We'll be lucky to get off the field in one piece."

Murphy just stared at Hall, haunted by his words.

"Well, we gonna go running or what?" Hall prodded, evidently tired of monkeying with the foil-and-coat-hanger contraption the Murphy family called an antenna.

"Running? We just had practice."

Hall looked relieved. "You don't want to run, fine. I was tired anyway. I don't know why you like to freaking run so much…"

Murphy realized now that Hall wasn't sent over to get *him* to run, he was sent over to run *with* him. And he suddenly remembered not only that he did it every night after dinner during the season—but why he did it.

"It clears my head," Murphy said as he stood up, walking toward the door. "Let's go…"

Hall followed him outside. Murphy sized up the future NFL Hall-of-Famer, wanting to put something to bed he'd been wrestling with his entire life.

"Who's faster? Me or you?" Murphy added, stretching his future bad leg.

Hall chuckled. "Probably me." You didn't make it to the NFL without being cocky. And fast. Murphy was nervous, but excited to see.

"Let's find out."

"What? You wanna *race?*" Hall questioned, worried, but also eager in his own way to prove himself.

"To the end of Robinson Road," Murphy said, calculating it was about two football fields from the spot where they were stretching.

"You sure, man? Sprinting? I don't think we should overexert ourselves," Hall added defensively, inching toward the road.

"Come on," Murphy pressed. "I want to know." And he did. If this was a dream and he didn't wake up in the same body tomorrow, he wanted to at least have had a go at it. And he couldn't think of a better way to spend a school night than beating a soon-to-be millionaire in a footrace. It was wired into his hardscrabble DNA.

"Nah, man. I can't. It's getting dark, and I have a butt-load of homework," Hall mumbled as he nonchalantly walked down the driveway.

Before Murphy could argue, Hall shouted, "Go!" and took off down the road. "Ha-ha! Sucker!" he added, putting twenty yards between them.

Murphy smiled to himself as he raced after Hall, legs pumping.

He didn't want to slip on the gravel and pull anything, so he waited until they were on the cracked asphalt straightaway to really turn on the jets. Hall's legs were longer, and there should have been no way Murphy could catch up to him. Not with the head start he had and the pace he was running.

But somewhere near the end of Robinson Road, Murphy pulled up alongside Hall, who gave it all he had, but still couldn't break past Murphy, who still had another gear.

Murphy turned it up around the final turn and crossed the imaginary finish line ten yards in front of the man who would become one of the highest-paid receivers in the NFL, a player who was known for his breakout speed.

"Okay! You beat me!" Hall yelled as he jogged to a stop near the rusted street sign.

Murphy just kept running.

Chapter 29

HE RAN ALL OVER Coldwater. Across the covered bridge near Butler Pond. Down to the old metal clock on Main Street. Past the old feed mill. There was no rhyme or reason; he was just running for the pure joy of it. And his young body was in such good condition that when he finally quit, it wasn't because he was tired, it was because it was getting late.

He came to a stop at the top of the hill, a perfect vantage point to look out over the rolling valley that held the village of Coldwater. He saw two possible futures spread out before him. To the right, the one he'd already lived, represented by the three tall smokestacks of the cement factory. To the left, the pure white glow of the Coldwater High School football field.

The lights were still burning bright despite the cost of keeping them on, because it was tradition. They always kept the lights on around the clock during the week before a big game. So the angels could find the field.

If Murphy had to choose between a life lived in the dark and dusty confines of a cement plant or on the green grass of a brightly lit football field, it was no contest.

He just hoped he woke up tomorrow.

Chapter 30

MURPHY'S EYES SNAPPED OPEN as his alarm clock sounded. He sat up, gasping for air like a drowning man. It took him a moment to adjust to his surroundings, but he saw he was still in his trailer. A quick glance at the mirror next to his bed told him he was still young.

A smile broke across his face. *Maybe this is real.*

He spent Tuesday in a blur of distraction. Murphy neither cared about nor could follow any of his classes. He spent most of his time staring out the window, distracted. The last thing he wanted to do with his second chance was learn algebra. If this was real, he was one hundred percent certain he wouldn't ever need it. And wasting your dreams or the afterlife on math seemed like a mortal sin to him.

When the time for practice finally arrived, Murphy ran the team hard. He threw some particularly tough passes in front of Rodriguez, who pulled a muscle trying to bring one in. Coach replaced him with the only spare receiver they had—Gig.

Coldwater was a community in the truest sense of the word, and if you belonged to it, no one really cared what color you were. They did, however, have a slight prejudice against boys in the prime of their lives who couldn't throw or catch a football. The town had a very small pool of male recruits of football age and couldn't afford any weak links. Gig's lack of production on the football field had, at times, made him a target of ridicule.

Though Murphy had joined in a few times to razz him as an adult for being the one receiver on the team who had never caught a ball in a game, he was fond of Gig. When he thought back, he could never quite remember why Gig had never reeled one in. Maybe he'd never thrown the ball to him?

When he saw Gig break wide open over the middle, he sent one right to him. It was on target, and timed so perfectly to his route, Gig would be hard-pressed *not* to catch it.

The ball bounced off his face mask and dropped him to his knees.

As the rest of the team broke into fits of laughter, Gig popped up, flabbergasted. "Since when does he throw it to me? He doesn't ever throw it to me!"

Rodriguez limped back on the field, ready to go again. As he waved Gig off, he slapped him on the shoulder pads, sniping, "Don't worry, Gig. You'll catch one someday!"

Murphy suddenly remembered why he'd never thrown a ball to Gig.

He couldn't catch to save his life.

Chapter 31

MURPHY'S MOM HAD WORKED late on Tuesdays for as long as he could remember. "Double-shift Tuesday," as it was affectionately called, was when he and Coach Hand spent the evening watching *Matlock, Roseanne,* and *Coach.* And even though Murphy had never set foot on the high school field again after his injury, he had rarely missed Tuesday nights with Coach Hand. Ever. It was just the two of them, at Murphy's house, like it had been since Murphy was a boy. Coach would heat up some Hungry-Man dinners and they would break out the aluminum TV trays and hunker down. Sunday was the Lord's day, but Tuesday was man's day. A sacred bonding time with the only father he had ever known. It was also the only time in any given week when Murphy didn't have to share Coach Hand with the town, the team, or the fire station, and he cherished it.

Coach Hand was a farm boy who had left Coldwater, seen the world from behind an M-16, and realized the best place on the planet, for him at least, was the town where he had been born and raised. "Sometimes you have to leave home to really appreciate it," he always said. He came back to Coldwater to teach English and coach football and hadn't left since. Except for away games. He'd come back to Coldwater worldlier and with more love than ever for the town—but also with a hidden pain behind his eyes. He'd lost his best friend in Vietnam, and though he never had much say in the matter, he'd never forgiven himself for it.

As they sat on the couch, watching a rerun of *Roseanne*, Murphy was pensive. He was pretty sure he could get out of Coldwater this time around by *not* breaking his leg, and he was determined to take as many of the people he really cared about with him as possible. "I'm gonna go up for the draft early."

"Finish school," Coach said, and then downed the last of his beer.

"I can finish school anytime. If I go pro sooner, I can start getting paid and help my mom out. She needs to stop working so hard." Murphy paused. "And I need to get her out of Backwater," he added.

"Hey. What did I tell you about that?" Coach shot back. Angry. Murphy knew he hated it when anyone disparaged the town. Besides, that was what all the city kids called Coldwater when they came to play football. Coach Hand usually made the offending team leave with their feelings hurt. In fact, one particular offender—Moeller, out of Cincinnati—had painted "Backwater" on one of their banners. Coach Hand beat them so soundly and so mercilessly that reporters compared him to the famous Ohio State coach, Woody Hayes. Once, when the Buckeyes led their hated rival, the Michigan Wolverines, 44-14 late in the fourth quarter, instead of going for the customary one-point kick after a touchdown, Hayes ran for a two-point conversion. Reporters who believed it unsportsmanlike called him to task, asking "Why did you keep going for two-point conversions when you were so far ahead?"

Hayes had glared and said, "Because I couldn't go for three." And left it at that.

"I can probably get you out of here, too, Coach." Murphy tried another tack. "I could get Ohio State to bring you on as an assistant offensive coordinator or quarterback coach."

Coach smiled, shaking his head as he collected the TV-dinner trays.

"I appreciate that, Big Time. I really do. But Ohio State already offered me a job," Coach said, walking to the sink.

Murphy stood up, stunned. If this was true, Coach Hand had never mentioned it to him, not once in his almost-forty years. "What? When?"

Coach thought hard, trying to recollect. "Back in '85 when they wanted Tommy Jaeger. When we won sectionals in '87. And pretty much every year since then."

Murphy walked into the kitchen, his mind reeling.

"How come you never took it?" Murphy asked. It probably paid ten times what Coach made as a high school teacher, and was way more prestigious.

Coach Hand rinsed their forks and knives under the faucet, unusually quiet. As if he had something to say, but wasn't sure how to say it. The water ran for what seemed like forever.

Coach finally just turned off the tap. "They've got enough coaches at Ohio State," he said as he turned to find his coat.

Eighteen-year-old Murphy wouldn't have thought anything of that answer, but the Murphy who was pushing forty inside could read more between the lines. He watched the man grab his work coat, studying his face for subtext, and caught him glance over at the snapshot of Murphy's dad standing beside him in Vietnam. It was all Murphy needed to know. Coach Hand didn't turn down those jobs because Ohio State had enough coaches. He turned them down because Scott Murphy didn't have enough fathers.

"You know," Coach said, heading for the door. "When I was your age, I really was just like you. Stubborn as all heck. And so ready to get out of this damn town. But when I did get out, and saw what I saw, and did what I did…" Coach trailed off and Murphy knew from the hollow of his voice he wasn't just talking about war, or killing another human being. He was talking about watching Murphy's father, his own best friend, die. "I couldn't run back here fast enough," Coach Hand finished, buttoning up his jacket.

Murphy didn't know how to respond. He seldom did with Coach. The man was a mystery to him, and their relationship was simple, but complicated.

As he watched Coach walk out into the cold, Murphy thought

he looked frail and old. The thought of the inevitability of Coach's demise brought him back around to his mom. He knew the exact day and time of his mother's death. He also knew enough about the relentless nature of her disease to understand that he couldn't extend her life even one second, no matter how much money he had. All he could do was make the time she had left a little better. And the way he saw it, working twelve-hour shifts in the state hospital was no way to live your life. He had to get her out. And to get her out, he had to get himself out. He had to avoid his injury and play professional football so he could take care of Thelma. And nothing and no one, not even Coach or Macy, was going to hold him back from doing that. His mom had given him everything. He owed her that.

Chapter 32

"FATE" WAS SCRAWLED ON the blackboard in big letters. And if that wasn't bad enough, Mr. Greenway underlined it five times as he lectured. Murphy was as focused as he'd ever been in class, which was about half as focused as he usually was on the football field. It wasn't because he didn't like Greek literature, it was because he just didn't understand half of it, nor was he able to pronounce the damn names.

Despite his opinion of the subject, Murphy was sitting in the front row, rapt. The story Mr. Greenway was talking about was different from the other ones he knew. Or at least it was different to Murphy this time around. And luckily, Chris Hall had lent him the *Cliff's Notes* in first period so he actually sort of knew what Mr. Greenway was talking about.

"Oedipus knew every bad thing that was going to happen to him. The oracle told him what his destiny—or fate, as the Greeks called it—would be. He was going to kill his father and marry his mother. It doesn't get much worse than that, people."

Nervous titters of laughter spread through the classroom.

"So what did Oedipus do?" Greenway asked.

Murphy looked around, hoping to see someone smarter than he was answer the question. He heard a grunting noise from behind him and turned to see Todd White's hand eagerly raised and swinging in the air like he was bidding on the hottest girl alive.

"Todd," Mr. Greenway called, pointing at him with his nub of chalk.

"He tried to get as far away from his mother and father as possible," Todd offered.

"Exactly. He did what anyone who knew something bad was going to happen to them would do. He tried to stop it. He ran, far, far away. He got as far away from his mother and father as he could. But did that solve his problem? Did that save him from his fate?"

Todd's hand darted up again.

"Someone else answer one. Mr. Murphy?" Greenway said, breaking Murphy out of his reverie. "Thanks for joining us." The students broke out into laughter; Murphy was notorious for cutting this class. "You seem unusually attentive today. Perhaps you'd like to chime in. Did he solve his problem?"

Murphy stared at the four bold chalk letters on the blackboard, haunted.

"No. It all ended up happening. He couldn't change it."

Mr. Greenway circled "FATE." "Precisely. He tried to change it, but no matter what he did, he couldn't!"

Mr. Greenway scrawled a new word on the dust-covered board: "DESTINY."

"Now. What about Rilke? What were his thoughts on fate, or what he called destiny? Anyone besides Todd?"

Greenway nodded to someone else in the back with her hand up. As the person leaned out to answer, Murphy saw it was Macy. He'd never realized they had a class together.

She hesitated with her words, a little embarrassed to find the whole room staring at her. "Rilke said that you should look inside yourself and figure out what you really want, then set every part of yourself toward getting it. He thought you should make your own destiny."

Murphy stared at her, amazed.

Greenway elaborated. "Yes. So, Rilke would say that Oedipus wasn't a victim of some gods on Mount Olympus, he was a victim of something within himself. He would argue it was Oedipus's own pride, not fate, that caused his downfall."

Murphy's eyes lasered back in on the board as Greenway underlined "DESTINY." He felt like there was an answer for him in this, some kind of hope or lesson. He just couldn't put the pieces together.

"So, what does that mean? What do these authors seem to be saying when it comes to fate or destiny? Mr. Murphy? Do you know?"

Murphy shook his head and looked back to Todd, whose hand was flailing again.

"Todd..." Greenway nodded.

RRRRRING. The class bell sounded and the entire class jumped up. Except Murphy. He watched in horror as they collected their things and piled out the door. "We'll pick it up tomorrow!" Mr. Greenway yelled at the students.

Murphy saw Todd duck out and disappear into the crowd. He raced after him.

Tomorrow might be too late.

He caught up to Todd near the intersection of the main halls. School was over, and while most kids were heading outside, Todd was staying inside. Murphy was sure it was chess club Todd was going to, or something stupid like that. He finally caught him by the library and spun him around by his backpack.

"Hey, wait a second. Todd!"

Todd threw his algebra book up in front of his face in a defensive posture, cowering in front of the lockers.

"Whatever I did, I didn't mean to!" he shouted, trying to wriggle away.

Murphy relaxed his grip on Todd and smoothed out his coat.

Todd's eyes slowly opened and he stared at Murphy, surprised not to be in pain.

"I just want to know what you were going to say before the bell rang," Murphy asked, trying not to sound too anxious.

Todd narrowed his eyes, suspicious. "Is this some kind of elaborate ambush? My geek sense is tingling."

DON HANDFIELD

"It's not an ambush. I want to know what you were going to say about fate and destiny. What Rilke said…"

Todd gave him the same look any self-respecting nerd would give a low-IQ quarterback trying to hold a serious conversation about literature. "Now I know this a joke…"

"I'm serious, Todd." Murphy couldn't believe he was begging. "You're smart and I need some help."

Todd must have seen the desperation in Murphy's eyes. "What? Do you need a certain grade to get your scholarship?" Todd inquired. Why else would Murphy care?

"Yeah," Murphy said. "I need to get a good grade."

Todd seemed relieved by this answer.

"Rilke was saying screw fate. Choose who you really want to be and go for it."

Murphy felt some hope.

For the first time in twenty years, he thought that maybe his fate wasn't in the hands of some cruel god. Maybe it was in his own.

Maybe it's a choice. Maybe I can have it all.

Chapter 33

A TRUCK FROM THE cement plant was backed up to the edge of the football field and a few gray-dust-covered workers were unloading wooden beams. Murphy stared for a long moment. He knew why they were there, but none of the other players appeared to notice or care. Murphy knew almost all the workers by name because he'd labored alongside many of them at the auto plant. They looked younger, and different. Like they thought they had jobs that would feed their families forever. Like they still had futures. Kind of like Murphy right now. *The factories are gonna close down. No changing that.*

Murphy wondered if his own life would suffer the same fate. Or if he could control his destiny.

The players started mumbling when Coach went over to talk to their foreman. He was pointing to each end zone.

"What the hell is going on?" Hall asked, worried.

Murphy knew, but felt no need to answer. They'd find out soon enough.

"All right, guys, bring it in," Coach yelled as he blew his whistle softly. "Take a knee," he added.

The players gathered around him, expectant. Nervous. There was some heavy machinery being unloaded from the truck behind them. This football field hadn't changed in fifty years and it was unsettling.

"I've got some bad news. And I've got some good news. Bad

news is, we're not playing at Ohio State on Friday night."

A collective groan spread through the team. Only Murphy wasn't surprised.

"What? Why not?" Hall stood up, protesting.

"Ohio State went from turf to grass last year. It 's about fifty grand per game to repair. And we didn't sell enough tickets to cover the cost," Coach replied, failing to mask his irritation.

"We didn't sell enough tickets to use the grass?" Rodriguez asked, stunned.

"Everyone in town bought two, but we didn't sell enough to use the lights. They said we could play there if the band didn't march at halftime, but I told them that wouldn't work..."

"We're not playing in the Horseshoe because of the *band?*" Pierson asked, incredulous.

The grumbling rose to a crescendo. Ohio Stadium held over a hundred thousand people, and while they wouldn't fill the stands, they all felt like they'd earned their right to play in a big venue.

"They're part of our town. And they're part of our team, Pierson. If they can't be there, then we aren't going."

Hall slammed his helmet onto the ground, kicking it. "What's the good news?"

"The good news is we won the coin flip. We're playing right here! The aggregate company agreed to build us more bleachers so we can get everyone in," Coach added optimistically.

"That's the good news? No recruiters are gonna drive all the way out to Backwater!" Hall kicked his helmet across the grass.

"Maybe not as many. But we've got home field advantage." Murphy could hear Coach's ire growing.

"Yeah, some advantage. Maybe they'll trip over a cow patty. They didn't give us the field because they think we're gonna get killed."

The team grew silent as the truth of Hall's statement hung in the air. They'd all read the papers. They knew how mismatched the Saints and the Cavaliers were.

"You know what? You might be right. And you can get down,

because some accountant somewhere doesn't believe in you. Or you can look around and be happy that the hardworking people who live here, who can't afford a fancy hotel in the city, can now come out and watch your sorry ass play!" His last words lingered. Most of the players knew this reality. Their parents were among the ones who couldn't afford the trip to Columbus.

Murphy and the team looked out at the ghostlike cement workers toiling for them in the hot sun. Free of charge. Hometown people. People like them.

Chapter 34

MURPHY SAT IN THE bleachers post-shower, going over the playbook for Friday. He did it before every big game, in the exact same spot. He liked to look at the field as he read the plays and ran them in his mind. Cymbals crashed below him and Murphy was annoyed to see the marching band clomping all over his imaginary line of scrimmage and blowing his concentration.

He gathered up his playbook, about to stop for the day, when he saw Macy in the middle of the scrum, playing her clarinet.

He'd always ignored the band. He wondered how many times Macy had walked by him in his past life without him noticing her. The question puzzled him, because now he found it next to impossible to take his eyes off her. It wasn't her falling out of step every now and then, or even bumping into the bass drummer—it was actually something else that threw Murphy for a loop. Macy, for brief and blessed shining moments, had absolute grace and rhythm. And the marches were complex, and she had to do the steps while she was playing music. More than that, her joy was what really caught Murphy's eye. Every note, every stumble, every near collision with a band-mate was *fun* for her. It was infectious, too, as it seemed to delight everyone around her.

Murphy had always seen his wife as practical. He'd never seen her as smart or talented. But here it was, in front of him. Living proof.

Macy Edwards was special.

After the band was done practicing, Murphy fell into step with Macy as she walked across the field, breaking down her clarinet.

"Hey," he said, happy to have her alone.

Macy looked around to confirm he was talking to her, and then gave a tentative reply. "Hey."

"I never realized how complicated those marches were. Kind of like trying to play music and run for a touchdown at the same time," Murphy smiled, meaning it.

"Yeah? Well, no one is trying to tackle you."

"I don't know. That tuba player got a little too close for comfort a few times."

Macy laughed shyly, blushing just a bit.

"You're good," Murphy added, "I was surprised."

"Uh. Thanks. I guess."

The moment that followed was awkward. Murphy felt like Macy was waiting for him to do something. Stay or leave, he couldn't tell.

"Hey, Scotty," said a voice behind him. "Good luck at the game on Friday." Murphy stared, trying to place the kid. He was a little dorky, dressed head to toe in acid wash, with sunny blond hair and one tooth that hung out at a different angle from the rest. Norman Something. Murphy had always called him Stormin' Norman after the Desert Storm General Norman Schwarzkopf. It wasn't out of respect, but it wasn't necessarily a put-down either. It was just a simple moniker because the kid was in ROTC and wore a uniform to school some days.

"Thanks," Murphy said, wondering why Norman was still standing next to him. They weren't exactly friends.

Norman turned to Macy, nervous. "Hey, you uh, working at the Dairy Queen tonight? I was gonna come in with my parents later."

Macy moved with friendly excitement. "Oh, great. Make sure you sit in my section."

Murphy stood there a moment, watching them make eyes at

each other, and realized the kid wasn't there to talk to him. He was there to talk to Macy.

He's hitting on my wife right in front of me.

Murphy was about to step toward Norman with ill intent when the kid waved and walked away. Either he sensed Murphy's ire, or didn't want to jinx Macy's invitation with any further chatting.

"Is that your high school flame?" Murphy demanded, jealous.

Macy looked at him, confused. Her face told him exactly what her mouth was too polite to say: What's it to you?

Murphy stared at her, unsure how to answer that question. "I thought you worked at the hospital in Celina tonight?"

Macy looked at him quizzically. "That's volunteer, DQ pays. How'd you know I work at the hospital?"

Murphy had probably said too much already. He was relieved when he saw Pierson and Hall walk from the locker room.

"Small town," Murphy said, walking away.

Chapter 35

MURPHY WASN'T GOING TO go running tonight. He had more important things to do. He had a question. And he needed an answer. His mom would be getting off a fourteen-hour shift, and while she normally made him dinner when she got home without complaint, this time would be different. This time he was going to make her dinner.

He wasn't going to win any awards for what he was cooking, but it did have significance. It was the same meal she made him every Friday he had a game, just two nights early.

Though his mom never went to games, they did have a pre-game ritual. She would always make him the same thing, SpaghettiOs and green beans. If it was an away game, they ate early, Murphy in a shirt and tie, Thelma in her nurse's outfit. Coach made the whole team dress up for away games; he said they were representing not just a school, but a community, and he wanted them to look their best. If it was a home game, Murphy dressed more casually with his jersey over a flannel shirt.

They never talked about football at these pre-game meals. Not once. They weren't the usual dinner conversations about nonsense, either. They were more serious. They were life conversations.

After his injury, Murphy never went to another football game, but he and his mom did continue their ritual, every Friday night, without fail.

Murphy went into a tailspin most Friday nights after his

mother died. His heart really couldn't bear losing her and football. He developed a new ritual—he would drive to the Indian liquor store up in Chickasaw and buy a fifth of Jack Daniels. He always made sure to pour half of it out, knowing he wouldn't be able to stop himself from finishing whatever was in the bottle. The half he kept, he drank slowly. By the time it was gone, he felt he was still functional, Irish sober.

Coach Hand had gotten wind of it and in his own gruff, fatherly way put an end to Murphy's sulky Friday nights. He'd shown up unannounced on a Thursday and asked Murphy to reenlist in the Coldwater Volunteer Fire Department. Since everyone else was at the games on Friday night, they needed someone to hold down the fort.

Murphy had refused, at which point Coach Hand, knowing him probably too well, said that was fine, because he was worried Murphy would no longer be able to complete the physical he had once set the town record for at age sixteen—recruits had to carry a one-hundred-and-eighty-pound dummy up and down three flights of stairs.

Murphy showed up at the station first thing the very next morning and passed the test straight out.

The scanner on the refrigerator squawked. Murphy knew all the codes by heart and this was nothing to worry about. A 10-91B. Noisy animal. It was the Rothenberger's German shepherd again. Thelma always kept a police and fire scanner on, even though she worked twelve-hour days and sleep was a precious commodity. She didn't read the newspaper. She didn't watch the news. And besides, she didn't know any of those people anyway. She could learn everything she needed to know about everyone she knew, and everyone she cared about, from that scanner, the hair salon, or the diner in town.

She would ignore the simple stuff—the 10-68s, tree limb down, or the 10-75s, a hole in the road. Sometimes, however, the scanner would report something horrible and she'd casually turn down the volume because she didn't want her son to know about it. Even though he didn't recognize all the codes when he was a kid, he could still always tell when it was bad news—like the 11-79s that announced a car accident, or worse the 11-44 that called for the coroner to drive down from Celina. When those kinds of calls came in, Thelma wouldn't react, she would just curl her worn hands around her mug and dip her tea bag over and over again, as the lines of her face pulled together in sympathy and worry.

For a village of around two thousand people, any tragedy within the town limits was a hard blow to take. These weren't strangers. These were people she knew, people who had at one time or another relied on her, or she had relied on them. When someone died in Coldwater, you didn't just lose a neighbor, or a friend. You lost a member of your family and a piece of yourself, too.

Murphy was thinking about this as he finished setting the table. When his mom walked in from work, exhausted as usual, she saw the full dinner on the table and was immediately concerned. Her son had *never* cooked her dinner before.

"What happened? What's wrong?" she asked as she looked around. She'd come home once to small craters in the living room carpet when he and Chris Hall had learned how to light matches. She'd gone to church every Sunday since, convinced the only reason the house didn't burn down with her precious son in it was divine intervention, and she figured she owed Him one.

"Nothing, Ma. Sit down," Murphy said as he pulled out her chair.

She looked into his pupils to see if he was drunk or high, and then put her hand on his forehead, checking for a temperature.

"Did you get suspended from school?"

"No, Ma…" Murphy noticed the gauze bandage taped under her forearm as she raised it to his head. He knew exactly what it meant.

She'd been bitten again.

Thelma Murphy got off easy most nights with just a scratch on her arm, maybe a bruise on her leg. Tonight, they got her good, though. Bit clear through her skin. Thelma must have hastily bandaged it herself between shifts because the wound was red and swollen, well on its way to infection. Murphy made her sit by the kitchen sink as he cleaned and re-dressed it. She never reported these incidents, because she didn't want to go to the infirmary instead of working. She never wanted to lose the paycheck.

The place Thelma worked—Mansfield Hospital—was a state-run institution for the mentally retarded. Those last two words had fallen out of favor in Murphy's time, but that's what it was called then and he didn't know how else to describe it. There were thirty to a room. Thelma was one of many orderly nurses in charge of feeding, changing, clothing, and caring for patients. These were adults—from ages thirty to seventy—many with the strength of grown men and the mental capacity of infants. Sometimes, they got violent. Thelma said it was part of the job. Much like Murphy coming home bruised and battered from football, it came with the territory. Nothing to make a big deal about.

And just as Thelma didn't like Murphy getting beaten up playing football, he couldn't stand his mother coming home with teeth marks on her arm. Or scratches. Or bruises on her shins from where she was kicked repeatedly by heavy-soled boots.

He wanted her out of there. He wanted her to be able to quit her job. Which was one of the reasons this dinner was so important. He was working on his Coldwater escape plan. He was going to beat fate and get everything he should have had the first time around. He just needed some advice first.

Murphy waited until they were on dessert to ask her. He'd spent most of the dinner building up his nerve. The subject of his father was a touchy one, and he wanted to tread that ground carefully.

"Mom? What if you had a chance to do your whole life over again? What would you do differently?" Murphy asked, running lines through his vanilla ice cream with his fork.

Thelma looked at him as if the whole notion was an impossible fantasy, and therefore really not worth discussing. "Nothing."

"Nothing? Come on. I'm serious."

"I don't know." Thelma added, "Finish high school!" Then

she broke into a boisterous laugh. Murphy smiled at his mom's exuberance, and then let the silence and crickets take over for a few more moments before he dropped the bomb.

"What about Dad?" This was what he'd been waiting to ask. The whole reason for the dinner.

Thelma's face went slack and Murphy felt himself drowning in the pool of silence that washed over the table. Even the crickets shut up. All he could hear was the ticking of the antique cast iron novelty clock on the kitchen counter.

"What about him?" she finally answered.

"Would you still have married him?" Murphy asked.

The look she gave him stopped him short, but he needed an answer, dammit. His life might depend on it. His future certainly did.

"Would you still have married him, knowing…knowing it wouldn't work out?" Murphy pressed on. Saying "didn't work out" to describe the young love of her life full of bullet holes, face down in the mud in some far-flung rice paddy, was the understatement of the century, but Murphy was trying to be sensitive. It was the first heartbreak of her life and he needed to know if she'd risk going through it again.

Thelma looked at him, brow furrowed, as if she was genuinely concerned not just for his life, but for his soul.

"Of course."

Murphy had his answer.

Chapter 36

THAT EVENING, MURPHY DROVE through town, feeling the itch to talk to somebody, anybody, about what was happening to him. He kept checking in his pocket for a cell phone that didn't exist yet so he could call someone to discuss everything. If this was a second chance and he was going to make a brand-new life out of it, then there was really only one person he felt like he had to reckon with first.

He pulled down Prineville Road and headed for the lights of the brick-and-shuttered Dairy Queen where he knew Macy worked.

He parked his truck and tried to figure out what he was going to say to her. He had no idea how to explain to his wife-to-be that he was from the future, and what he really wanted to do was make sure the accident that brought them together didn't happen again. It sounded crazy to him, he was sure it would go over no better with her.

But the fact of the matter was, Murphy was lost and for once in his life, he realized he needed help. Todd's technical explanation about the inevitability of fate had made his head spin and he was going to try to go with his heart this time. And that's what told him that the right thing to do was to talk to the person in the world who knew him best. Macy.

He shut off his engine and after the first few friendly waves had turned into conversations and even a couple of autographs, he restarted his truck and drove over to the outskirts of the parking lot. He ducked behind the dash, just low enough that if someone glanced over they would see an empty truck, and just high enough that he could see into the restaurant.

He caught glimpses of Macy's dimples as she passed by in her polyester uniform with its small apron, her hair in a hairnet, smiling cheerily to a customer or a co-worker. She took so much joy in everything she did—even helping the busboys clean off the tables.

Murphy realized as he watched her that she had never really known him as a football player. Despite the small size of the school, she was a year younger than Murphy and they had hung in different crowds. And back then, she was so far off his radar it wasn't even funny.

Murphy ducked lower as he heard a familiar rumble and saw Hall's primer-colored '68 Camaro coast into the lot. So many football players rolled out that it looked like a clown car. Winton, Hall, Pierson, Rodriguez, and Bird, all wearing their letter jackets, strutted toward the restaurant like five bantam roosters.

Murphy ducked down as they glanced his way, hoping they didn't see him.

As he rose up from the seat, he saw someone behind the car next to him doing the exact same thing. The guy had on a backpack and was crouched low, and when the coast was clear, he started sneaking across the parking lot. It wasn't much of a sneak—he was too uncoordinated to be stealthy. Murphy recognized Todd White, his future mailman, and wondered what he was doing there.

When Todd neared the front door of the restaurant, he realized too late that he was on a collision course with the five football players. Murphy watched it unfold.

"Whoa! Whoa! Hey. White Urkel—what the hell are you doing here?" Rodriguez said, squaring off in Todd's path.

"We told you never to come back here," Winton added, flanking him.

Todd sidestepped them, inching toward the door, which was blocked by Pierson.

"You know you were banned, freshman," Pierson said. "Under threat of extreme bodily pain."

"This is a public venue, I have a legal right to be here," Todd said, voice cracking.

"What about our rights, chump?" Rodriguez shot back. "And our lefts. And our uppercuts."

Todd stared at them like a pissed-off deer in headlights. "That's cool, you know. I wasn't that hungry anyway," Todd said as he backed away, right into Murphy. He turned around and tried to bolt, but Murphy grabbed his backpack and held him in place.

"Oh no…" Todd said. He was scared before. Now he looked doomed.

"What the hell is going on?" Murphy scowled.

"We caught him trying to break the ban," Pierson said helpfully.

"I wasn't sure if it was every night or just weekends…now I know, I'm clear. It won't ever happen again…" Todd trailed off as he tried to back away but Murphy held on to him.

Rage welled up inside Murphy. He'd become particularly defensive of those less able since his injury. Fat jokes, cripple jokes, racism, all of it made his blood boil. He stared at his five teammates, furious. "Who banned him?" he demanded.

Hall, Rodriguez, Pierson, and the rest of the players all stared back at Murphy, flummoxed.

"What?" Hall mumbled.

"Who the hell banned him?" Murphy pressed, getting in their faces. He was ready to fight any of them or all of them.

They exchanged puzzled glances, each trying to figure out who would answer, when the reply came:

"You did, Murphy," Hall said, matter of fact.

Murphy stared at them, his rage turning to shame as the realization sank in.

I banned him.

"OK. Well. He's unbanned now. And we're working on something together, so from now on, leave him alone." Murphy said as he adjusted Todd's backpack strap on his shoulder. "Come on, Todd. Let me buy you a sundae."

The restaurant grew quiet as Scott walked in, then after a brief moment, most of the customers started to clap, greeting him like a war hero. Murphy flushed, embarrassed, and hurried past the *Please Wait To Be Seated* sign as he led Todd over to a booth in the corner.

"You seriously want to eat with me?" Todd asked.

"Yeah. And get whatever you want, because if I remember right, I get free ice cream here," Murphy said, covering his face with the menu as he watched Macy across the restaurant, talking intently to two boys from their school. He recognized one of them as Norman, the boy she had been talking to after band practice. A pang of defensive jealousy rose up in Murphy's stomach as he felt certain that Mr. Tuba must be the high school flame she had been so reluctant to name.

He doesn't look like much. Then Murphy checked himself. Hell, the guy had both legs, which was more than Murphy ended up with. Besides, Macy liked them weak. That's why she fell for him, wasn't it?

"No, I actually...I can't really eat ice cream. I'm lactose intolerant."

"You're what?" Murphy asked.

"I'm allergic to milk," Todd explained.

"I know what it means, Star Trek, but if you can't have milk, why the hell did you risk getting your butt kicked to come to an ice cream parlor?"

Todd's pale cheeks flushed red in patches and he tried to push his unruly spectacles back up onto his nose. Murphy followed Todd's gaze over his menu to the waitress station.

Sasha elbowed past two of her gabbing skinny co-workers on her way to the drink machine. "Move it, pixies. Real woman doing real work here..."

He watched Todd watch her, smitten. It all came together: why Todd was always making the extra effort to find Sasha when he delivered the mail. Why he was always dropping by for two and

144

three mail runs when Sasha was over watching the kids. Murphy didn't know why he'd never noticed it before. Actually, he did know. He was too busy with his own life-and-death worries to dwell on the crushes of the town geek.

"You like Sasha?" Murphy uttered in disbelief. His mom had always said, "There's an rear end for every seat," but Murphy couldn't imagine anyone falling for Sasha.

It meant that as far as Murphy knew, Todd White had been in love with her for over twenty years, and he had never once acted on it.

"Sasha! Come here a second!" Murphy yelled. She was godmother to his girls, and he might not like her but he knew her well enough to at least provide Todd with an introduction. Besides, he was going to need Todd's help with this time-travel thing, so if he could do something to grease the wheels, so be it.

Sasha ambled over, snorted at him, and breezed right past.

"Stuff it, jock itch, you're not in my section."

So much for that.

"The direct approach doesn't work with her," Todd said. His tone was matter of fact, as if he knew everything there was to know about Sasha.

"You got a better idea?" Murphy asked.

"Take it slow. Bide my time," Todd responded.

Murphy knew Sasha well enough to realize that Todd had never once made any kind of move on her. In fact, he remembered at least seven specific conversations between Macy and Sasha in his kitchen that put Todd at the top of the list of people in Coldwater who might not be interested in women at all.

"Look, Todd. I can tell you your way definitely won't get you anywhere for at least twenty years…"

Murphy held up his arm to wave for Sasha and Todd tried to push it down.

"No. Please. Don't. I didn't come to talk to her!" Todd protested, blushing.

"Then why the hell are you here?"

Todd stared down at the menu and shrugged his shoulders.

"I don't know. I guess I just came to watch her."

Murphy fell silent as he looked over at Macy taking an order at a nearby table. He understood completely.

He overheard a customer asking Macy what was good and he was captivated by her honesty as she answered him in an unabashed, nonjudgmental way. "The Philly cheesesteak is good. It doesn't have enough cheese for me, so I can ask them to put more on it for you." Murphy got lost for a second trying to figure out what he loved about her so much. She wasn't nearly the beauty Jenny was, not by a long shot, but there was something so honest and fresh about her. What you see is what you get. That's what she was. No pretense.

Todd saw him staring and leaned in conspiratorially. "I heard a rumor that a few of the Dairy Queen girls go to Butler Pond and skinny-dip after work."

Murphy snorted. "Yeah, well, Beth Lammers and Martha Lotti will take it off whenever and wherever..." Murphy trailed off, taking a swig of ice water.

"No," Todd interrupted. "Not them. Sasha and Macy Edwards. I brought binoculars, if you want in..."

Murphy choked on his water and coughed a spray down onto his placemat.

"What?" he choked out between coughs.

"I heard some of the band guys talking. They said Macy had nice..."

Smash!

A plate broke on the floor nearby. Murphy spun his gaze to see Macy wheel out of the kitchen, smiling sheepishly. "Sorry," she said to no one in particular. As she knelt down to clean it up, a waiter backed out of the kitchen with two plates of food. He hit her and fell over, sending a Kicking Buffalo chicken salad and a bowl of clam chowder flying at Murphy and Todd.

The Macy he knew was just as klutzy as the one carefully and good-naturedly picking pieces of salad out of Mrs. Johnson's perm. But she would never, ever, under any circumstances, take off her clothes and swim naked with another guy.

But he was going to take Todd up on his offer, just to be safe.

Chapter 37

HALF AN HOUR LATER, Todd was sitting in Murphy's truck in the shadows of the Dairy Queen parking lot. He was still cleaning off his baby blue Member's Only jacket with disposable wipes. It was just a cup of clam chowder he'd been doused with, but it got him pretty good.

Macy skinny-dipping?

Murphy still found it hard to believe. As far as he knew, she was a virgin when they got married. But then again, he'd never really asked her. He banished the thought from his mind.

"You don't need binoculars, Todd," Murphy said, annoyed. "They're twenty feet away."

"Binoculars aren't easy. I'm practicing," Todd responded.

Binoculars aren't easy? Murphy wondered how this kid made it through the day alive.

"Here they come!" Todd wailed, ducking down under the dash.

"Here who comes?" Murphy demanded, seeing the girls still in the restaurant, cleaning up. He followed Todd's gaze to a blue 1984 Caprice Classic station wagon as it rolled into the lot. Behind the wheel was Norman, and with him was his *compadre*, a greasy-haired guy with a molester mustache. *Perfect for Sasha.*

"Who is that guy?" Murphy said.

"One of the Ponts brothers," Todd replied.

Murphy had no love for the Ponts brothers. They were violent hillbillies and had been since elementary school. He'd heard one of them had gotten a girl from a nearby county pregnant in eighth grade. He wondered what Ponts was doing hanging out with a band geek, and then checked himself. He realized that in the pursuit of women, men could make strange allies. Case in point: the chowder-scented geek next to him.

Murphy stared, perplexed, as the station wagon parked in the back of the restaurant. The DQ's back door opened and Macy and Sasha walked out and got into the car.

"Told you," Todd gloated.

"They're probably just getting a ride home." Murphy hoped.

He started his truck and followed them out of the lot, and his heart sank as he saw the car turn right, toward Butler Pond, instead of left, toward Macy's house.

Murphy wondered what he would do if he caught his wife in the arms of another man. Then he realized how crazy whatever he did do would seem to a girl who had no idea they had ever been together.

Love and time travel are complicated things.

Murphy turned off his lights as he rolled past Gig's house and coasted his truck onto the edge of the field on the west side of Butler Pond. He could see the still water rippling in the moonlight. There was a natural hot spring that bubbled up from the bottom of the pond, making a small section of it swimmable, even in the dead of an Ohio winter.

A covered bridge spanned a brook that fed the pond. The black water was blanketed in a late-night mist. Murphy took a turn at the binoculars without bothering to remove them from Todd's neck, yanking him over so he could get a better look.

He saw them all sitting near the dock in a circle around a campfire, smoking a cigarette. Cigarette? His wife hated cigarettes. He focused in for a better look. Yes, he was sure that wasn't just cold air coming out of Macy's lungs. He handed back the binoculars.

But smoking or not, she certainly wasn't getting naked. They were just talking.

"They're just hanging out and smoking cigarettes. Now, come on. Let's go. I feel stupid sitting here spying on them," Murphy said. "I told you, Macy Edwards doesn't skinny-dip."

Just then Macy stood up, spinning and dancing in circles down the dock as she peeled off her jacket and threw it toward the hood of the station wagon, laughing.

"Um. Dude. Those aren't cigarettes."

What the hell? Murphy's mind reeled. Macy getting high? He suddenly wanted to start the truck and drive over and kick all of their butts, but checked himself. His wife might have smoked a little wacky weed, but he was still confident that she didn't take her clothes off outdoors in the company of strange men. She'd never do that.

Murphy started the truck and shifted into reverse, ready to back away from the scene of the crime.

"Wait! Wait a second! My God! They're coming off!" Todd said as the gaiety on the dock increased exponentially. Sasha made the boys turn around as she peeled off her parka.

Murphy slammed on the brakes and Todd yelped as the momentum smacked the binoculars into his head. Murphy jammed the truck into park and grabbed the binoculars so hard Todd's whole body jerked across the seat toward him.

Murphy put the binoculars to his face in time to see Macy shimmy out of her skirt, skin pimpling with goose bumps in the chill air as she stripped off her bra and dropped her panties on the dock. Her perky C-cup breasts didn't give when the bra dropped, and her figure was free of the stretch marks of two pregnancies he called her tiger stripes.

"Damn, dude. I don't even need binoculars to see those," Todd said, awed.

Murphy dropped the binoculars and slammed his foot down on the accelerator. He shifted into drive and peeled out on the gravel as he sped toward the dock in a fury.

Macy and Sasha pressed their naked bodies together under a quilt as they shuffled toward the end of the rickety old dock. Each giggle sent sputters of foggy breath into the air as they neared the water.

"Okay, you can turn around now!" Macy said as the girls dropped the blanket and jumped in the water together, naked. They gasped and splashed as the cold water took their breath away, and came up laughing.

Norman and the Ponts kid had torn off almost all of their own clothes when headlights raced across the meadow toward them. The guys froze like half-naked deer as high-beam headlights blasted across them and Murphy's truck skidded to a stop a few feet away. They looked up, frightened, as the door opened and Murphy jumped out, pulling off his letter jacket as if he was preparing for a fight.

Teenage Murphy might have thought of that as a viable first solution, but Scott Murphy was a parent now. He didn't ball up his fists; he just reached in the truck bed for an old horse blanket and went down the dock to retrieve Macy.

"You guys get dressed and get the hell out of here," Murphy said angrily.

Everyone just stared at him, stupefied.

"Get the hell out of here before I call your parents!" Murphy yelled, and the guys gathered their clothes and scrambled into the station wagon.

Norman started the station wagon and yelled out to the girls, "Call you guys tomorrow." He and Ponts peeled away.

Murphy stormed down the dock with the blanket and held it open toward Macy.

"What the heck are you doing out here, Macy?"

"Swimming?" Macy answered, her teeth chattering as she dog paddled in place next to the dock.

"Back off, meathead," Sasha yelled.

"Shut it, Sasha! This has nothing to do with you!" Murphy spoke with authority. Then he turned his wrath on Macy as he waved the blanket like a bullfighter. "Macy Lynn, get out of there right now and get dry before you catch pneumonia." Murphy spoke with such concern, familiarity, and utter certainty that Macy seemed to see no other alternative other than to obey him. Sasha watched in disbelief as Macy climbed up the dock ladder into the blanket.

Sasha smacked the surface of the pond, sending a stream of water at Murphy. "What are you? The swimming police?"

"Mind your own business, Sasha! Come on, Macy," he added as Macy turned in circles, wrapping herself up in Murphy's wool blanket.

"What are you two doing? You should be ashamed of yourselves," Murphy said. "You're naked, for God's sake!" Murphy rubbed Macy's shoulders to warm her up.

"That's how you skinny-dip," Macy replied, staring at him in confusion. "And since when do you care, anyway?" she challenged, her dripping hair steaming in the night air.

"Maybe I shouldn't," Murphy said as he pulled a wool cap down over her wet head.

"Hello?" Sasha said from the water. "What about me? Am I supposed to just come out naked?"

"Please don't!" Almost seeing Sasha naked once was bad enough.

"I got it," Macy said as she pulled away from Murphy and stepped to the edge of the dock. She opened the blanket and as Sasha got out, Macy wrapped the blanket around her. The two girls shuffled toward the still-burning fire.

"Is this what you two do in your spare time? Get naked together?"

"Is this what you do in your spare time? Stalk us? Freak," Sasha shot back.

Murphy stumbled over his words as he tried to compose an adequate response. "I wasn't stalking you. I just happened to be driving by with my friend Todd…"

"Your friend who?" Sasha asked as they looked over at his truck. It was empty.

"Todd! Get out here!" Murphy yelled into the night.

Nothing. No movement or sign of Todd at all; just the silent crackle of the fire.

"Todd! Come out or you die!" Murphy yelled again.

They heard grass shuffle and saw Todd step awkwardly out from behind the truck, addressing Sasha. "Um, hi. I sit behind you in civics class. You uh, always come in at the bell, and your hair is always wet from gym class. I can see your freckles, like now."

Todd stopped, frozen in embarrassment. He'd revealed too much. Murphy expected Sasha to crush his poor little heart, but she softened, sensing his vulnerability and affection.

"Since when do you hang out with this bonehead?" Sasha questioned.

"I don't really know him that well," Todd said, distancing himself from Murphy. "I was just uh, helping him out with his schoolwork."

"With binoculars," Sasha added skeptically.

Todd stared down at the binoculars around his neck, busted. He devised a plan of action to save himself from further embarrassment and threw Murphy to the wolves. "He likes Macy and was afraid she might be skinny-dipping!" Todd said, wagging an accusatory finger in Murphy's direction.

Macy blushed and Sasha stared at him, flabbergasted.

"What?" Murphy said, surprised to hear Todd diming him out. "No. He likes Sasha and I caught him outside Dairy Queen, spying. You guys are surrounded by perverts and I saved you—you should be grateful!"

"You came to spy on Macy!" Todd shot back.

"I wanted ice cream!" Murphy said.

"So did I!"

"You're lactose intolerant!"

Murphy felt a shove on his shoulder from two small hands and then was airborne. The next thing he knew he was underwater. A second splash a moment later told him that Todd got the same treatment. Murphy came up in time to see the girls giggling as they jumped in after them.

"It's freezing!" Murphy yelled as he treaded water in his jeans.

"I thought you were supposed to be some kind of big tough football player," Macy said flirtatiously as she swam toward him. He could see her ample bosom floating just beneath the surface, the silhouette of her youthful Rubenesque body under the water.

He'd never encountered this Macy.

What else don't I know about my wife?

"I thought you were supposed to be this innocent little band girl," Murphy retorted.

"Well, I guess you learn something new every day." Macy gave him a devilish grin.

Todd was still sputtering as he struggled to stay afloat. "Is this supposed to be fun? Because I feel like we're all going to catch pneumonia. Or possibly giardia," he added.

"Oh, relax, you'll get used to it," Sasha told him as she grabbed his head and dunked him under water.

When they were all near freezing, they got out. Murphy stoked the fire, and helped hang Macy's clothes on a tree limb to dry. He felt oddly at ease here in the woods with her and Todd and Sasha. All of them were in his clothes—Todd in his gray football sweats, Sasha in his farm coat, and Macy wearing his letter jacket. It looked right on her. For a moment, Murphy felt like a king as he saw everyone around him warmed by his belongings. He was able to clothe, feed, transport, and take care of four people he cared about.

He just hoped he could make it last.

Chapter 38

MURPHY THREW THE TRUCK into drive and cast sidelong glances at Macy wrapped in his letter jacket, sitting in the passenger seat. He cursed himself for wishing she was buckled in right next to him in the middle of the bench seat, the way she always rode. Her hair was still wet and her cheeks were flushed red from the cold. Sure, Jenny looked like she belonged on the cover of a fashion magazine, but Macy looked timeless, pure, like a girl in a fairy tale. He hated to admit it, but he missed her. He looked back at Todd and Sasha lying on the squashed bales of hay in the back of his truck, chatting away.

"Looks like he's doing okay back there," Murphy said, trying to start a conversation.

"I know. Did you hear him? He knows all these cute little things about her, even though he's never really even talked to her. That's so romantic."

Macy's smile lit up the cab. Murphy stared at her, and immediately wanted to tell her some of the million little things he knew about her.

"Drive slow, alright?" Macy said to him.

His heart jumped as he took his foot off the accelerator.

"I just want them to have a little more time to talk," she added.

They rode on in awkward silence for a few moments, until Murphy broke through it. "I'm playing football again," he said.

"I didn't know you'd ever stopped," she replied, not particularly interested.

"It's all I've ever been good at, Macy. And it's gonna get me out of here. It's going to get me out of Coldwater, once and for all."

"Out of Coldwater? You say that like it's a prison or something."

"Come on. Don't tell me you don't want to get out of Backwater someday, too."

Macy's lips tightened. "It's Coldwater. With a C," she scolded. "And no, I have no intention of ever leaving. I love it here."

"Love what?" Murphy shot back. To him, being stuck in his tiny hometown had always been his accidental future. He could never imagine living here by choice.

Macy stared out the window as she spoke. "The fields...the trees," she said as she took them in, shining in the moonlight all around them as they drove.

"They have fields and trees everywhere, Macy."

"Butler Pond. They don't have that everywhere."

"Yeah, but if you're that into skinny-dipping, I'm sure there's other places you can find to take your clothes off and swim."

"Not just that. In the winter, it freezes and people ice skate. And if you stand on the hill over it and look down, it looks like an old painting." She sounded wistful.

"You can ice skate other places, too."

Macy got quiet and just stared out the window. For a moment, Murphy felt like he might have won the day, until she spoke again.

"This town is small enough that it feels like one giant family. But it's still big enough that someone you thought was one way, turns out to be entirely different when you get to know them." Macy smiled at him and then turned to stare out the window again. "That's what I like about Coldwater."

Murphy stared at her reflection in the window, dumbstruck. A profound realization swept over him in that wet moment in his truck cab with the heater blasting warm air at them both—he was in love with his wife.

Perhaps for the first time.

There were only two days until the game on Friday. He had

only a few hours to convince Macy, his future wife, to spend the rest of her life with him. And he felt like now might be his best chance to do so.

"Macy," Murphy said, pulling over and putting the car in park. She looked at him with immediate distrust.

"Things are going to be different," Murphy continued, earnest. "I'm going to go to college. I'm going to play football there. Then I'm going to play in the pros and they're going to pay me a lot of money."

"That's great, Scott. Good for you," she said, staring at the back of her hands.

She twitched when Murphy moved his hand from the gearshift onto hers.

"It's not just good for me, Macy. It's good for both of us. I can take you with me. I can get us both out of here...."

"Oh, my God!" Macy broke into giggles, placing his hand back on the gearshift. "Do girls actually fall for that crap?"

Murphy stared at her as she wriggled out of his letter jacket.

"Free sundaes at the DQ, people worshipping you. I guess you're just used to it."

"Used to what?" Murphy asked, incredulous.

"Things coming easy to you. I mean, you just decide you like someone or you want something, and that's it? You think it just happens?"

"Nothing in my life has ever come easy!" Why was he so angry with her?

Macy stepped out of the truck. "Come on, Sasha, we can walk from here!"

Sasha nodded goodbye to a crestfallen Todd.

"Hey," Todd yelled in protest as the girls started walking down the side of the road. "I'm not with him! We're not really friends."

Murphy shut him up with a sidelong glare.

As Todd got in the cab, Murphy was fuming. Not at the turncoat nerd, at Macy. He pulled up alongside the girls, pacing them as he yelled out at her over Todd.

"You want to stay in this stupid town, Macy? Huh? You'd rather spend your life scrimping and struggling in Backwater, living in a trailer home?"

"I bet I'm happier scrimping than you are with your millions!"

"No, you won't be! The best you can do here is be broke and miserable on a stupid farm in a broken-down house! I don't want that life anymore, Macy. I had it once. I'm not gonna be a cripple again. I'm getting out of this town, Macy. With or without you."

"What? Whatever. Good riddance! Now leave me alone."

Murphy floored it and his truck roared off into the night.

When they got to Todd's house, Murphy sat back in his seat as the truck idled.

"Did you see that? I talked to her," Todd said eagerly.

"Who does she think she is?" Murphy was still smarting from Macy's rejection. "I have the best girl in the whole country. Probably in half the state! Jenny's gorgeous. She's smart. She's ambitious. She's...coordinated!"

"We were in the same water," Todd said dreamily, staring out the window as he basked in the memory.

"All I ever wanted to do was play football, Todd. And now that I have a chance to do it again, I'm not giving it up!" Murphy punctuated his statement by jamming the heel of his hand into his steering wheel.

"That means water that touched Sasha naked, touched me naked," Todd said, looking at Murphy with a lopsided, goofy smile. The stadium lights in the distance glinted off his braces and caught Murphy's eye. The field was still aglow.

"I'm getting out of Backwater, Todd. I don't care what it takes, or who I have to leave behind."

No one was going to stop him from getting out of here this time, he swore to himself. Not even his future wife.

Chapter 39

THE SUN WAS UNUSUALLY bright in Coldwater the next morning. Murphy drove through town, happy to see the place so alive. A lot of these businesses would be shuttered in twenty years, but for now the little town was doing okay. He made a mental note to pump some of his future NFL earnings back into the local economy. He turned his truck toward Jenny's house, right off Main Street, and among the largest and nicest houses in Coldwater. Old Victorian homes, left over from the boom days when Coldwater was one of the only railroad stops in Ohio.

Jenny bounced toward his truck like a happy kitten, jumping in on his side and clambering over his lap, as was her custom. Murphy was getting used to it again. In fact, he had half convinced himself he didn't need to feel guilty anymore for wanting to be with Jenny. Macy wasn't his wife yet. And that life was starting to feel more like the dream, and this one more like reality. Here he was, only eighteen, with his whole life ahead of him. He was allowed to live a little. Wasn't he?

Then why haven't I had sex with her yet?

Murphy pushed the question from his mind. He had a game on Friday. That was the reason for his chastity. He hoped. Because being faithful to a woman who wouldn't even give him the time of day seemed kind of stupid. Sure, they had been married in one possible future, but that future was an accident. It was based on a cosmic mistake that had sent his life into a twenty-year tailspin.

God willing, he would be able to set things right this time.

What good was having a second chance if you didn't do things differently?

Murphy was walking to his first-period class with Jenny when he saw Macy out of the corner of his eye. He looked over at her and knew she could see him. You couldn't help but notice Scott Murphy in the Coldwater High School hallway—he was the Elvis of this small town. His presence sent a ripple of congratulations, high fives, and good lucks, especially now, when they were just a day away from the biggest football game in history.

He could get anyone's attention.

Except for Macy's.

Chapter 40

MURPHY WAS ON HIS way to gym class with Hall, Pierson, and Gig—he'd become such a solitary man, he'd forgotten what it was like to always travel in a group. He listened to them celebrate the growing swarm of media coverage descending on their small town. Satellite trucks lined the end zone of the football field, and clusters of photographers with long lenses were waiting for them to step onto the field for practice.

"Game is gonna be on TV, man!" Pierson said. "I can't believe it!"

"Local TV," Hall corrected, "But the *Sports Illustrated* guy came in this morning, and that's nationwide."

Murphy wished they were more focused on the game and less on who was going to be watching. His own teammates were still not convinced they could beat Versailles and that troubled him. Deeply. He knew he couldn't do it alone.

"Hey! Watch it!" a girl exclaimed as she collided with another kid and two sets of books tumbled to the ground, papers flying everywhere.

The two accident victims were virtually ignored as the stream of students continued around them, but Murphy paid attention.

"I'll meet you guys there," he said, letting his teammates walk on.

Macy was at the center of the commotion, and probably the person at fault. As she knelt down, collecting the books and papers of the girl she had bumped into, she was apologetic. "I am so sorry..."

"Watch where you're walking," the girl snarled. Murphy remembered her—the bank girl again. She was semi-popular, and had dated a few guys on the football team.

"Hey, listen," Macy pitched nervously as she scooped together the girl's belongings. "While I have you down here, would you mind signing my petition? It's to save the marching band..."

The girl snatched her last book from Macy's hand and stood up, giving her an icy glare. "Drop dead."

Macy's face shattered but Murphy could tell that she was trying to stay positive as she started to collect her own papers, which were still scattered across the hallway. People were stepping on them and Macy was getting bumped and shuffled as the crowd started to walk through her instead of around her.

But the stream of students parted as Murphy knelt down to help Macy collect her dignity along with her books. As he handed her the last belonging, a tattered clipboard, they stood up together. She was genuinely grateful as she blew an errant strand of her bangs out of her face. "Thanks."

"What are you doing?" Murphy asked.

Macy responded sheepishly, like a salesman who has had doors shut in her face all day and is starting to doubt both the product and her sales technique. "It's a petition. To save the marching band. Because if that goes, then 4-H club could be next, and then all this town will be is one big sweaty locker room. With no music..." she trailed off, realizing she was pitching this angle to the wrong audience.

Murphy could tell she was close to giving up. Murphy had heard rumors of budget cuts for the arts and knew they were contemplating canceling music classes at Coldwater High altogether. He never remembered giving it much thought in the past, because while the band was great for a few minutes before every game, and after every touchdown, he didn't consider it a necessity. The only music he cared to listen to was Bruce Springsteen, John Mellencamp, and

Hank Williams.

"How many do you have?" Murphy asked, reaching for the clipboard and pen.

"Four," Macy said.

"Four pages? That's a pretty good start," Murphy said, proud of her.

"People," Macy corrected. "Band's not as popular as football."

Macy tried to grab the clipboard back, but Murphy kept it, looking down at the four names. Sasha, one dork, Macy, and him. It was pitiful. And it made him angry that people were ignoring Macy. Whether he ended up with her or not, she was still the sweetest human being in Coldwater and she deserved better. He undid the top of the clipboard and took out the stack of photocopied sheets, moving through the mid-bell crowd.

"Hey! Everyone! Listen up. Take this and sign it. It's a petition to save the band," Murphy shouted, handing out the sheets one by one. "Take one, sign it, and pass it around," he added, giving a few to another person. Soon, the intersection of the two main hallways was packed with people clamoring to sign.

"Hey, I need one!" a kid from the periphery called out, reaching for his own paper and running off with it. "Here, take more." Murphy passed out the last of Macy's petition sheets. As kids swarmed him, Macy was pushed down the hall, jostled away from her own petition by people who had snubbed her not twenty seconds ago. Just when it seemed like she might get swept away, Murphy pulled her back toward him.

The crush of kids around them was a maelstrom of flailing elbows and shoving hips, but Murphy protected her. The space around him, around them, was calm and open. Like the eye of a storm.

"You all right?" he asked her.

She nodded up at him, speechless. He handed her a petition sheet. He'd already gotten fifty signatures. She would have five hundred within another few minutes.

"Thank you," she said softly. As he looked into her grateful

163

eyes, the world seemed to shift on its axis again and that timeless recognition floated in the space between them.

"Scotty!" A voice rang out, springing them back to the present. Jenny slid through the bustle of kids, winding her way between Macy and Murphy. "What are you doing?" she asked with a smile. There wasn't a trace of jealousy in her voice.

"Nothing." Murphy handed the clipboard back to Macy and took Jenny's outstretched hand.

"Come on, let's go," she said, linking her arm through his.

Murphy looked back as they rounded the corner to the science room. He saw Macy standing alone in the middle of the crowd. She was still looking right at him. And for the rest of the day, all Murphy could think about was that familiar sparkle in her eyes.

Chapter 41

MURPHY KNEW THAT HE needed to use whatever advantages were available to him for the game on Friday night. Whether he was dead, or dreaming, one fact remained constant—he was locked in his own past, in the year 1991.

He'd not only lived his own life in the future, he'd seen the future of the game of football. So he spent all of sixth period filling his notebook with all the play schemes he could remember from throughout the years to come.

After school, he carried the tattered notebook into the small closet off of the locker room that Coach Hand called an office.

Coach Hand stared down at the elaborate schemes drawn out on loose-leaf paper. They weren't just crazy. They were freaking genius. Things he had never seen. It was like he'd gotten a peek into Bill Walsh's playbook for the next decade. Some of these were things even Bill Walsh hadn't dreamed up yet.

"Where'd you get these plays, son?" Coach Hand demanded.

"Super Bowl XXVII, mostly. Some of them are older stuff. Bill Walsh, Steve Young."

"Young?" Coach Hand demanded. Steve Young was still a backup in 1991 and had been 4-4 in his first eight games before getting injured. He was not yet a legend.

"We're not running these plays. We're sticking with the ones that got us here. Besides, you might be able to run some of these, but most of them are too damn complicated for this team. This ain't the pros, son."

Murphy didn't fight it. He knew Coach was right. He also knew to pick his battles.

"Okay, Coach. I'll give them up. But I just have one request to make."

"What's that?" Coach Hand replied.

"I want to pick the last play," Murphy said. Dead serious.

"What?"

"The last play of the game. I don't care what we run during the game. But the last play. It has to be up to me."

"Son. You want me to hand over the last play of the biggest game this town has ever played, sight unseen, before we even start the damn game? Are you out of your mind?"

"Just want one play, Coach. You can have all the rest," Murphy said, not letting go.

Coach Hand fixed a steely gray-eyed stare at Murphy and stood up to his full height, like a silverback rising up to face a young gorilla trying to challenge his position in as leader of the troop.

"You want the last play, son? You're gonna have to earn it."

Chapter 42

MURPHY AND HIS MOM piled out of her Pinto and walked toward Jenny's house. Murphy had on the only blazer he would ever own, the same corduroy one he'd worn to the bank, but the elbows hadn't been patched over yet and it wasn't as threadbare.

The Clearys lived in the nicest house in Coldwater. It was a historical home, and supposedly Abraham Lincoln had given a speech there once. Mr. Cleary was very wealthy, very patriotic, and a bit of a history buff. Between the columns of the porch hung red-white-and-blue banners designed to match those in the grainy black-and-white photo he had found at the Ohio Historical Society. All that was missing was old Abe himself. Mr. Cleary worked as a lawyer in Columbus, but he had built up his practice to the point where he could live where he wanted, and he, like most city people, thought small towns were romantic.

Which they are if you're rich—if you're poor, they can seem about as romantic as a state prison.

Murphy couldn't help remembering with shame the first time they'd done this dinner. He'd been so embarrassed by it all. Embarrassed by his mom's discomfort at the Cleary's wealth, her outdated polyester outfit, by her contribution to the meal—a casserole in a chipped dish (the best one they had) with lumps of chicken grease congealing at the bottom.

His attitude back then made him blush with anger now. He vowed to do more than football differently this time. He knew his mother was someone to celebrate, not be ashamed of. All he saw was her strength and how beautiful she was, as the sun reflected down on her through the oak trees that lined the walkway.

"This porch is bigger than our house," she said to no one in particular.

"In a few years, I'm going to be able to buy you a house three times as big as this," Murphy replied, meaning every word of it.

Thelma's mouth looked at him like he was crazy. If she hadn't been holding the casserole dish, she probably would have given him a light slap.

"What the heck would I do with a house three times as big as this one?" she asked as if his suggestion was the dumbest thing she had ever heard. "Save your money," she added as the door creaked open and Mr. Cleary stepped out, throwing his arms wide.

"Momma Murphy and Mr. Football!" he proclaimed, his cheeks red and his mood loose from an afternoon cocktail or two. "Come on in!"

He glad-handed Murphy, slapping him on the shoulder, and then turned to usher Thelma inside.

"Have you been here before, Thelma?" Mr. Cleary asked to set the stage for his favorite speech—the lofty "Abe Lincoln spoke here" pronouncement, followed by a tour of the premises.

"Yep," Thelma said, not adding another word.

Mr. Cleary stopped in his tracks, surprised. Murphy was, too.

"When?" they both asked at once.

"Memorial service," she replied. "The judge who used to live here let us use it for my husband's—Murphy's father's—wake."

"That's right," Mr. Cleary said. "You know, I do some work with the historical society and I've seen that little plaque they have down at the fire station. I was thinking they could do something bigger. Maybe a statue."

"It's big enough. I'm sure people got better things to do with their money," Thelma said. She was referring to the idea of building a statue of her dead husband, but as she spoke, Murphy saw her nod imperceptibly at the mounted animal heads—everything from zebras to elk to moose—that seemed to be watching them from the walls of the Cleary house.

"Scotty!" Jenny said as she scampered down the stairs in a pair of short shorts. She leaped up on him, wrapping her long tanned legs around his waist. The familiar scent of tea rose perfume drifted over him and with it a flood of memories. Climbing up the poles of her front porch and sneaking across the roof into her window. Making love to her quietly in her four-poster bed, wondering when her parents might burst in through the lockless door. Sweaty, furtive, window-steaming sessions in his truck at the drive-in.

It all came back to him and with it a dread of his daughters reaching puberty. He made a mental note to dig the shotgun out of the attic and find a prominent place to display it when any of their guy friends came calling. Murphy was so caught up in this thought that the fact that he was tangled up in the arms of a woman who would not, and could not, give him those daughters was completely lost on him.

Jenny planted a kiss on Murphy and he blushed. Mr. Cleary didn't seem to care, but Murphy's mom was glaring disapproval. Murphy extricated his limbs and tried to present Jenny to his mom like a lady.

"Mom, you remember Jenny," Murphy said.

"Jennifer." Murphy's mom smiled politely and handed her the chicken casserole. Jenny stared down at it like it was a dead animal.

"Mom! MOM!" she yelled. Mrs. Cleary came from the kitchen, harried, potholders flapping as she made her greetings and took the food.

Jim Spangler, the Buckeyes' Offensive Coordinator, was the guest of honor that night. Jenny had taken it upon herself as Murphy's self-appointed agent-in-waiting to arrange the dinner at her parents' house, rather than asking Spangler to crowd into the Murphy trailer.

"Great chicken, Thelma," Spangler said with genuine appreciation.

"I tried," Thelma said. Murphy heard only "I failed."

Jenny reached for the salad dressing that was perched precariously at the edge of the table and Murphy's fork clanked hard onto his plate as he dropped it and shot his hand out to stop her from knocking the bottle onto the floor.

She held it securely and stared at him, puzzled.

"Sorry. Thought it was gonna drop," Murphy said sheepishly, retrieving his fork. If that had been Macy, he would have prevented a certain disaster, but Jenny was a bit more sure-handed. She gave him a scolding look like he was misbehaving in front of their important guest.

"I heard Notre Dame and Penn State are still coming after you. I hope you told them that you're set on being a Buckeye," Spangler said, half serious.

"Yes," Murphy answered with certainty. "I'm going to Ohio State, for sure. I want to be near my mom." It was really no contest. Not only were the Buckeyes his favorite football team, Columbus was relatively close to Coldwater, and he wanted to be as near to his mom as possible. Her time on Earth was limited and he wanted to make the most of it.

"Aw, you're so cute," Jenny said with a smile.

"Well, thank you very much, Thelma. For keeping him close to home." Spangler raised a toast to her with his Diet Coke. Jenny's parents joined in a little too enthusiastically—clearly their drinks had more kick.

"He don't have to go nowhere for me," Thelma said, turning to her son. "You go where you wanna go and don't worry about me."

Murphy saw she meant it; she genuinely wanted him to do what was right for him, and leave her out of the equation. He appreciated the sentiment, but it didn't change his mind.

Spangler misinterpreted the moment of loving silence that passed between mother and son as disagreement and spoke up nervously. "Don't you want him in Columbus so you can come see his games?"

A silence fell over the table. Everyone but Spangler knew that

Thelma hadn't seen him play a game since seventh grade.

"She doesn't come to games," Jenny spoke carefully. She'd never understood it herself.

"She works nights," Murphy said in her defense.

"I don't like watching him get hit," Thelma added nonchalantly.

Spangler was incredulous. "He's the best prep quarterback in the state. Probably in the entire country. You have got to come see him play. He'd make you so proud."

"I'm already proud of him." Thelma eyed the clock on the mantle. Murphy had never, in his entire life, heard her utter these words out loud. He was moved. "I have to get to work, so I'm gonna leave y'all to it. Nice meeting you, Mr. Spangler."

Murphy walked his mom to her car. Jenny had driven his truck home from school in anticipation of this dinner and his mom having to work, so it was sitting there gleaming in the driveway. Murphy thought it was a travesty that he was driving a fancy truck they could barely afford while his mother drove fifty-some miles to work in a car that was falling apart.

"Why don't you take the truck tonight? I don't need it," Murphy suggested.

"I'm not driving that big thing all the way to Russell and back," she said as she pulled open the Pinto door. Murphy stopped her.

"You're the one working, you should be driving the nice car."

Thelma nudged him aside and got in. "My car works just fine. Go back inside and finish your dinner," she said as she started up the Pinto.

Murphy didn't want to let her go. Not without saying something they had never said to each other. "Mom. I know we never say it…"

Thelma stopped him with a look. "We don't have to say anything. It's in what we do."

Murphy and his mother exchanged a long look, and Murphy realized she wasn't scared to say the words, she just didn't think they did the feeling justice.

Chapter 43

"TELL YOUR MOTHER AND the Clearys thank you for me again. And do me a favor," Spangler said on his way to his rental car. "Take it easy on Versailles tomorrow night. A lot of those guys are your future teammates."

"Yeah? Well, I was kind of hoping they would take it easy on me," Murphy said, knowing they would do anything they could to hurt him.

"Me, too," Spangler said, worry creeping at the edges of his eyes. "You know, I've seen all your tapes and everything on Versailles, too. And I've seen your linemen play a few games…"

"Yeah?" Murphy inquired, unsure what he was getting at.

"Look. I'm not your coach yet, but I will be, so I'm gonna give it to you straight. Your line plays hard. They've got heart. But, son…they aren't gonna be able to protect you worth a damn tomorrow night."

"I know," Murphy said. The second half of the game was a hazy fog to him, but he remembered the first half well enough. It was too painful to forget. He was sacked more times in two quarters than he had been in his entire career.

"What you've done with what you have backing you up is unbelievable. And we're excited as all heck about having you on the Buckeyes' roster next year."

Murphy stared at him, feeling like this was all leading up to something.

"What I'm trying to say, son, is we don't *need* to see you play any more football. We're sold. And we wouldn't fault you one bit for sitting this game out."

His words stung Murphy's ears and made the noise of the crickets seem even louder. This man was about as big an expert on the game of football as you could be, and he was genuinely afraid for Murphy's well-being if he stepped on the field tomorrow night.

"Either way. Good luck," Spangler said as he got into his car and drove away.

Murphy watched him go. He realized that Spangler wasn't just offering him a warning. He was offering him a way to guarantee his scholarship to Ohio State and the brighter future he'd missed out on the last time around.

If he didn't play in the game, he couldn't get hurt.

Chapter 44

MURPHY SAT WITH JENNY on her porch swing in the dark, contemplating the fallout from this dinner. What would the town think if he didn't play? How would Coach react? Jenny had other things on her mind.

"Do you ever think about us, Scotty?" she asked, nuzzling into his shoulder.

"Yeah," he answered truthfully. "Pretty much every day."

"I can't wait for us to get out of here together. For all those things we've always talked about to finally be real…"

Murphy stared off into the night as he thought about this. At one time in his life, he would have done anything to be where he was—on this porch swing, with this girl, his future so bright. But now, he felt trapped. Jenny was wonderful, and on paper, she was the perfect woman. She just wasn't the perfect woman for Scott Murphy. Not the man he was now.

He loved Macy. And he loved football. And he didn't see why he shouldn't be able to have both.

First thing in the morning, he was going to tell his future wife everything.

Chapter 45

MURPHY PARKED HIS TRUCK a ways down the road from Macy's trailer for safety. He knew her dad well enough to know that a boy showing up first thing in the morning wouldn't go over well, and while he wasn't worried about himself, he certainly didn't want the old man going off on Macy on account of him.

She'd be midway through her chores by now. Macy and her parents worked Old Man Kelly's farm, and in return they got a small plot of land, a trailer to live in, and a few stalls in the barn for their own livestock. They were essentially modern-day sharecroppers.

Murphy sneaked around the silo to the back of the barn. He knew the way by heart. The surroundings haunted him with their familiarity. New, but old. Old, but new. Eighteen years from now, he and Macy would buy this farm. Owning it had been Macy's lifelong dream and Murphy had been happy to help her make it come true with the money his mom had left them when she passed away.

But it didn't work out.

And in Murphy's mind, it was time to try a new dream. Murphy had hope. If he said the right thing, made all the right moves, he could have Macy and a football career. And that was why he was here. To sell her his dream. No more being poor. He could give his wife anything she ever wanted.

Anything but this damn farm.

He wanted no more of it, a feeling driven home as he gazed out across the large round bales of hay that spotted the freshly mown field like yellow freckles. The last time he'd laid eyes on this tract of land, it had been full of his rotting soybeans.

A calf brayed in hunger and Murphy almost jumped out of his skin, thinking it was Macy's dad or Old Man Kelly about to pelt him with buckshot.

Murphy heard a clatter in the barn and turned to see Macy stumbling out, carrying two buckets of silage for the cows.

"What are you doing here?" she demanded, looking around to make sure no one had spotted him. "My dad will kill you if he sees you."

"He's on the south field. And I parked down the road. Don't worry."

Macy seemed comforted enough by this to continue with her chores, perhaps hoping if she ignored Murphy he might leave her alone. Her bovine charges had gathered at a rusted trough, shoving past each other with their powerful necks as they angled for the best position to get to the sweet fermented corn mash.

She softly admonished the more pushy cows by name and they became calm and more polite. Murphy was caught up in her awkward charm for a moment, but when she turned back to him with empty buckets, she clearly wanted him gone.

"You can't be here. We can talk at school."

She didn't just seem scared; she seemed self-conscious. He could tell that she hadn't showered yet, her hair was tousled, and she wore her dad's manure-covered mud boots and an old torn-up farm shirt. Murphy felt a glimmer of hope that perhaps it wasn't that she didn't want to see him, but that she didn't want him to see her like this.

"I have to talk to you. It's important," Murphy said, searching her eyes for some hint of the glimmer of love they would eventually hold for him.

She considered him for a long moment, and then relented.

"Okay. Come in here. And be quiet!" she added, ducking through the door and into the shadows of the barn.

Macy patiently poured out feed for the five calves in the stalls. She seemed much more relaxed here.

"Thanks. For helping out with the petition. The entire school signed it."

"No problem," Murphy said as he started to help her through the rest of her chores. He backed off when he saw she was getting spooked after he took down the pitchfork from the hook where it was hidden under the rafters as if he'd done it a hundred times before.

He had.

"So, what is it?" she asked, when all the calves were fed. "What's so important?"

Murphy stopped and caught her gaze. The morning sun filtered onto her porcelain face through the ancient windows covered in decades of hay dust. She looked as beautiful as he'd ever seen her.

"Us," he said.

Macy rolled her head, trying to act as if she thought he was crazy. But the way she stood, not moving away, told him something else.

"You have a girlfriend," she said, searching his eyes, perhaps hoping for some new development.

"I don't marry her. I marry you," Murphy said.

And with that, Macy snapped back to reality. "Did your friends put you up to this? Because it's not funny."

I'm losing her.

"Look, I have a lot of chores to do…"

This calls for desperate measures.

Murphy grabbed her and kissed her for all he was worth.

She gasped as his lips hit hers and sat stunned for a moment, then fell into it, kissing him back, until reality set in and she froze up and pulled away.

She stared at him, eyes wide, furious.

Whap! She slapped him across the cheek and touched her own lips in contemplation as if they were still burning from his kiss. Then she climbed up through the hayloft, as fast as her feet would take her.

"I hate you, Scott Murphy!"

So much for that approach.

Murphy followed her into the hayloft. He had to get through to her. He had to get her to understand. Murphy wanted it all. He wanted Macy *and* football. And he knew the only way he could make that happen was with the truth.

"Your grandmother had a cabin in Mann's Choice. And when you were a little girl and used to visit her, you two had a game. You'd make a wish and write it down on a piece of paper and put it into a knot in the wood floor. She told you if you did that every year, and if every year it was the same wish, it would come true."

Macy stopped sweeping hay down the chute to the calves and stared at him like he was a ghost.

"I know what you wished for."

"No…" That was impossible. Murphy knew that she'd never told anyone but him, not even her grandmother.

"You wished that one day you could buy this farm you and your parents work on."

Murphy walked closer to her. *It was working.*

"Your dream came true, Macy. We get married and we buy this farm. And we have two kids…"

Tears welled up in Macy's eyes. It was too much.

"Two little girls. Krista and Jamie—named after your aunts!"

Macy dropped the broom and headed for the door. Murphy ran to intercept her, putting his hand firmly on her shoulder.

"Stop! Why are you doing this?" she protested.

"We end up together because I get crippled in the game tonight. But I'm gonna change things. If I don't get hurt, I can go to college and in a few years, I'll be making a lot of money. I can finally take care of you, Macy. I can buy you all the things you've never had…"

"Stop. Stop talking. And please, just leave me alone."

Murphy held her firm. Both of their lives depended on it.

"We tried your dream, Macy. It didn't work out for us. And I'm not gonna end up here in Coldwater working at a factory or broke, with a bum leg and two kids I can't support. I'm not doing it again!"

"I'm not asking you to!" Macy yelled back.

"I'm asking you, Macy. To come to Ohio State with me next year."

"What are you talking about?" Macy wasn't scared anymore. She had a spark of hope in her eyes. Some part of her seemed to want this, too.

"We weren't supposed to be together. We were an accident..."

And with that the spell was broken. The hopes in Macy's eyes shattered and were replaced by an infinite sadness. The sadness of a woman who knows she'll never really be loved the way she needs to be loved by the man she loves with all her heart.

"But I'm saying it doesn't have to be like that," Murphy said, trying to recover.

It was too late.

"Relationships aren't accidents. They're decisions. And if you make one you're not happy with, it's called a mistake. So maybe you're better off without it," Macy said as she pushed past him toward the barn door.

"What do you want, Macy? To be married to a cripple who can't pay the bills? Are you only attracted to losers you can feel sorry for, or what?"

She turned back to him, her sadness now colored with pity.

"I don't think I could ever feel more sorry for you than I do right now."

"What is that supposed to mean?"

"It means I hope what you're telling me isn't true," she said, and somehow her sorrow softened her words. "Because I don't want to end up a consolation prize. Not for anybody. Not even the star quarterback. And I hope I never marry a man who thinks making money and being famous is what he needs to do to take care of a woman. Or a family."

Macy's anger faded and as her eyes met his, that timeless recognition took hold. For just a moment, they weren't two teenagers locking eyes, they were two old souls who had lived and bred together staring deep into each other's hearts. They both couldn't help feeling they weren't quite adequate and didn't exactly fit what the other person was looking for and deserved. There was sadness to it, but also understanding—if it wasn't meant to be, it simply wouldn't happen.

"If you want to change things so badly, then they must not have been that great. Right? Did you ever stop to think that maybe you never really wanted that life in the first place?"

Murphy stared at her, a quarterback without a play.

"Goodbye, Scott Murphy. I really hope you get exactly what you want," Macy said as she gave him a gentle kiss on the cheek. Her touch lingered as he watched her walk out of the barn.

He called after her, but it was half-hearted. Deep down in a dark part of his heart, he feared she was right.

Maybe we weren't meant to be.

Murphy realized this was far more than two high school kids breaking up.

It was two souls saying goodbye.

Chapter 46

FEAR AND WORRY WORE at Murphy's gut the whole day as he pretended through six periods of high school education. The hallways were covered with construction-paper reminders of his impending doom; he couldn't walk down a hallway or peek into a classroom without seeing a "Go Coldwater!" sign or a banner with a football on it urging "Win States!" It's hard to concentrate on Greek literature when you're scared out of your mind.

High school wasn't fun anymore. The nostalgia had worn off and even the thought of playing football that night made his heartburn act up. *Heartburn? I'm eighteen damn years old. How can I have heartburn?* Did his forty-year-old mind full of worry so corrupt his soul that he'd turned his insides old?

He remembered when he was a kid and they'd had to put his grandmother Eunice in the nursing home. Eunice, like her daughter, had lost her husband young, and bore the weight of that heartache through her entire life. It had taken its toll on her body and soul and she eventually started losing her mind. She'd try to drink the ketchup, or talk about the fifth-wheel trailer she slept in outside like it was in another town. She seemed to be going backward in her life, rather than just losing it, because eventually she kept asking Murphy and his mom to play hopscotch and marbles and stickball. Murphy was a latchkey kid who was on his own after school because his mom worked. Thelma not being able to afford a babysitter was one thing, asking a ten-year-old to be a babysitter to a senile senior citizen was another altogether, and that's why his grandmother had to go in the home.

The crazy part was that Mémère was in the nursing home for six years before she died. And while she was there, Murphy witnessed a miracle. When she entered the place, she wore Coke-bottle-thick eyeglasses and was stooped over like a hunchback from osteoporosis. By the time she died, she had 20/20 vision and stood stock straight. The doctors couldn't explain it, but it made perfect sense to Murphy. She was six years old in her mind. No bills, no taxes, no failures, no resentments, no heartaches, and no heartbreak. Just fun, all day. She thought young, so she became young. And here Murphy was, thinking old, and getting ulcers.

Can't wait until this is over.

Murphy knew there was only one course of action now. The only way he could be sure that he wouldn't break his leg was to not play in the game. And there was no way he was not going to suit up if he set foot in that locker room. And if he suited up, there was no way he was not going to play. And if he played, he figured the cosmic arithmetic would lead to him getting his damn leg broken again. He wasn't gonna let that happen.

Murphy figured the only surefire strategy was to get as far away from Coldwater as possible while that game was going on. If he had to look even one villager in the eye, they would know he wasn't playing.

And he *wasn't* going to play.

There was no more debating that for him. He had his game plan, now he just had to execute. First, he needed to figure out what he was gonna do instead of play that game. Half the state of Ohio would be in Coldwater, and he couldn't show his face anywhere in the damn county. Not tonight. In fact, it probably wouldn't be advisable for the next few months, but that was okay with him. Once he started winning again in Columbus, the locals would forgive him for not playing in the biggest game his small town had ever seen.

At least he hoped so.

Murphy finally decided he was gonna drive his truck to the airport and watch the planes take off. Not the little puddle-jumper airport up in Celina or the little one up in Auglaize. He was going to drive over to the big airport in Dayton. Big to him, anyway. Scott Murphy had never been on an airplane in his life. And he figured if he was going to be playing at Ohio State, he needed to get used to them, starting right now.

Murphy figured he was actually a little more nervous about *not* playing than he had been about playing. Probably because he was a lot better at football than he was at wordplay. And Murphy wasn't sure there would ever be anything harder for him to do than to tell the only father he'd ever known that he wasn't going to suit up for him tonight.

Maybe I can still convince him to come to Ohio State. Maybe I can convince him there will be bigger games.

Murphy thought he might be getting better at lying to himself, but he still wasn't convinced. He knew the old man pretty well and knew that what he was about to do would probably take a few years off Coach's life, but he was caught. He needed to take care of his mom, she was number one, and a cripple can't do that. A loser can't take care of anyone.

He'd purposely planned to wait until just before sixth period, the last class of the day. That way Coach wouldn't have a lot of time to chew him out before the bell rang and class started. Then he'd go his own class near the front of the building and race out right after the last bell and drive out of town before anyone found out and tried to talk him out of it.

As he did his death-row walk toward Coach Hand's classroom, it dawned on Murphy how ridiculous it was that he was actually wearing his jersey under his letter jacket as he went to tell Coach he couldn't play. He'd formulated his plan long before he got dressed for school that morning, but wearing the jersey was a game-day tradition and if he'd showed up without it, the jig would have been up long before he'd built up the nerve to explain.

Murphy paced in front of the lockers down the hall from

Coach's classroom, waiting for the crowds to thin out just before the bell. He didn't want an audience.

"Good luck tonight, Scotty!" some freshman kid shouted with a metal grin.

Murphy nodded, embarrassed, and then caught Coach Hand as the bell rang and he was reaching out to close his classroom door.

"Coach, wait," Murphy said.

"Class is starting," Coach said, about to close the door in his face. Scott Murphy might be the star quarterback, but everyone was equal in Coach's eyes. If a third-string freshman benchwarmer got caught smoking in the bathroom, the old man grumbled and complained about it for days, as if it were his own son. Murphy used to think he was just naturally a little grouchy, but now he understood the gruffness for what it was. He cared.

Murphy had learned from experience that caring isn't an easy thing. Caring is why you get hurt. Caring is why you suffer.

"This is important." Murphy pleaded with his eyes.

"So are they," Coach said, nodding back to his classroom full of kids as he once again started to shut the door on Murphy. "Come back after class…"

"This can't wait." Murphy shoved his toe in the door, stopping it.

Coach Hand sized him up, as if wondering if he should be angry or concerned. It must have been the desperation in Murphy's eyes that made him turn to his students. "Everyone open your dictionaries and flip through until you find a word you don't know. Write down the word and its definition, then write five hundred words on it."

Five hundred words? He must know it's serious.

Coach Hand stepped out into the empty hallway, gently shutting the door, brow furrowed with worry. "What is it, son?"

Murphy searched for the right words. Words so poetic and true that they would make the old man understand. But the words never came.

"I can't play tonight," he finally blurted.

He expected fire and brimstone. He only got love and concern.

"What happened? Did you hurt yourself?" Coach said, looking at him for some sign of injury. From his face, Coach half expected to see a limb missing or a pool of blood on the floor from a black-market organ theft. He couldn't think of anything else that would stop Scott Murphy from playing football.

"No. Not yet..." Murphy said, realizing too late he should have just gone with it. He'd never thought of faking an injury, but it would be hard to argue with. Perhaps because injuries weren't pretend in his mind, but instead morbidly real.

"You're not hurt?" Coach said, at a total loss.

Murphy fumbled over his next words, realizing they wouldn't make sense. "No. But if I play, I could get hurt."

Coach Hand looked at him, incredulous, as Murphy pressed on.

"And if I do get injured, I'll lose my scholarship. So I can't play tonight."

"You're not playing tonight, because you're afraid you *might* get hurt?"

"We're too small to be playing this team! Everyone knows it," Murphy said, referring to the news articles that had been coming out in the *Cleveland Plain Dealer* and the *Columbus Dispatch* about the game. There were state legislators down at the capitol building right now, drawing up a bill to prevent this kind of physical mismatch from ever happening again. They were going to create divisions between schools based on student body size, something Ohio had never done up to this point. There had never been a reason to—no small school had ever done what Coldwater had.

"What in God's name has happened to you?" Coach barked at him. "Two weeks ago, if I'd said we were playing the Cincinnati Bengals, you would have felt sorry for them because of the beating you thought you could give them. Now you're telling me we're too small and you're quitting?"

"I have to," Murphy said, knowing Coach would never understand, and that maybe that's where he had to leave it.

"Well, what do you want me to say, son? It's okay? I'm happy? Your teammates are gonna be just fine?"

All of these things couldn't be further from the truth. The last one in particular hit home. If Murphy was the best quarterback in the state and Versailles could break his leg, what were they gonna do to the spindly-legged freshman quarterback, Bobby Holliday?

"I'm not throwing my life away for a high school football game. I have a future!" Murphy shot back.

"You know what the future is? The future is just a bunch of what you're doing right now, strung together. And right now, all you're doing is giving up, and trust me, there's no future in that!"

The old man's words stung, because for the first time since he'd tried to kill himself, Murphy realized that what he had done could be interpreted as just that—giving up.

But I wasn't giving up. It was a Hail Mary. And so is this.

"I hope you don't give up this easy on life, son. Because it gets a heck of a lot harder than football!" Coach shouted as Murphy walked away down the hall.

Murphy glanced back and caught the disappointment in Coach's eyes. Murphy knew the look well. It was the one a man wore when he felt like his life's work was a complete failure. He had seen it every day of his adult life in the mirror.

Murphy turned the corner toward his class, one period away from freedom. This didn't feel like a victory, though. He was comforted only by the fact that he reckoned that he was committing the lesser of two evils. Murphy committing suicide on Homecoming by asphyxiating himself in his truck in twenty years would surely hurt the old man far worse than him sitting out some stupid state championship game.

Chapter 47

SCHOOL WOULD BE OVER in five minutes. Murphy eyed the clock nervously, knowing he'd have to make a hasty exit. Gig, Rodriguez, Hall, and Pierson all shared sixth period with him and they usually skipped it to drive to the skating rink in Celina or swim at the rock quarry up in Dexter. Today, though, all were present and accounted for, because Coach had a thing about game days. If you don't come to school, you don't play.

But I'm not playing. So why the hell am I still sitting here?

Gig squealed from his desk on the far side of the room, waving them over.

"Guys! Look. Look!" he said, gesticulating out the window.

Murphy craned his neck and saw three shiny tour buses pulling into the school parking lot. They were here early to warm up, probably because their coach, unlike Murphy's, didn't really give a damn about sixth period.

Look at those buses.

They weren't mix-and-match take-what-you-can-get school buses like Coldwater drove to away games; they were tour buses—with bucket seats, tinted windows, and air conditioning. And since interstate gas stations were too dirty for the Saints' lily-white asses, their buses had bathrooms. Murphy reckoned they probably had double-ply toilet paper, too. Murphy remembered the crappy bus Coldwater had, and how often it broke down en route to a game.

"They're here," Gig announced to the room in a hushed

whisper. Hall jumped up from his desk, pushed out the window, and wagged his middle finger at them.

"Murphy, check these chumps out!" Hall called to him with an air of false bravado.

Murphy couldn't help it. He had to see them, even though he didn't *need* to see them to remember them. Alex Washington, one half of the duo that broke his life in two, had gone on to NFL fame that far eclipsed Chris Hall's. But he wanted to see the others. He wanted to see if the Goliaths he'd beaten once in the arena were really monsters, or if they too had been shrunk to normal size by the perspective of manhood.

The fancy hydraulic door hissed open and a teenage behemoth stepped off. At least 6'4" and close to three hundred pounds. Acne pushed through his cheeks the same way his muscles threatened to burst through the white leather sleeves of his letter jacket. He didn't look like a high school student—he looked like a Neanderthal serial killer with a crew cut.

Nope. Still monsters.

"Damn," Pierson said, his face full of fear. "Look at the size of their lineman."

"That's not a lineman. That's their quarterback," Murphy said, voice low. Five three-hundred-pound beasts stepped off the bus behind him. "Those are their linemen."

Pierson swallowed hard.

As Murphy watched the rest of the nightmares exit the tour buses, his heart sank. When the whistle blew, the Versailles Saints would have eleven Goliaths on the field at once—all of them hell-bent on destroying the village of Coldwater.

And David was gonna be a no-show.

Chapter 48

MURPHY TURNED THE RED fabric over in his hands, enjoying the texture. There, on the back, in bold white letters: MURPHY. The scarlet jersey had gray stripes on the arm and a big number 13 emblazoned on the chest and back. His Ohio State jersey. He was holding his future.

"Well? What do you think?" Jenny asked.

"It's great. Thank you," Murphy said, troubled. He was still unsure of his decision. When he thought about it logically, it made perfect sense. Skip the game; don't get injured. When he listened to his gut, something about it seemed dead wrong.

He'd had to bolt out of school right after the bell and disappear. His teammates were gonna find out he'd deserted them any second now.

Jenny wrapped her arms around Murphy and pulled him in for a wet kiss. It felt as good as he remembered, perhaps even better, but Murphy was distracted. Out of place. He could see the glow of stadium lights over the trees and hear the marching band practicing as they tapped out the war cry of his hometown. His best friends and the only father he'd ever known were getting ready for battle.

And I'm here. Being a chicken.

"Stop worrying about it," Jenny said, tugging him closer by the lapels of his letter jacket. "If there is even a remote chance of you getting hurt, don't play. End of story."

Murphy stared into her blue eyes. They shone with that special light a woman has when she looks at the man she loves. It was a look Murphy had already seen fade once—and he never wanted to see it happen again.

"I know. It's just…they're all counting on me."

"I know you, Scotty. All you've ever wanted was to take care of everyone." Her gaze bored into him. "And when you go pro, you'll have enough money to do that."

Murphy nodded as her words sank in. She was right.

"No more night shifts and double shifts for your mom. And no more *trailer*," she said with a derisive glance over at the double-wide. "You can get her a *real* house."

Murphy felt a protest rise up from his gut. His mom was proud of her house. It was clean and well kept, and she wouldn't cotton to anyone looking down on it simply because of its size or its value. But Jenny had a point. And Murphy had seen firsthand what Chris Hall was able to do for his family with his football riches. And Murphy knew he was better. He could do more. He could get his mom a lake house and a fancy Cadillac. Hell, even if he didn't end up with Macy, he could still take care of her too. He'd send her a check anonymously and buy her that farm she'd always wanted outright if he had to. It was all starting to make sense. Jenny was more than beautiful—she was smart and business savvy. "You're right," Murphy said with a smile. "You're right."

"I know," Jenny shot back, crinkling her perfect nose into his. "And you'd better get used to that. Because after the game, you are mine." She gave him a final sensual kiss, and then backed away and got into her shiny red Mustang.

As he watched her drive off, he decided to go by the hospital with dinner and surprise his mom. And he was even going to splurge and buy restaurant food, because they had something to celebrate. He wasn't going to play this football game, which meant he wasn't going to get injured. He'd go to college, and then go pro.

The Murphy family was going to be rich.

Chapter 49

THE IDEA OF BRINGING his mom some food from a fancy restaurant died pretty quick. Not only was Murphy broke, he also had forgotten to take into account the horde of people descending on his small town. Any restaurants within a fifty-mile radius were closed or full.

His truck was the only vehicle driving out of Coldwater that evening. He reckoned he passed more than a thousand cars heading into town with their lights on, even though the sun was still not fully set.

It looked like a funeral procession.

Murphy thought of it as the end of his old life, and this dinner with his mom was a chance to celebrate the new one he was going to start living right after the game.

He settled for some subs from the hoagie place up in Hawthorne. The guy behind the counter was listening to the pre-game on the radio and his eyes almost fell out of his head when he saw who was buying the sandwiches.

"You know who you look like?" the man asked, unwilling to believe he could actually be Scott Murphy—the kid he thought *was* football in this part of Ohio. The idea of Murphy buying sandwiches at a gas mart in another town when he was supposed to be suiting up for the state championship was as unlikely as seeing Santa Claus sunning himself on some South Padre Island beach on Christmas Eve.

"I get that a lot," Murphy said as he paid for the sandwiches.

"That kid's a phenom. Gonna drill those rich city kids a new one and send them packing!" the man exclaimed, beaming a hopeful grin.

Murphy wondered which of his futures would disappoint the man more—him being a no-show for the state championship, or breaking his leg trying to win it.

As he started his car, he forced the thoughts from his head. His job was to take care of his mother, not some gas-station worker in some no-name town like the one he grew up in.

Mansfield Hospital was a drab brick affair built in the late fifties to care for the wounded of World War II. Not the guys who came back with visible wounds, but the guys with the kind you couldn't see. Not at first anyway. They called it "shell-shock" back then.

Now Mansfield was home to mental patients, mostly the mentally retarded, or mentally challenged, or whatever the latest term for it was. Political correctness was an odd thing in Murphy's mind. To him, it wasn't what you said; it was how you said it. He'd gotten in plenty of fights as a boy when other kids had found out where his mom worked and used the word "retard" as playground ammunition. They weren't coming from a good place and Murphy had scuffled in the gravel under the jungle gym plenty of times in protest. But he thought it was silly to think that changing a word, or finding a new word, would make a difference. You need to change the people, and then the word won't matter. But if you just change the word, without changing the people, things don't get better—it just gets harder to figure out who the real bastards are. And then they just hid in plain sight and inevitably found a way to corrupt the new word just like they did the old one.

He'd learned the weight of words firsthand after his injury. He'd started out a cripple. Then he became handicapped. Then he was physically challenged. It was as if people wanted words to distance themselves from the reality of Murphy's situation, something he could never do. And their attempts to find the right word and their discomfort at getting it wrong made Murphy uncomfortable. He was crippled, inside and out. And he didn't give a damn what word was used to describe it, only the emotion with which it was spoken. The teardrop-shaped scar on his cheek was from a bar fight in Dayton when Murphy deemed someone's inflection off. He didn't like to fight, but he had a mean streak when it came to bullies. He figured that of all the lame, he was more capable with his fists than most and thus nominated himself to deliver a few butt-kickings to some idiots with a superiority complex. He did so in the hopes that they would think twice before picking on someone less fortunate ever again.

When his mom said the word retarded, it was just a descriptor—a simple statement of fact, uncolored by hate or judgment. She cared for the men and women in her charge, and did so with the patience, firm hand, and toughness of a single mother. She didn't take guff from her son, and didn't take any from her charges at work either. She was respected and known for being a hard worker.

Murphy didn't want to create any hubbub walking in the front door, so when he saw Mitch, the burly black orderly, smoking by the side entrance, he figured he'd go in that way.

"What the heck you doing here, sonny? Don't you have a game tonight?" Mitch asked.

"Brought dinner for my mom," Murphy said, waving his bag of subs as he skated past Mitch and into the hospital.

Murphy was surprised to find his mom mopping an empty hallway, listening to the football pre-game on the radio as she cleaned. The reception was spotty and as he walked toward her, he saw her worn fingers fumbling with the dial whenever it started to go out. There was no mention of Murphy's absence as far as he could tell, but the game was still at least an hour from kickoff.

He never knew she listened to his games.

He did learn after his injury that his mother had been close by. She had explained that in the third quarter, when it seemed like Coldwater might have a chance of winning, her boss had sent her home, with pay. She had protested, upset at what she saw as charity. She finally agreed to it when he threatened to fire her if she *didn't* leave. She said she had parked on the radio tower hill a half mile from the game to watch—close enough to see movement, far enough away not to have to witness any of the violence. She'd always said getting the night off was a blessing, because she wasn't forty minutes away from her son when he needed her most. It only took her two minutes to get to the field. He only remembered flashes of it, but he would never forget his mother in the ambulance with him, holding his hand, her firm grip and unwavering gaze carrying him through the horror of that night.

"Mom," Murphy said as he got close. She almost jumped out of her skin as she turned around, surprised and clearly more than a little concerned to see him. It was like the deli guy, but with his mom, the look wasn't so much about football as it was physics. It was impossible for a person to be in two places at once.

"I brought you some dinner," Murphy said, holding up the subs.

"Don't you have a game tonight?" she said, concerned. She, like Coach, thought the only way he would miss a game was if he was physically incapacitated or deathly ill.

"I'm not playing," Murphy said as he walked into one of the nearby break rooms and spread out the feast of subs on the table.

"You're not?" Thelma asked, searching his face for the real answer.

"No. And things are gonna be different after tonight, Mom," Murphy said with determination and hope. "From now on, I'm gonna be taking care of you."

He held out the plastic chair for her. Thelma stared at him and sat, but it wasn't to eat. She waited for him to sit down across from her, and then spoke. "You don't take care of me. You take care of yourself. I'm fine," she said in a firm tone.

"I can live cheaply next year, and start sending you some of my scholarship money so you don't have to work so much," Murphy went on, unwrapping his mom's hoagie.

"Save your money. I don't need it," Thelma said, ire rising.

"Also, that truck. It's nice, but I don't need it. We should sell it. I can run to school or get a ride with Jenny."

"Sell it? I just bought it!" Thelma exclaimed.

Murphy remembered it was a present for his eighteenth birthday, just a few short months ago. "You could take the money you put into it and take a nice vacation or something."

"I don't need a vacation. And I don't need you telling me how to manage my money," she shot back.

"It's a waste, Mom, I don't need it!" Murphy said, trying to make her understand. The thought of her driving that worn-out Pinto to work while he tooled around in a fully restored truck rubbed at his soul. He didn't deserve it. She did.

His mom narrowed her eyes and pointed one of her slightly crooked fingers at him, the way she did when it was lecture time and he was to do only two things: shut up and listen.

"Hey. Some people spend their money on fancy trips. Some people go gambling. I don't like any of that. I like to spend my money—and I ain't got much—on you. You never had much of anything growing up and you never complained. Now I want you to have something nice and that truck's gonna take care of you for a long time. Longer than I'll be around, if you take care of it."

The truth of her statement made Murphy's mission to make her understand even direr. He wanted her to start living now. There was no time to waste.

"Mom. I'll be able to buy as many trucks as I want when I'm making money after college. Right now, I'd rather you use that money from a truck I don't need to go somewhere or buy yourself something nice."

"Things don't make me happy. Vacations don't make me happy. You being happy makes me happy."

"I am gonna be happy. And things are gonna be different! No more trailer. No more double shifts…"

Thelma slapped his hand away from the sub he was picking at. He looked up at her.

"No more trailer? Things are gonna be different?"

He'd never seen her look so disappointed in his entire life. He thought it might be the trailer comment, but this look wasn't anger. She looked concerned for his soul. When she finally spoke, her voice was quiet and quivered with an uncharacteristic level of emotion.

"What's so wrong with right now, huh? What if this is it? What if this is all you get, kid?"

"I've done that life, Ma. It was a nightmare."

Murphy felt his mother's hand hard against his cheek. He stared up at her and saw angry tears brimming at the edges of her eyes. He'd never seen her cry. Or get this angry.

"It seems like nothing is ever enough for you. And if you can't be satisfied with what you have, right here, right now, then you're never gonna be happy. No matter what you get."

Murphy dropped his head in shame. His words had hurt her. She'd worked her entire life to give him the best life she possibly could, and here he was telling her how bad it was.

Her voice softened and turned wistful. "You asked me if there was something I wished I could change about my life? If there was something I would do different?"

Murphy remembered the question he'd asked her over dinner a few days ago. He thought she hadn't paid too much attention to it at the time, but apparently it stuck with her.

"If there was one thing I *could* change," she went on. "That would be it."

Murphy remembered hearing an adage that you can only be as happy as your least happy child, and now, having been a father, he completely understood.

Murphy had never been much of a crier either, but he had almost forty years bottled up inside him and once the dam burst, it was a deluge. He broke down, his chest heaving as sobs racked his body. All the things he'd never said to her, all the goodbyes, and I love yous. And here he'd thought he was going to make her happy, and he'd never felt more like he'd failed her in his life.

"I'm sorry...I can't even take care of my family. I can't do it again. Not going back. So what if I don't play a stupid football game…" After a few minutes of blubbering, he realized she'd come over to his side of the table and was holding him. His tears weren't falling on his cheeks anymore—they were being absorbed into the clean linen of her work scrubs. When his chest finally stopped heaving, she pulled him upright.

"Hey," she said, snapping him out of his somber reverie. "What do you want, son? What are all these tears about? Huh?"

Murphy wiped his face and looked at his mother, caught in waves of uncertainty. He hugged her again, and this time held on. There was a chance he might not ever see her again. Not as he remembered her, anyway.

Thelma in a mansion was a different woman to him somehow, and though he wanted and planned to deliver his mother a better life, he would miss this hardscrabble no-nonsense woman. He met her gaze, making sure to memorize every line, every wrinkle of her face.

"It's just… You won't be there." Murphy said.

"Just because I'm not there, doesn't mean I'm not there," she said, eyes on his.

Murphy remembered all the times he'd imagined her sitting in the broken-down Pinto at the edge of his bean field. The time he swore he could *feel* her watching over him, long after she'd been buried. Her statement rang true. As long as his heart was beating, his mother would be with him, whether she was alive or not.

As he thought back across his journey to this moment, part of him couldn't help but wonder whether the whole thing might have been her doing. She'd spent her life fulfilling her son's wishes, breaking her back working every day in the hope that he found happiness.

"I just want to make you proud. I just want to make everybody proud. But I don't know what to do…"

She stared at him, intent on getting her point across. "Stop worrying so damn much about doing what is gonna make everyone else proud, and do what's gonna make you proud. You get that?"

Murphy was quiet, not fully comprehending.

She simplified. "You want to make me proud? Make yourself proud."

Thelma grabbed his chin, raised it, and locked her eyes onto his, the way she always did when she wanted him to understand something. She knew the only two openings into her son's thick skull were through the soft parts—his eyes.

"And I'm not talking to Mr. Football, neither. I'm talking to Scott Murphy."

Chapter 50

SCOTT MURPHY SAT ALONE in the dark bedroom of the double-wide trailer he grew up in. Through the sheer curtains of his window he could see the glow of the stadium lights radiating through the rustling trees. He could hear the drums of the marching band in the distance.

All he had to do to guarantee his college education was play one down at the college level. All he had to do to achieve that was to sit here for two more hours.

No victory. But no injury.

What his mom had said to him over their hoagie dinner kept running through his mind: *"Make yourself proud."*

His mom told him to do what was right for Scott Murphy and not Mr. Football. At first it seemed like exactly what he wanted to hear. Forget football. Protect yourself.

But as he sat on his old bed replaying the interaction in his mind, he realized that wasn't what she had meant at all. She meant that it wasn't about football; it was about who he was as a human being.

So what would Scott Murphy think was the right thing to do?

Which Scott Murphy? The eighteen-year-old buck or the scar-faced alcoholic cripple?

He realized whatever the right answer was, it would be the same for either Scott Murphy. The flesh might change, but the soul remains constant.

Murphy looked around his room and in that moment realized that everything he had—everything that he had ever had—was given to him. His father gave him his name. His mother gave him his home, his truck. Even his football prowess was a gift from his mother working double shifts so he could practice instead of getting a job and Coach Hand teaching him from a young age. And then he realized just how much Coldwater had given him. When his mother died, there were more than two thousand shoulders at her funeral he could have cried on. He thought about the forty-two guys standing on the sidelines of that football field without him.

Part of him wanted to stay right here on the couch.

Part of him wanted to go play football.

Which part was right? Which part was Scott Murphy?

How can I do what would make Scott Murphy proud, when I don't know who he is?

The wind in the trees and the sound of the drums that echoed from the stadium faded out, and he was left alone with himself in a sea of silence.

Murphy realized that as he'd been talking to himself, someone inside had actually listened. He figured the one doing the listening must be his heart. Or the little piece of God we all carry inside our chests.

That's Scott Murphy.

Having found himself at last, he posed the question again.

The answer came quickly and without effort. Scott Murphy would never be proud of Scott Murphy if he just sat here and waited for destiny to pass him by. If he was going to make a different future and change his fate, he would do it on his feet, under the lights, in front of the people he loved. Not huddled in some teenaged boy's bedroom like a coward.

Scott Murphy owed this town something. Not a victory. That was something he owed only to himself. But at least he owed them a chance.

Scott Murphy never backed down from a fight.

Chapter 51

THE TEAM WAS DRESSED and ready when Murphy walked into the locker room, but the pre-game feeling was as somber as a morgue. By the looks he got when people finally noticed him, he realized Coach Hand must have told them he wasn't coming. Hall was sheet white when he met his gaze, and a few guys were purple, as if they were literally holding their breaths, trying not to explode.

His battered helmet was on top of his open locker, where his lifeless jersey hung inside like an old ghost. Coach turned from the clock on the wall and met his gaze. Stone cold silence fell over the room. Saying you weren't gonna play was one thing. Showing up after a stunt like that and expecting to be welcomed back was another.

Murphy met the old man's gaze and said the only thing he could think to say. "Sorry I'm late."

His words hung in the air. The air got thick with tension as the two men stared each other down across the locker room.

It felt like the old man could see the fear in his eyes, and knew that he was still scared, but that he wasn't here for himself. David was here to do battle for the people he loved.

"Get dressed," Coach said, heading back into his office.

Murphy's teammates all stood up to greet him, slapping him on the back. Relieved.

Chapter 52

"SCOTTY?" HALL YELLED, BANGING on the bathroom stall.

Murphy knelt on the floor and sweat beaded on his brow, as he filled the toilet with the remnants of the submarine sandwich. He couldn't help but notice that the lettuce and meat held up pretty well, considering how violent the process was.

Murphy could count the number of times he'd thrown up in his entire life on one hand. It just wasn't something that happened to him. He always figured the extra liver he got because he was Irish came with a cast-iron stomach. His gut would rust up with ulcers, twist in knots of worry, resentment and fear—but it wouldn't give up on the job and throw honest work the wrong way back up the assembly line. For a moment Murphy hoped he was only kissing porcelain right now because his body figured it had more important issues to concentrate on than digesting food. Like playing football.

But this wasn't efficiency making him lose his dinner. It was just honest-to-goodness fear.

As the realization knotted up his stomach and he dry-heaved into the toilet, he couldn't help but feel optimistic. He was sure he hadn't been scared like this the first time he'd played this football game. And he figured if that was different, maybe everything about the game could be different, too.

Maybe I can change the future.

Chapter 53

AS THE CAVALIERS WAITED in the school parking lot to take the field, Murphy had to lean over the rusted-out '69 Pontiac Firebird frame parked on blocks near the high school auto shop and puke his guts out again. For the first time, he understood what it was like to be a soldier heading into a battle knowing there was a good chance he wouldn't make it back in one piece.

He felt close to his father in that moment. The first time Murphy played this game, he was all pomp and circumstance. He was afraid of nothing, and his eighteen-year-old mind had figured that was what courage was—lack of fear.

Now he knew that was just being a dumb kid. Nothing brave about it.

But this time he understood what he would suffer if he couldn't change the future. The pain of the injury. The months of surgeries. The rehab. The beginning of the slow death he would die for the next twenty years if this game didn't come out right.

He was scared for his life. Like his father must have been in Vietnam.

Thelma never talked about how his dad died. Murphy had pressed hard one summer as a kid when he still thought war was romantic. Coach Hand had told him the story. Before he heard it, Murphy, like most people, figured soldiers died on the battlefield out of bravery, or fear, or were killed out of hate or anger by the enemy. Coach Hand's version was different. He said every man he ever saw die on the battlefield died out of love. Sure, they sometimes got cut down trying to take some meaningless unnamed hill. But most of the time, they were dropped trying to save someone they cared about. The old man could barely get the words out when he talked about what Patrick Murphy did. How he led a group of men across a rice field to save another group of men, even though they knew it was most likely a suicide mission. Murphy's father had sacrificed himself to save others.

Murphy knew that was what bravery was. Tasting the fear rising up in your stomach, feeling the world go silent as your heartbeats hurt your ears, the flutter of adrenaline, every bone and vein in your body telling you to run away from something—to *not* do something—and then doing it anyway.

Doubt swarmed Murphy's mind and he felt his insides roiling again. He squeezed the pennies he was going to plant at each end zone tight in his fist to try to calm himself down.

That's what this game is. A suicide mission.

Chapter 54

MOST HIGH SCHOOL FOOTBALL games, for the kids not on the field, are simply social events. Teenagers have hormones and other interests besides watching something that may or may not impact their lives, and besides, it's Friday night, time to hang out. It's the end of the school week. They talk to each other, they flirt, they run the bleachers, or they loiter by the snack bar. Very few watch the field.

But then there are games that matter. Games where each person in the stands and each person on the sidelines is keyed into every play. Every human being gathered is focused on the field—their hearts and minds hanging on every moment. The combined intent of so many souls focused on one singularity makes the air electric. The crowd inhales and exhales as an entity. Every person in the stadium becomes connected.

This was one of those games.

Satellite trucks lined the edge of the field with reporters in pancake makeup staring into the lenses of cumbersome video cameras. The new bleachers were packed to capacity, with more people present for this football game than had ever set foot in the town of Coldwater. Despite the fact that the town population had decreased by a third in the last century, there was a bigger crowd here to see Scott Murphy play football than there was to see Abraham Lincoln give his speech.

Murphy crowded behind the large paper Cavaliers banner with

his teammates, waiting to break through when the time was right. He saw Jenny on one of her cheerleading teammate's shoulders, holding the top of the banner. Despite her support for him not playing, he could tell from her face she was proud to see him here. Murphy pushed her out of his mind, as he always did before a game. He needed to think about football right now, not girls.

Murphy might be physically a little rusty—but he had twenty years of knowledge on any player on the field. The game had evolved dramatically since his high school career—and despite never setting foot on the Coldwater High School football field since his glory days, he'd watched NFL games every weekend, every chance he could get. And while seeing guys he used to run circles around, like Chris Hall, making millions had made him bitter, watching players like Joe Montana, Steve Young, and Brett Favre had made him better.

The announcer's voice echoed through the stadium as the Versailles Saints ran on the field. A chorus of cheers erupted from the visitor's side of the stands. From the home side, the only thing heard was silence. The Coldwater crowd would never boo an opposing team, it was considered bad manners, but the absolute stillness of an entire town sent a clear enough message.

When Murphy peered from behind the banner the rush of sights and sounds was overwhelming. The flashbulbs. The surging crowd. The girls who had come from the next county to stand on the sidelines and watch him play football because they thought he was cute. The *Sports Illustrated* reporter here to write a feature about him. The NFL films cameraman on the sideline. Murphy didn't care about any of it. All that mattered to him, all that had ever mattered when he was playing football, was winning. Because he knew that the world was a different place for winners. Whenever anyone tried to tell him otherwise, he knew they were lying.

Winners can feed their families. Winners don't shop for clothes at Goodwill. Winners' moms don't have to drive thirty-some miles each way in a broken-down car to work a fourteen-hour shift and come home with bite marks on their wrists. Winners don't have to actually kill themselves to keep a roof over their heads.

He heard the cheers crescendo and saw the closest thing any high school kid could have to a mortal enemy running across the field. Alex Washington. Number 54. He was known as the most devastating linebacker high school had to offer at that point in time. To Murphy, he was simply the man who broke his leg—the person who ended his life.

No one present but Murphy knew it, but 54 would go on to be one of the most famous and highly paid defensive players in the history of the NFL. He was so quick, so relentless, and so punishing on opposing quarterbacks that he single-handedly changed the way the game of football was played.

The irony of this bitter rivalry was that Alex Washington and Scott Murphy were very much alike. Both had grown up without a father in the house. Both had single mothers who worked relentlessly to provide for their children. Neither of their mothers liked the violence of football. And both boys played football as if their lives depended on it.

When Scott Murphy or Alex Washington stepped onto the football field, they weren't there for a game. They were there to put food on the table. They were there to feed their families. And if you got in the way, they would do anything they could to destroy you.

Alex Washington had ended up in a rich city school because he was good at football. He had no illusions that when he was no longer good at football, they'd bus him and his mother right back to the Cleveland projects without a second thought.

But Murphy's knowledge of their similarities came from the future, and right now he had to be in the present, so there would never be any love between Alex Washington and Scott Murphy. Nor could there be. There could only be one Mr. Football. There could only be one Ohio High School State Championship football team. Alex Washington was unquestionably the physically superior athlete, while Scott Murphy was better at the things that couldn't be measured. Things like effort, leadership, and ability to perform under pressure—the things coaches called intangibles.

Last time they met, Murphy won the day, but went home in pieces. Washington went home a loser, but went on to become a superstar.

Murphy's mind trip was cut short by a sharp slap on his helmet and he turned to see Hall, grinning. "You ready to make history?" he shouted.

"Change it, at least," Murphy said as he snapped his chinstrap.

Time to break through the banner.

Chapter 55

MURPHY AND WASHINGTON SQUARED up in the center of the field like two prizefighters before the title match. They each had co-captains with them, but they might as well have been alone—each of them knew this game was about him.

Damn. He's bigger than I remember.

"You ready to die, Backwater?" Washington said, grinning death at him from behind his face mask.

Murphy didn't respond—he was too busy trying to figure out what to call in the coin toss. The first time they'd done this, he was pretty sure they hadn't won. Murphy knew this because he always chose heads, and when the flip went his way, he always chose to be on offense. Every time. But he distinctly remembered his team had started on defense because he remembered watching the Versailles running back return the opening kickoff for ninety-six yards and a touchdown. Those kinds of things stick in your mind.

Murphy didn't know if he should call heads because odds were it wouldn't come up tails again like it had the first time, or if he should call tails because this was a repeat and the flip would be the same as twenty years ago. It was like playing rock-paper-scissors with himself. Todd White would know what to do, but at this moment Todd was running like an idiot down the sidelines in the school's mascot costume.

The ref flipped the coin and as the silver dollar spun through the air, Murphy made his decision. "Tails," he shouted as the coin spun upward and then bounced across the grass, landing near Washington's shiny new red Nike cleats.

It was tails.

Murphy had won the toss. He was about to ask to receive when Pierson, his co-captain, spoke up before he could get the words out.

"Kick! We wanna kick!" Pierson shouted quickly.

Murphy turned to him, incredulous, protesting, but it was too late. "Coach said if we won to kick it," Pierson explained when he saw Murphy's anger.

"Coldwater is kicking!" the ref shouted.

Murphy realized he had more than Alex Washington and the Versailles Saints to contend with if he was going to succeed in his plan to change the future. If he was going to win without getting hurt, he needed to take control and call the plays. But Coach Hand had his own game plan in mind, and the old man wasn't exactly a pushover.

Versailles picked the side of the field that would give them the wind at their backs.

Washington bumped Murphy as he made his way back to his sideline. "Gonna break every bone in your body, sucker," he said through clenched teeth.

Murphy smiled and gave Washington a sarcastic "Good luck." But jogging toward the sideline a few moments later, he was haunted by the statement.

Not every bone, but enough to ruin my life if I don't change things.

Chapter 56

MURPHY STOOD BY THE battered metal water cooler and watched Versailles run the opening kickoff back ninety-six yards for a touchdown. Just like they had done in 1991.

Dammit.

For twenty years, Murphy had dreamed about getting an opportunity to play this game again, but now that he was here, lining up to take the first snap, he realized he was fighting a war on three distinct fronts: one against a football team called the Versailles Saints; a second against the pitifulness of his own team; and a third against the cosmos itself. He suspected that while he looked for an opportunity to make things different, the universe, or fate, was going to do everything in its power to put things back the way they were meant to be.

And while doing battle with the cosmos might seem daunting, Murphy was most concerned about Versailles right now. Their defensive linemen averaged three-hundred-and-twenty-five pounds each. To the gathered spectators, they comprised a front line of the best defensive players high school could offer. Murphy, with twenty years of Sunday and Monday night football under his belt, saw them not for what they were, but for what they would be—future professional football Hall-of-Famers whose salaries could buy the town of Coldwater a few times over.

All Murphy had going for him was the fact that Chris Pierson, the left tackle, still had both his testicles. In his farm-boy prime,

TOUCHBACK

Pierson was a bit of a behemoth. Six foot five, three hundred pounds, Pierson was charged with protecting the quarterback and making sure Murphy didn't end up in the hospital before the game was over. He failed at that mission the first time, and Murphy knew if he didn't do things differently this time, he would in all likelihood fail again.

Murphy also knew that even in his prime, Pierson was still no match for #54 Alex Washington. His blindside pass rush was so devastating that Murphy had seen games where professional quarterbacks forgot the snap count when he glared at them across the line of scrimmage. The best Murphy could hope for was that Pierson could buy him a second or two.

"Red Twenty-six! Red Twenty-six!" Murphy shouted, calling out the first play of the game. It was a short screen to Hall across the middle. "Set! Go!"

Murphy took the ball and dropped back, counting silently in his head. *One one-thousand, two one...*

Bam! Wham! Murphy felt two impacts, the first was #54 hitting his blindside like a locomotive, and then a half-second later, another impact as he was slammed into the ground.

As Washington got off him, he gave Murphy an extra push into the ground.

And though it hurt, Murphy popped right up. He had to. If Washington knew how badly that had hurt him, the game was lost. Murphy's ears were ringing and he saw particles floating around in his field of vision.

Damn.

Less than two seconds. He had somehow remembered it being more than that. Maybe Pierson just wasn't ready for how fast he was.

"The pain's coming all night, Backwater!" Washington said, getting in his face.

Backwater.

Sure, Murphy had called Coldwater "Backwater" a hundred thousand, probably a million times. It was his crap little Podunk

212

town and he could call it anything he wanted, but when someone else said that word, he felt the blood start to boil up into his head.

Murphy played by rhythm, which meant that he was throwing the ball on a count, not a look. His receivers simply ran the pattern and turned at a certain point and found the ball—usually already hitting their chest pads. He was deadly accurate and as long as someone could give him a look, he could thread the needle and put the pass where it needed to be.

The problem was that receivers needed time to run patterns to get open. And he hadn't even gotten to a two count before Washington was on his back. And even the fastest man alive can't get more than fifteen yards in that kind of time.

Coming into this game Versailles knew that Murphy would only have a few seconds of pocket time before he got hammered. So that was all the time Murphy's receivers would have to run downfield. About twenty yards was all that Murphy could expect, which would limit his passing offense to short passes. In fact, Versailles was so confident, they'd spent the entire two weeks before this game practicing only one key defensive scheme—a short-pass defense that could convert to contain Murphy if he took off running.

It had taken Murphy a whole quarter to figure this out the first time he'd played this team. But not this time. He was going to do things differently. No down-to-the-wire finishes. He was determined to get so far ahead of Versailles by the fourth quarter that he could just take the bench and let the chicken-head freshmen players take a knee to run out the clock and win the game.

Even if Pierson could only slow Washington down long enough to buy Murphy a half second, it could still be enough, because football was as much a chess game as a wrestling match. If someone does the same thing every time, you can find a way to beat it. And if Washington was anything, he was consistent.

To beat them, he needed to go long—throw deep passes.

To go long, he had to beat Washington.

To beat Washington, he needed to figure out his rhythm.

Which meant he had to take one more devastating hit.

"Fifty-four Right! Fifty-four Right!" Murphy yelled as he stepped to the line to let Pierson know where 54 was. He needed that extra second.

"Twenty-four! Twenty-four! Red! Set!" Murphy shouted as he knelt behind the center. He flicked his wrist and the ball came up into it. He moved back. Seven steps this time. He wanted to see what he was working with. In his mind, he kept the rhythm: one one-thousand…

He scanned. No one open.

Two one thou—Wham!

A Mack truck with a #54 license plate hit Murphy from the side. Washington slammed his arm down on Murphy's helmet like a battle-ax and then picked him up, lifting him up in the air, then slamming him down hard.

Bam! Murphy's helmet popped off and rolled across the ground. The collision was so violent that a few people in the crowd almost fainted, thinking it was his severed head. Murphy struggled to stand up, body aching. He shook his head, trying to shake away the swirls of star-like motes that floated in his vision. He was sure he had a concussion.

Murphy had taken two of the hardest hits of his life, but with the pain, he had been delivered valuable information. He now knew exactly how long it was taking Washington to get through Pierson—just under two seconds both times, like clockwork.

And now he had to put this information to use. It was third down, so Murphy only had one chance. He slapped Pierson on the helmet, hoping the big man didn't get lucky and slow down Washington more than usual and mess up his count. His friend had to get bowled over just as fast on this down as he had on all the others. Everything depended on it.

Murphy went into the huddle. His ears rang and his heart pounded as he did the calculations in his head. Washington would take one second to bowl over Pierson, and then another half second to reach him. That gave Murphy almost two seconds to get out of the pocket or get rid of the ball. If he held onto the ball or stayed in the pocket any longer than the two-second mark, he was going to get his clock cleaned again. And no one could stand too many hits from Alex Washington.

At least, that is what they assumed.

Washington smiled again. It was a razor-blade smile, below the eyes of a mass murderer. Washington hated Scott Murphy—the little farm boy who stole his Mr. Football medal. To him, he'd lost out from the same old bias—stats favored the offensive player over the defensive player. Quarterback success was easy to quantify, it was measured in yards and points. Defensive success is harder to measure, and Washington felt shortchanged.

"Red Eighty-one. Trips right. On four." Murphy said in the huddle.

"You wanna throw a bomb? Are you crazy, man?" Hall protested. "You won't have enough time…"

"Let me worry about my time. You just get your ass open and catch the ball…"

Murphy left the huddle early, confident, as he always did. He led; he didn't B.S. Plus, he wanted to set a fast pace from the start. They needed to outwork these guys if they wanted to win.

"Red Eighty-one! Red! Eighty-one! Hut! Hut! Hut!" Murphy called from behind center.

Smitty fed him the ball and Murphy did a seven-step drop, counting in his head.

One one-thousand. Two one…

Murphy leapt forward and spun right at that exact moment and Alex Washington found his arms grabbing nothing but cold Ohio air.

Three one-thousand…

Murphy scanned downfield and found Hall. He was covered—two men deep. He wasn't open.

Four one-thousand. Five…

The other linebacker dove at him. Murphy slipped the tackle and pumped it to Bragdon. Hall's coverage bit on the fake and ran to cover this new target. Hall kept running for the end zone, wide open.

Six one-thousand...

Hands raked Murphy's jersey and he was yanked back hard as he released the ball.

Wham! He hit the ground hard and Washington glared down at him. Apparently he'd recovered and hunted Murphy down for revenge.

It was probably the second hardest hit Murphy had ever taken, but he thought he heard the cheers of a Coldwater touchdown just as he blacked out.

Murphy came to a few seconds later with Coach Hand looking at him, concerned, and Doc Salisbury shining his little penlight into Murphy's eyes.

Damn. Don't remember this.

"What did you say, son?"

"I didn't realize I said anything."

Murphy was beginning to think that changing this game could have some unforeseen negative consequences. But that was okay, because anything was better than spending the rest of his life crippled in Coldwater.

As they helped Murphy to his feet, the crowd went bananas. He checked the scoreboard and realized they had scored a touchdown. Hall came back to Murphy and threw him a penny that Murphy caught in mid-air. He realized he *had* shared his secret with one person, his boyhood friend Chris Hall, and he had not only understood it, but had cherished it as much as Murphy. And just like that, for the first time in twenty years, Scott Murphy and Chris Hall were best friends again.

Murphy smiled as he walked to the sidelines. He distinctly remembered that they hadn't scored on the first drive the last time he played this game. He had changed something.

Washington muttered under his breath as Murphy jogged by.

"You're dead, mother—"

Murphy gave him a canary-eating grin. On the contrary, he'd

never felt more alive.

This is going to be easier than I thought.

Chapter 57

WHEN ALEX WASHINGTON RETIRED from football in 2009, Bob Costas asked him to name the best quarterback he had ever played against, and Washington had replied, without hesitation, "Number thirteen. Scott Murphy."

Costas had never heard of him. He shuffled through his notes, scanning his encyclopedic sports brain for some clue about Scott Murphy, and panicked. Was there some legendary football great he had never heard of?

"Who?" Costas finally asked, a little stunned.

"Some cat I played in high school. Small town. Beat us in the state championship. No one I ever played was as good as that kid."

Relief flooded Costas's face. High school.

His relief was quickly replaced with scorn. He pressed Washington for a better answer, skeptical. "Steve Young, Brett Favre, Tom Brady..." Costas went down the list. "You've played against them all. And you're saying a high school quarterback was *better*?

"Hey, man," Washington shot back with a thin smile, folding his huge championship-ring-covered hands together. "You asked who was the best."

"Okay, well, if Scott Murphy was such a great quarterback, why didn't he play in the NFL?" Costas came back.

The Cheshire smile faded from Washington's face. "Because I broke his leg."

No one outside of Costas, Washington, two cameramen, a sound technician and the segment editor ever heard that answer. The idea was so outlandish, and Costas was so flummoxed by it, that it landed on the cutting-room floor.

Chapter 58

MURPHY'S VICTORY WAS SHORT-lived. Fourteen seconds, to be exact. That was the amount of time it took for Versailles to march down the field and score. That was all the recovery time Murphy got before he had to go back into battle.

The scoreboard was a grim reminder of his predicament. Coldwater trailed 21-7 and it was only a few minutes before halftime. Whenever Murphy figured out Alex Washington's rhythm, Washington changed it.

"Slowing down, huh, Backwater?" Washington said as Murphy staggered to his feet after yet another devastating hit.

"I thrive on pain," Murphy shot back tiredly.

"I hope so, sucker! Cause it's coming all night!"

"Your mom said the same thing last night," Murphy yelled back. Washington stared at him, incredulous. Washington was jumping out of his skin with anger as Murphy led his team into the huddle. His teammates struggled to hold him back.

"What did you say about my momma, Backwater? Huh? I'm gonna kill you, sucker! You understand? You're done!" Washington yelled, still trying his best to break free and kill Murphy.

Murphy had nothing against Washington's mom, and would have reacted even more violently if anyone had said the same about Thelma. But desperate times called for desperate measures and he needed to get under Washington's skin.

Pierson pulled Murphy back to the huddle, eyes wide with fear.

The game wasn't even halfway over and the big lug's uniform was already covered in dirt and blood.

"Settle down, Murphy. You're pissing them off and they're taking it out on me," Pierson said through heaving breaths.

Murphy felt his head get light—his vision still hadn't cleared. He put his arm over Tony Kascek, the tight end, to keep his balance. He needed a few more seconds to recover.

"I need him mad, Chris. I need him to make mistakes," Murphy said.

"You're trying to rope-a-dope him, Murphy? Are you crazy? Stop standing up to him and get your ass out of the way or he's gonna light you up!" Hall cautioned. He was referring to the boxing strategy where a fighter purposely allows himself to get pummeled by a stronger opponent to tire him out before turning the tables.

Murphy might not remember the second half of the championship, but he remembered the first, and he had seen enough games of Alex Washington's to know he had no chance playing him conventionally. Washington was bigger, faster, and stronger than Scott Murphy would or *could* ever be. To win, Murphy had to outthink, outlast, and outwork him. It's not the size of the dog in the fight; it's the size of the fight in the dog.

And Murphy wasn't going to give up.

He also had no intention of having his leg broken again. Murphy knew the play that had injured him was "Black Seven," a quarterback bootleg option. He also knew that if worst came to worst, he could simply call an audible at the line and change the play if it came down to that. As long as he didn't run that specific route as the final play, he wouldn't injure his leg. Or so he figured.

Todd White, the smartest kid Murphy knew, had said that he might be a victim of fate and might have no choice in what happened. Murphy had never, in all his years of being crippled, thought of himself as any kind of victim. Cursed, yes; unlucky, yes; miserable, perhaps. But never a victim. His mother had raised him too right for that. So the fact that Fate was trying to make him a victim, forced to relive the worst moment of his life, made Murphy even more determined to change his future.

"Black Seventeen on three!" Murphy called. Black was their code for a quarterback option play. Option plays gave the quarterback just that—the option to hand off the ball or keep it himself. "On three" meant to go on the third hut.

"Black Seventeen! Black! Seventeen! Hut! Hut! Hut!" Murphy called from behind center. He took the snap and rolled out right. It was a designed running play, but out of habit he looked downfield for any open receiver. As usual, there were none.

He saw Alex Washington closing in on him near the sidelines and calculated that he would knock him out of bounds just shy of a first down. That wasn't good enough.

Washington's eyes went wide as he saw Murphy spin and duck. At first he must have thought Murphy was doing what every other quarterback did when they heard his footsteps—duck and cover to ease the pain. Washington realized too late that Murphy wasn't trying to avoid him to lessen the impact—he was turning into him to *increase it.*

This had never happened to Alex Washington. No skinny little quarterback had ever bucked up and stepped into him. For a split second, he had absolutely no idea how to react. That split second was all Murphy needed to get low and blast Washington's diving legs out from under him.

Washington's momentum did the work and he flipped up over Murphy's back and briefly saw sky as he went inverted and then slammed down hard onto his back.

Without looking back, Murphy tucked the ball and raced downfield.

Seconds later he danced across the goal line. The stands erupted in pandemonium. The Versailles Saints had never been scored on twice in the first half, all season.

Any other quarterback in the state would have spiked the ball, pointed to friends, knelt in prayer, done something in celebration of doing the impossible, of scoring such a massive touchdown in such an important game.

Murphy never celebrated in the end zone. He believed that scoring a touchdown was like getting invited to a fancy party. If you acted like you'd been there before, and behaved politely, you'd be sure to get invited back.

He respectfully handed the ball to the ref, and then went to the edge of the end zone and knelt down as if to tie his shoe. He grabbed one of his lucky pennies and stuck it in his sock.

As he jogged back to the sidelines, he saw Jenny shouting his name and kicking her perfect legs into the air. He would have cracked a smile if he hadn't seen the girl in the marching uniform and goofy hat standing with the band behind her—Sasha. And if Sasha was there, Macy wouldn't be far. He scanned the faces and finally found her, talking to the tuba player. She didn't seem one bit interested in him or the game.

Good. It's better that way.

Pierson jumped on him as he reached the sidelines, shouting in his ear, "Nice work, baby!"

Murphy pushed him away, unsure why he was so upset at the world right now. He told himself it had nothing to do with Macy's disinterest and everything to do with the fact that despite his best efforts, his team was still trailing by a touchdown. Just like they had the first time around.

"It's happening again!" Murphy grabbed Pierson's face mask and shook it, shouting, "We trailed them the whole game! We gotta get ahead! You hear me? We gotta get ahead!"

Murphy screamed at the defense as they ran onto the field. "Get me the ball back!"

Time was running out.

Chapter 59

WHEN THE WHISTLE BLEW and Murphy led his battered team off the field for halftime, he stared up at the old Coca-Cola scoreboard. A few of the bulbs were burned out, but he could still read the score: 21-14. Coldwater was behind by a touchdown, and despite Murphy having played this game before, he hadn't managed to change anything, not really. The score was still exactly the same at this point as it had been twenty years ago.

He was consumed by dark thoughts about his failure to noticeably change his destiny, when a flash of gold caught his eye. He turned and saw the marching band walking past in formation. He stared over at Macy, holding her clarinet as she marched, trying as best she could not to look in his direction.

Murphy tuned out the beginning of Coach's halftime speech. He was locked in his head, floating somewhere between the future and the past, which were kind of the same thing right now. It was all muddled. Every time he had scored earlier or called a different play, it hadn't made a difference. The points on the scoreboard at halftime, to the best of his memory, were the same they had been twenty years ago. For all intents, he had altered nothing.

Maybe Todd was right. Maybe he couldn't change it.

Maybe I am about to ruin my life all over again.

Murphy saw that Coach Hand had the dictionary out again. Coach had a habit of turning halftime speeches into English lessons. Murphy had always thought the dictionary bits were silly and remembered ignoring them during games, but this time he figured he might as well pay attention. It was either do that or worry about a future he couldn't seem to control.

"Champion," Coach read from the dictionary. "Who can tell me what it means?"

The kids in the locker room shifted uncomfortably, sensing a trap. Coach Hand taught English, and words had meaning. He could get from the dictionary as much profundity and spiritual insight as some people could from the Bible. His lessons were often hard to grasp and he would get in your face to make you understand them if he had to.

"No one here can define the word 'champion'?" Coach shouted, incredulous.

"A winner," Pierson offered hopefully.

"What else does it mean?" Coach asked, more urgently. Silence fell over the locker room, punctuated by shuffling cleats and the heavy breathing of the overweight linemen still recovering from the first two quarters.

"Murphy!" Coach yelled, snapping Murphy to the present.

Murphy looked up. Unsure of the question.

"What's another definition of 'champion'?" Coach asked, eyes boring into him with unusual intensity.

Murphy shrugged, wiping sweat from his nose, rankled. Not a vocabulary lesson. Not now. And he hated roundabout lessons. Question-asking teaching—or Socratic crap, as he called it—tired him. If there was something someone was trying to teach him, he preferred they just hit him in the forehead with it instead of beating around the damn bush.

"I don't know, Coach," Murphy said tiredly. He was, for the first time since going back in time, feeling like he was pushing forty again.

"The guy who's the best?" Gig threw out, trying to be helpful in some way, since he hadn't yet set foot on the field and didn't expect to anytime soon.

"That's still the first definition," Coach responded, peering down his nose through the narrow glasses he needed for reading. When he was a kid, Murphy had never understood why people did that; he'd taken vision for granted. But the second he hit forty, he too was holding menus at arm's distance to see what he was gonna eat.

"A person who has defeated or surpassed all rivals in competition," Coach read, with emphasis. After that sank in, he went on.

"Who knows what the second definition of the word is?" Coach asked, looking right at Murphy.

Murphy felt there were a lot of other words Coach could be drumming the team with right now. Like "protect": to keep from harm. As in protect the damn quarterback. Or "pocket": the safe area around the quarterback created by his offensive linemen. As in, it would be nice to have a pocket to stand and throw from for a change, instead of getting hammered every down.

"Murphy?" Coach pressed.

"Is there gonna be a test on this later or something?" Murphy responded sarcastically, falling into his old patterns. He wasn't a brain guy and resented being put on the spot.

Coach didn't care, as usual, when he was trying to teach him something. "Yes, son. There's gonna be a test on this, every damn day for the rest of your life!" He yelled as if turning up the volume might hammer it into Murphy's thick skull. He punctuated his point by throwing down the dictionary hard at Murphy's feet, where it landed with a thump.

"Pick it up," Coach said. Murphy was in no mood, and it more than crossed his mind to ask the old man to step outside. The locker room grew dead quiet. The rattle of the marching band out on the field filtered through the school halls, ghostly.

Murphy sank his anger back down into his belly and reached down, picking up the old Webster's. The cover was half torn off, and the pages were dog-eared.

"Page two hundred forty-six." Coach broke the silence.

Murphy flipped through the dictionary, drops of sweat tumbling off his brow onto the pages as he scanned through words he would not, or could not, make himself ever care to know— abactor, badious, cachexia. He finally got to the offending page and saw the word in question circled carefully in red pen.

"Read the first definition again, please," Coach said.

Murphy was great at reading coverage on a football field. Words on a page made him nervous. He wasn't stupid, but he wasn't exactly Einstein either. He didn't even like to say some words out loud because he didn't like how they sounded. They sounded stuck-up. At the diner, when he'd order salad and they'd ask him what kind of dressing he wanted, he was never sure what the difference was between French dressing and Thousand Island, and both sounded equally pretentious—so he'd always just ask for the orange one.

"Champion," Murphy read. "First definition. A person who has defeated all opponents or surpassed all rivals in competition."

"Great. Now read the second one," Coach added.

"Second definition," Murphy said, reading the words by rote, without really absorbing their meaning. "A person who fights for a cause or on behalf of someone else."

A wave of understanding swept through the room, and as usual with this kind of teaching method, it was lost on Murphy at first.

"Do you understand the difference?" Coach inquired.

Murphy watched as heads nodded.

"The first kind of champion? You can only be that kind of champion part time. Because no one, no matter how good, wins forever. And when you aren't the champion by that definition, what are you?"

"The loser," Murphy spoke, finally getting it.

"One of those champions fights for himself. The other one fights for someone else. If you're gonna fight for yourself, by yourself, you have to win to be a champion. If you fight for someone else, with someone else—if you work together as a team, for a cause bigger than each of you is individually—you will always be a champion. No matter what the scoreboard says."

The kids took this in. They understood the significance. Each of them had "COLDWATER" emblazoned on the front of his jersey in big letters. They knew who they were fighting for.

"Winning isn't what makes a champion. Fighting is. Never giving up. Never backing down. It's standing up for what and for whom you believe in. It's protecting the ones you love and the ones who love you. Do you understand that?"

Coach Hand called them to gather around him. It wasn't the pep rally Coach usually did to fire them up before games. It was more of a prayer circle. Quiet, meaningful, and powerful. He spoke softly, looking each of the sons of Coldwater in the eye.

"If you go out there to fight for what you love, I promise you will be a champion—not just tonight, but for the rest of your life."

Coach's words had an odd resonance for Murphy. He figured he'd probably heard them once before, twenty years ago, but completely ignored them. But they had meaning for him this time. He knew what it was to love and to lose. He had only ever thought it was possible to be a champion of the first definition, and the fact that there was another way to that kind of glory was something he still couldn't quite fathom.

"Murphy, hang back a second," Coach said as the team filed back out into the parking lot.

"What?" Murphy replied defensively, expecting to get chewed out for mouthing off.

"I've never seen you play like this."

Murphy bristled. "I'm doing the best I can, Coach."

"It's the first time I've seen you playing for the name on the front of your jersey and not the one on the back." Coach said.

Murphy couldn't believe the old man was praising him. He felt his play was inadequate at best. They were, after all, still trailing by seven points.

"But," Coach continued with a pregnant pause. Murphy was almost relieved.

"But what?" he asked, almost eager for the normalcy of an ass-chewing.

"You've got ten other guys out there. Stop trying to do it all by yourself."

The last thing Murphy wanted to hear was the old man's "spread the ball out" speech. Did he want to win or not?

"I'm just trying to win, Coach," Murphy said, looking toward the distant lights of the field. The halftime show was winding down. Almost time to go.

Coach Hand put a hand on his shoulder and gently turned Murphy to face him. He wanted him to hear this. "You didn't carry this team here, son. You led them. And these boys may not be the biggest or the best. But they're farm boys. They're tough. Lean on them. They won't break."

Chapter 60

MURPHY COULDN'T REMEMBER THE second half at all. According to the doctors, the chemicals that flooded his brain after such a massive injury had effectively erased his memory of the moment of injury and everything leading up to it. It was too traumatic.

Any advantage of hindsight he might have had in the first half would be gone. In the twenty years since the accident, Murphy had never once watched a tape of the game, either. He'd had no desire to see it. He did, however, ask what play he had run that had led to the injury. He wanted to know the name of the last play—the one that had ended his football career, and for all intents and purposes, his entire life. *Black Seven.* An option bootleg.

His decision to run that play, though he didn't recall it, had haunted him his entire life. He had secretly thought it was a horrible decision, to call a running play with so much field left to get to the end zone. He thought it was a miracle he scored the touchdown at all with such a bad call. Deep down, he harbored a secret resentment toward Coach Hand somewhere in his heart, but it never came to the surface. Murphy knew that if Coach Hand had called Black Seven and Murphy had really had a problem with it, he would have done what he always did—change the play at the line of scrimmage with an audible. He'd tap his helmet, yell "Check!" and then call a new play.

But here he was, the game halfway over, and he wasn't even sure he could change anything.

He might be trapped. He might have no choice.

Coach Hand's words about using his team resonated. Murphy looked over at the sidelines and saw Gig, sitting on the bench, playing with his cleats. His laces were pure white and his uniform unsoiled, a stark contrast to his teammates who were covered in a red, brown, and green mélange of blood, mud, and grass stains.

It gave Murphy an idea. He might not remember the second half of the game—but he knew one thing for sure. Gig had never caught a pass in a game. Hell, Murphy was pretty sure he'd never caught a pass in practice either.

There were less than two fifteen-minute quarters left before the worst moment of his life and he needed to know if he could control his destiny. He needed to know if he could change his life. Otherwise, his football career—and any hope of a future free from struggle—would be dead in just under half an hour of playing time.

Murphy approached Coach as Versailles kicked an extra point. They were now leading by fourteen—two touchdowns. *Desperate times call for desperate measures.*

"Put Gig in," Murphy said.

Coach did a double take. "What?"

"You want me to use my team. Put Gig in." Murphy wasn't leaving the sidelines until he did.

"You want me to pull a receiver who can catch and replace him with Gig?" Coach was all about teamwork, but this was no time for suicidal charity.

"No, just put him in as a fourth wide-out. We can spread the field," Murphy explained.

"Son, if I put him in as a fourth receiver, that's one less body back on the line protecting you," Coach warned.

"I know," Murphy said as he pulled on his helmet and tightened his chinstrap. He was going to need it.

Coach considered for a long moment, but after the halftime speech and Murphy's determination, he had to at least give it a go. But he looked none too pleased about it. It really had nothing to do with whether they won or lost, at this point, it had to do with exposing Murphy to even more of a beating than was already well underway. "Gig! You're in!" Coach shouted.

Gig looked up at him in disbelief. "Me?"

Coach collared him by the shoulder pads and lifted him off the bench. "Yes, you. Now come on, get in there!"

Gig fumbled with his helmet, having trouble getting it secure. "What happened, Coach? Did someone get hurt?"

"No, get in there!" Coach pushed him out on the field, calling the tight end he was replacing back to the sidelines.

Gig jogged out, looking scared to death.

"Red ninety-two on one," Murphy said as Gig joined them in the huddle.

Murphy broke the huddle and grabbed Gig as they walked to the line.

"Get open, cowboy. It's coming to you."

"What? What? Murphy, don't mess around, man…"

Gig's pattern was a simple drag route for short yardage. He was supposed to run a few yards downfield, and then cut ninety degrees toward the middle of the field. Hall was going to run the post route long, which was going to draw the safety deep and clear out the middle of the field for Gig. It should be simple—pitch and catch.

Knowing Murphy's line was down one man, Versailles blitzed, and left Gig completely open.

Murphy rolled right and threw him the ball a half second before he got blindsided by Washington, who wrapped him up and suplexed him hard onto the turf, knocking the wind out of Murphy and almost putting out his lights.

The secondary groans of the crowd told Murphy all he needed to know. His pass had been right into Gig's hands and he'd dropped it.

Murphy felt like he just got run over by a freight train.

"What are you doing, Murphy?" Hall demanded back in the huddle.

"He was open," Murphy said, still shaken up from the hit.

"He's always open. And we never throw it to him, because he can't catch!" Hall shot back.

"How do we know he can't catch if we never throw it to him?" Murphy said in Gig's defense.

"No, Murphy," Gig interjected. "He's right. I ain't never caught one."

"I know. And we're about to change that, right now. Red ninety-two, split right ninety-two."

A murmur erupted from the gathered team—he'd just called Gig's number as the primary receiver on the next play.

"Are you crazy?" Hall asked, incredulous.

Murphy slapped him on the helmet and repeated the play and then they all clapped hands together and shouted "Break!" in unison to quit the huddle.

They might question the order when he gave it, but when it came time to execute, they'd do whatever Murphy told them. He was still the quarterback. He was still Mr. Football. And he was still their only chance of winning this game.

Chapter 61

GIG WAS ON A fly route, straight down the middle, deep.

Murphy was forced to roll away from Gig, and had to make a difficult throw, on the run, across his body, under pressure. He let it go as he was wrapped up, but still had a clear view downfield from under the pile of bodies.

It had been right in Gig's hands. And he'd done worse than miss it, he'd bobbled it, and it was almost intercepted by the Versailles safety.

If Gig had caught it, it would have been a touchdown.

Instead it was third and ten, and the hometown crowd was groaning and booing. Murphy was afraid if he threw it to Gig one more time, he and his mother might have to put the wheels back on their house and move out of Coldwater.

His team trailed by fourteen. If they didn't get a first down here, they would likely go down by twenty-one. And though he didn't remember the specifics of the second half, Murphy did remember the box score. They had never trailed by more than fourteen the first time they played this game. Murphy knew if they fell behind by three touchdowns in the third quarter and they were gonna lose this football game, no matter *what* Murphy did. He was good; he wasn't Superman.

And Murphy's own issues aside, he wasn't here for himself. And he wasn't here simply to not get injured. He was here to *win*. Coldwater raised him, and he knew what football meant to this community. He had seen firsthand how the people of this village would ride the hope-laden fumes of this state championship through two recessions and the second coming of the Great Depression. This victory would keep his town warm through two decades of long, harsh Ohio winters and cool through twenty years of hot, humid valley summers.

When they read the morning papers about the same magnates that had shut down their manufacturing plant taking their private jets to Washington to beg for a taxpayer bailout—secretly they would be proud. Knowing that their sons, kids with nothing, had kicked the stuffing out of the best high school football team money could buy on a cold winter night in 1991.

"Okay," Hall said as they came back into the huddle. "Amateur night is over. Now get me the ball so we can get a first down."

"Yes," Gig piped in. "Don't throw it to me anymore."

"Don't worry. It's not coming anywhere near you. Blue Thirteen on three! Break!"

Murphy saw the relief wash over Gig.

Good. He won't be expecting it.

Murphy knew Gig knew how to catch a ball. He'd been playing football as long as Murphy had. So if it wasn't a lack of know-how—Murphy figured it was an abundance of nerves.

Murphy had been sent to a sports psychologist his freshman year after throwing three interceptions in one game. Yes, that was uncharacteristic enough to warrant medical attention. His mom wouldn't take charity and could only afford to send him once, but he learned enough in that session that he never threw another pick. It was mostly a lot of scientific talk that was over his head, but Murphy understood the gist. When an athlete was learning a skill, he used a certain piece of his brain—the beginner part. This was the thinking part of the brain, which was essential for figuring things out, programming the body, so to speak. As he mastered the skill, his brain got rewired and another part took over—the master part. This was the part that did things without thinking. The brain became hardwired; the moves became instinct. Murphy threw three picks because he was *thinking* too much and his brain thought he was a beginner again, trying to learn.

Murphy was gambling that Gig had been so put down and ridiculed that he couldn't imagine himself as anything other than a beginner. He theorized that if Gig wasn't expecting the ball, he just might forget he was supposed to suck, and catch it.

At least he hoped so. Murphy's entire future was riding on it.

Gig's pattern was a curl route, or button hook. He was to run straight upfield until he got past the first down marker, then turn around and step straight back.

The moment Gig turned back toward Murphy, the ball hit him square in the chest. His arms instinctively went up and grabbed for it. He bobbled it up into his face mask, but managed to actually catch it before he realized what was happening. When he understood what he had just done, he dropped to his knees in disbelief, essentially tackling himself, but it was enough for a first down.

The crowd went crazy as the announcer's voice rolled through the stadium, "First down, Coldwater!"

Murphy saw a scrambled frenzy of paper shuffling up in the press booth as every single reporter up there had to double-check Gig's number, then look at the roster for his name. They'd been covering Coldwater football all four years Gig had been on the team and not one of them knew who he was.

Scott Murphy celebrated that first down with more exuberance than he'd ever shown over any touchdown or victory. He hadn't just helped out a friend. He'd just permanently changed history. He *could* win this and get home in one piece.

Gig held the ball up like it was a torch and the field was Ellis Island and he was a human Statue of Liberty. He screamed "Grandma! I caught one!" to his grandmother sitting in the stands wearing his white away jersey.

Murphy swore he even saw Coach Hand break a smile. Murphy figured Coach probably thought that if Murphy could get Gig to catch a pass, he should be able to beat Versailles with his eyes closed.

Chapter 62

"ALL RIGHT, RODRIGUEZ. IT'S your turn. We're gonna run a reverse with you up the middle," Murphy said in the next huddle.

"What about Washington?" Rodriguez asked as his face flushed pale with fear.

"I'll take care of Washington," Murphy promised.

Rodriguez didn't look convinced.

As Murphy started his cadence, Washington jumped at the line, taunting him. "I'm coming for you, Backwater! Gonna break you in two!" Murphy snapped it and faked the handoff to Winton as he rolled left. Washington wasn't fooled and neither was the rest of the line. They all rolled left in pursuit.

As Murphy passed upfield of Rodriguez, who was running right, he pitched him the ball. Murphy had the defense running one way, then tossed the ball to a guy going the other way, which is why they called it a "reverse."

Washington caught on first and actually had the quickness to intercept Rodriguez well short of a first down. He was almost on top of him when Alex Washington's legs suddenly weren't underneath him anymore. Scott Murphy had blocked him low.

Murphy's leg block was so fierce that Washington slammed forward headfirst onto the turf. When he stood up, he had a massive clump of Coldwater's finest caliche soil sod stuck in his face mask, partially blinding him.

Murphy was there to greet him when he stood up, helpfully

pointing at his own helmet to indicate where the offending clump was on his enemy's.

Washington pawed the clump of grass off and threw it to the ground. His eyes blazed murder as he heard the Coldwater crowd break into a frenzied cheer.

Rodriguez had just scored a touchdown.

"Hey, Washington!" Murphy yelled. "It's Coldwater. With a *C!*"

Chapter 63

THERE IS AN OLD tale about a stonecutter. He was working a large piece of granite into a block. He was adept enough, but he took no joy in his work. His demeanor was dour and businesslike. His face was tightened by strain. Asked why he was so tense, he answered simply, "I'm cutting a granite block."

A few feet down the road, there was another stonecutter, cutting a block of the exact same size, of granite quarried from the same pit. But there was something different about this man—the way his chisel hit the stone, the expression on his face, the confidence with which he landed each blow—this man was full of joy. When the same question was posed to him, he didn't say he was cutting stone; he said, "I'm building a cathedral."

Well, by the time the fourth quarter was winding down, twenty-one guys on Coldwater's football field were tired, sweaty, broken, and muddy. Tense. Worried. They were cutting granite.

But Scott Murphy was building a cathedral. He was erecting a monument to bravery, perseverance, and sheer athletic ability that would become legend in the state of Ohio and beyond.

The second half was actually fun for Murphy. Versailles had prepared only to stop one player, Scott Murphy. Their game plan involved double- or triple-teaming him—which always left one or two of Murphy's teammates wide open. And as long as he kept finding the open man, they kept moving the ball down the field. If Versailles tried to adjust and go back to man-to-man or zone coverage, Murphy simply took off running with the ball and made them regret it. As they entered the final minutes of the game, Murphy could see the fear pulling at the corners of his enemies' eyes—the exhaustion in their faces. At the end of the day, any sporting event has nothing to do with size or skill, it has to do only with one thing—will. And tonight Scott Murphy wanted it more.

The game was starting to become what he had always dreamed it could be—a bona fide second chance. Murphy was using his team, and perhaps for the first time in his life, he was okay with needing something from another human being, even if only for the few seconds it took them to catch a pass, lay down a block, or make a play—and he found that the more his confidence in his team grew—like magic—so did their abilities.

Chapter 64

WHEN THE TWO-MINUTE warning sounded, Scott Murphy had led his Coldwater Cavaliers to a three-point lead over the Versailles Saints.

The game was as good as won.

All Murphy needed to put it away was another first down.

If he managed that, he could then simply line up his team in the victory formation—the "prayer of thanks" offense, as some call it, because it consists of the quarterback kneeling right after he gets the snap. It was used to run down the clock. Versailles wouldn't be left with enough timeouts to stop the clock from running down. It would all be over. Total victory.

As Murphy took the huddle to call what he thought could possibly be the last real play in his high school career, he felt like he was forgetting something. A flash of metal in the end zone drew his eye and he saw what was niggling at him.

The marching band was sitting in the new end-zone bleachers that the cement plant workers had built for the game. Somewhere in that sea of black and gold was his future wife. Murphy scanned the crowd, wondering if she even knew what was about to happen. He spotted her near the top of the bleachers. She was beautiful, her auburn hair silhouetted by two car headlights from outside the fence. She looked vibrant, like she was in love.

The only problem was, she wasn't looking anywhere *near* Murphy.

She was holding hands with Norman, who was standing, rather than sitting next to her, due to the cumbersome bulk of his tuba.

"Come on, man," Hall said nervously. "What's the play?"

The play clock was clicking down. He didn't have much time.

Murphy snapped out of it and did what he usually did when they needed a big first down—he called his own number, with an option to throw it.

"Blue Forty-two, on two. Break!'"

Murphy was in the shotgun formation—several steps behind the line, because it gave him a few extra moments before he was swarmed by the Saints' defense. Pierson's snap was low and he had to kneel to pluck the ball off the dirt and almost got sacked. He ducked the tackle and rolled out of the collapsing pocket as the defense sensed a run and started to close in. As his lane flooded with crimson jerseys, he had to look downfield for an outlet. He saw Hall break toward the end zone, wide open.

Murphy cocked his arm to throw. And then he saw her.

Macy was looking right at him. And it happened again. The timeless recognition of two souls connecting on a plane that wasn't governed by time or space. Concern flashed over her face and she shifted on the bench, her gawky elbows accidentally knocking her clarinet off the bleachers.

Her focus was pulled away from the field, off of Murphy, and back to the boy next to her as Norman reached up and caught her clarinet and handed it back to her. To anyone else, this was a non-moment. To Scott Murphy, the universe froze for a beat. In that instant, he had a greater understanding of what marriage was, and what it meant, than he ever had before.

What he saw was more than his future wife falling in love with someone else. It was two paths through a time continuum that had once merged but were now unraveling—in both the past and the future simultaneously. Murphy believed he could actually see the wispy tendrils of their metaphysical connection unwinding and receding into the darkness above the halo of the brightly lit football field, returning to the nothingness from which they came.

And then he got hit by a truck.

Murphy flew seven feet as he felt his back buckle in. The ball stayed where it was for a moment, hanging in mid-air like Wile E. Coyote over a canyon, then dropped to the grass. A pair of hands swooped down and scooped it up without missing a step, heading for the Coldwater end zone, uncontested.

And just like that, it was happening again.

Chapter 65

MURPHY LIMPED TO THE sideline and collapsed in a tired heap on the bench as Versailles kicked the extra point. Murphy stared up at the scoreboard in horror.

I remember now.

Murphy suddenly realized the heft of that understatement. This wasn't memory. It wasn't even the worst case of déjà vu he'd ever had. This was reality, happening for the second time. Every smell, every sight, every face in the crowd, every blade of *goddamned grass*. He'd seen it before. He'd been here, in this exact moment, at this exact time. He was absolutely certain that he was reliving his fate.

And he only had thirty-five seconds left to change his life.

Chapter 66

MURPHY USUALLY DIDN'T RUN back kick returns, but he knew this might be his last chance to alter the course of history.

The thought of staying on the bench for the final series, and thus guaranteeing his own safety, crossed his mind, but it was never a serious option. The human being who would sit on the bench instead of trying to win this football game wouldn't be here. Not in Murphy's undersized body. What got him here had kept him in the game. It also destroyed him twenty years ago. He was consumed by the very thing that made him great.

No. I'm gonna beat these sons of bitches. And walk away in one piece.

Murphy caught the kick at the twenty-four-yard line and raced upfield. He could outrun his blockers, so he merely used them as visual cover for a few yards, then cut outside on his own, carving through the onslaught of defenders trying to take off his head.

He crossed midfield and thought he might make it all the way. He only had three guys to beat. One was the kicker, a non-issue. The other two were the best two players on the Versailles defense. The same two guys who broke his leg twenty years ago.

Two very big issues.

The three of them all collided near the forty-yard line and Murphy carried them five more yards before the laws of physics finally brought him crashing down hard at the thirty-five-yard line.

Murphy stood up, head ringing, and pulled the clump of grass off his face mask so he could see the scoreboard. Down by four points. Three seconds left. Fear knotted at the pit of his stomach as he realized it was happening again. It was all exactly the same.

The divots in the earth he'd just left with his body were the same he'd left here twenty years ago. The same clump of grass was on his helmet.

All of this happened before.

The world teetered as Murphy hobbled back to the bench. He remembered it clearly now. Versailles kicked off. He returned it to the thirty-five-yard line and called a timeout. Coach Hand called Black Seven. And Murphy ran that play and won the game, but lost his life and ruined his future in the process.

He was back in the nightmare and wasn't sure he could get out.

No. This can't be happening. Not again.

As he limped back to the sidelines, Murphy yanked his helmet back, ready for a fight. He knew the old man was going to call the play that broke his leg before, and he wasn't going to run it—no matter what.

"I'm not doing a bootleg!" Murphy yelled to Coach Hand over the roar of the frenzied crowd.

"What?" Coach asked, puzzled, as he worked to tuck Murphy's battered shoulder pad back into his torn jersey. He hadn't called a play yet. From the look on his face, he probably hadn't even decided on one yet.

"Black Seven! I'm not running it!" Murphy shouted back, preparing himself for the fight of his life. He loved the old man to death, but he wasn't running that goddamn play again. Even if it meant a brawl right here on the sidelines.

"Son, we need thirty-some yards in less than three seconds, why the hell would I have you run the ball?" Coach shot back to calm him.

"That's what I'm saying. I'm not running Black Seven! I'm not doing that play again!" Murphy said, Coach's words still not quite sinking in.

Coach Hand grabbed Murphy's face mask and pulled him

close.

"Will you listen to me for once? I'm not calling Black Seven!"

Murphy blinked. He felt like a matador who entered the arena prepared for the fight of his life and the bull was just rubbing his legs like a giant cat.

"What?" It was Murphy's turn to be confused.

"Let's go Red Forty-Four. Find Rodriguez or Hall in the corners."

Red 44 was a passing play. And with Hall's superior height on the Versailles cornerback, Murphy knew he could probably get him the ball high enough in the corner of the end zone that it would be a surefire touchdown. It would work.

Murphy was shell-shocked. He'd spent twenty years harboring a secret resentment against the old man for making him run the stupid play that got him injured. But here his Coach was, calling something completely different—a passing play that would enable him to win the game from the comfort of the line of scrimmage. No leg-breaking goal-line run needed.

"You want me to throw the ball?" Murphy asked, afraid he might be joking.

"Yeah. Unless you get to the line of scrimmage and see something you don't like, then change it. Audible," Coach responded.

"What?" Murphy stared at him, still stunned by this new development.

"You've played a hell of a game, kid. You call it," Coach Hand said, staring into his eyes with pride.

"You want me to run Red Forty-four or call it at the line?" Murphy asked.

"It's your choice!" Coach Hand yelled as he slapped his shoulder and sent him back onto the field.

Waves of elation swept over Murphy. He'd done it. He'd changed it. Flashbulbs popped from all over the stadium as he took the field for what would be the final play of both this game and his high school career.

Murphy had changed his future. He'd changed the final play

and it was something that he knew would work. He could win the game and get home to his mother tonight in one piece. He would get his scholarship. He would go to college. And God willing, he would play pro football.

He saw two distant yellow lights on the radio tower hill a half mile away. He knew his mom was there now, sitting in her Pinto. He imagined her weathered fingers dialing in the game on the car's AM radio. He wished she were here in the stands to witness this moment up close.

He was about to win them a new life.

Chapter 67

MURPHY KNELT DOWN BEFORE his teammates in the huddle, triumphant.

"You guys ready to win this?" Murphy said, smiling.

His battered and tired best friends all nodded. They had at least one more play in them.

"Red Forty-four on two," Murphy continued. "Hall, you're gonna be open in the corner. All you have to do is catch the ball."

This was it, the climax of the fairy tale. Scott Murphy, the poor kid from the small town, who was raised by that small town after his father was killed in action in Vietnam, was about to pay them back by winning the state championship.

He wasn't on the field right now for himself. He was on it for them.

He had become a champion in the truest sense of the word.

And the best part was that he knew he could give them a victory without breaking his leg and ruining his own life in the process.

The huddle broke enthusiastically and as Murphy walked toward the line of scrimmage, he glanced again at the two distant yellow lights on the radio tower hill.

His mom had said memory worked both ways but that it was just a lot clearer looking back than it was looking ahead. In this moment, Murphy found himself looking forward with that same backward clarity.

He would get his football scholarship to Ohio State. He'd break into the starting line-up as a true freshman, playing three years and leading the Buckeyes to two national championships. He would win the Heisman trophy, then enter the draft early and be taken as the first pick by the New England Patriots. His signing bonus would be seven figures. He would marry Jennifer Cleary, his high school sweetheart, who would rise to fame as a newscaster of her own accord.

He was going to be rich. He was going to be famous.

All that was left was the execution.

"Red Forty-four! Red! Forty-four!"

Murphy paused in his cadence. Something was wrong. He had a sense about these things. Shifting coverage by the defense. A missed blocking assignment. His eyes scanned quickly and saw everything was as it should be. It was something else.

Two little twirlers tossing batons in the air on the sidelines caught his eye. They weren't that dissimilar in age from his daughters.

The thought suddenly brought Murphy back squarely to the present. That was it. That was the flaw in this future—the chink in the armor of his master plan.

When he saw this future of football glory, Macy wasn't in it.

As he stood there thinking, in that frozen moment behind the line of scrimmage, he realized that his dream wasn't necessarily about football. All he'd ever really wanted to do was to take care of his family. And as he scanned the stands—he finally realized what he had been missing. The family he was supposed to be caring for didn't exist yet. And if he changed this football game, his life with Macy, his daughters, would all be erased from existence along with his failures.

The life he had with her, as tough at it seemed, was blessed with a foundation of love that was as real and true as he was ever likely to find in the universe.

No amount of material success could rival that. Ever. It wasn't about winning or losing, or breaking his leg or not breaking his leg, or being rich and successful or a poor failure. It was just about

Macy. Would he be with her or not? And when he realized that was really what it all boiled down to, it wasn't really a choice at all.

Murphy loved his wife. He missed his kids.

And there was only one way to guarantee he would ever see them again.

For the first time in his life, Murphy knew exactly what he had to do.

Chapter 68

MURPHY STOOD UP FROM behind the center, tapping his helmet to get his team's attention. "Check! Check!" He yelled to let them know he was calling an audible.

"Black Seven! Black Seven!" Murphy screamed, desperately changing the final play.

"What the hell are you doing, Murphy?" Hall protested. He knew Black Seven was a running play. Running that play from thirty-five yards out with three seconds on the clock and no timeout was madness against this defense.

It made perfect sense to Murphy.

He crouched back down behind the center.

"Go! Set! Hike!"

The ball snapped back into Murphy's hands just as the play clock ticked down to zero. Murphy turned and held out the ball to Winton, the running back.

He knew he could just hand off the ball and he'd be safe.

Murphy pulled the ball back into his chest and ran toward the sidelines, his eyes searching for the running lane to the goal line he knew would be there.

He saw Chris Hall in the end zone, arms up, calling for the ball. He was wide open. Murphy knew if he threw it, they would win the game.

He could still win this and walk away.

But I lose Macy.

He tucked the ball and cut through the opening in the line.

As he ran, he whispered a little prayer, not for himself, but for his old life. He hoped it wasn't too late to get it back.

Murphy broke a tackle at the fifteen-yard line, racing for the end zone.

He wasn't running to win a football game.

He was running because he couldn't stand to lose Macy.

Sure, he might be able to woo her eventually. But there was a chance that might not happen. And deep down, Murphy knew that the Murphy who never broke his leg wasn't worthy of the love of a woman like Macy. All the things that made him who he was led to them being together. If he changed one thing in that chain of events, he wouldn't be the same person. The Macy-Murphy he knew would, quite simply, cease to exist, and his kids would cease to exist with them.

The only way he could be with Macy, for sure, was to put all the shattered pieces of his life back where they belonged. He needed to take his perfect body, his college scholarship, his God-given football talent, and any dream of future NFL riches, and sacrifice them all on the altar of love.

As Murphy neared the five-yard line, he noticed the band bleachers just at the rear of the end zone. The world seemed to stall in its orbit as Macy pushed to the front of her cheering bandmates to look at him. As their eyes met in that moment, for just an instant, their souls touched—and they both knew the past and the future. All the pain, all the heartache, all the love, and all the joy they had shared and would share in their lifetime.

Murphy realized the life he had—crippled, broke, and nearly homeless—wasn't a curse. And Macy wasn't any kind of consolation prize. She was a goddamn gift. And he wasn't going to give her up. Not for anybody. Not for anything.

In that moment, Macy finally knew that Scott Murphy loved her more than anything. And Murphy knew she was worth his sacrifice ten times over.

Murphy saw the safety and the cornerback closing in on him.

He tucked the ball and said another silent prayer as he leapt toward the goal line.

Don't miss.

The safety hit his leg low. The cornerback hit his body high.

Crack! Murphy heard a pop like a gunshot as his leg broke in four places. His body slammed onto the dirt, hard, and he screamed. Waves of pain washed over him, pain so intense that he felt like he was going to throw up.

As he sat there, grimacing in pain, tears rolled down his face. Tears of joy. Tears of love. He'd just won his old life back.

Chapter 69

AS MURPHY LAY BROKEN on the turf, staring up at the stadium lights, his leg twisted under him at an impossible angle, he couldn't help thinking about the damn mutt back on his old farm that had cost him a new clutch. When they'd gone to the breeder to pick a pup, Macy and the girls had insisted on the runt of the litter. He was missing a chunk of his tail and one of his eyes was lazy. To Murphy, the damn dog was a complete rip-off. To the women he loved, he was perfect.

Murphy had *accepted* the dog, despite his shortcomings.

The women had *chosen* the dog because of them.

Acceptance is a willingness to tolerate a difficult or unpleasant situation.

Choice is picking something because you think it is the best.

Murphy had been accepting his life for almost twenty years.

This time he chose it.

And that made all the difference.

The tears Murphy shed that moment were tears of joy celebrating the future he had just won. Murphy wasn't accepting his fate as a crippled, washed-up farmer on the brink of bankruptcy. He was choosing the love of his life.

A scientist would say the elation that Murphy felt, as he lay crippled on the turf, was caused by the chemicals his body released into his brain in reaction to his injury. And they wouldn't be wrong.

A spiritual person would say the rapture Murphy experienced

was because, for the first time in twenty years, he felt like God was on his side again. He understood that there was a method to His madness. A purpose to this suffering.

That person wouldn't be wrong either.

Scott Murphy was neither spiritual nor a scientist. If you asked him, he would just say the world had opened up again. He didn't need the NFL. He didn't need the bank loan. He didn't need the farm. He didn't need any of it. He would survive. His family would survive. And they would do it for one reason and one reason only.

It's the same reason Murphy called the audible to break his leg again. It's why his dad laid down his life for his friends in Vietnam. It's why Coach Hand never took that job at Ohio State. It's why his mom worked so hard to keep him clothed and fed. And it wasn't any kind of ideal, or obligation. It was just an emotion, plain and simple.

He saw three of his magic pennies on the turf next to him. The copper tokens make him think of wishing wells, and the millions upon millions of wishes made with pennies. Murphy wanted to grab one. Not to make a wish. Just to give thanks.

He stretched his arm out for it as he started to black out from the pain—and found himself making a wish after all.

I want to go home.

Chapter 70

THE PICKUP'S TAILPIPE RATTLED against the hill as the cab continued to fill with haze. Scott Murphy's eyes rolled back into his head. He was an instant away from death.

A Hail Mary wouldn't do it. He needed an honest-to-goodness, walk-on-water-that's-turned-to-wine miracle.

And he got one.

The tailpipe rasped. The engine rattled, knocked, and then went quiet.

The blue vapor dissipated. Murphy's eyes fluttered open and then he blacked out.

Chapter 71

MURPHY HAD NEVER BEEN so cold.

Am I dead?

He tried to squelch the thought, but he'd been in a lot of hospitals and they weren't refrigerated. And hospital beds weren't slimy like whatever he was pressed up against.

He feared the worst as his mind reconnected with his body. He felt the familiar dull ache down the length of his left leg. He smelled the oddly comforting aroma of manure and oil. The slime his cheek was against had a texture—vinyl.

He sat up with a groan and winced as blood rushed back into his left arm. He'd passed out with it under him. The pain was almost unbearable, but it was nothing compared to how his head felt.

Maybe this is Hell? Stuck in a beat-up pickup with a permanent hangover.

His eyes were open but all he saw was darkness.

He heard crickets, a cacophony of crickets.

Murphy put his hand to his neck to check for movement. His skin was icy to the touch. No pulse.

He dug his fingers in a little deeper and felt the familiar *tha-thump* of his heart. He was alive.

Why?

The gas fumes should have killed him.

He sat up and tried to turn the key in the ignition but it was already in the "on" position. He cranked the starter and the big old engine tried to turn over…click…click…click…it wouldn't catch.

Murphy understood engines well enough to know they needed three things to work—air, spark, and fuel. The lights had come on, so it wasn't spark. He'd just changed his air filter last week, so he knew it wasn't that either.

Fuel. He couldn't believe it. He'd run out of gas.

He choked back a laugh as he realized that for once, Murphy's Law had worked in his favor.

But then, where was he? When was he?

He fumbled with the door handle—it was still jammed. He felt around on the carpet for the fallen Vice-Grips, clamped them onto the metal nub, and twisted them to open the window. When it was halfway down, he reached through and used the outside handle to release the door.

Murphy stepped out of the truck and, now unaccustomed to the delayed motion of his crippled leg, tipped forward and took a nosedive. He pulled himself up, covered in mud that stunk of cow manure.

Smells like home.

He stood and fished a horse blanket from behind the bench seat and cleaned up as best he could. The blanket smelled worse than the mud, but it was dry.

He *felt* alive, but he needed to see other people. Someone had to meet his gaze and speak his name so he could be sure he wasn't just a ghost. He looked toward the high school and saw the stadium lights still burning. Maybe he hadn't been knocked out for very long. Maybe he could catch the last bit of the game.

He limped down the gravel road out of the old quarry and cut through the graveyard toward the back entrance to the football field. As he lurched into the woods near the school, he realized something was wrong. Quiet. There was no crowd noise. No band. No game.

What the hell?

The lights were still on. But the field was empty. The bleachers were empty. The parking lot was empty. There wasn't another human being in sight. According to Murphy's watch, it was ten o'clock. He'd been in Coldwater long enough to know that games never shut down this early. Most of the town stayed to clean up.

Litter blew across the field. The scoreboard was still on, but it flashed all zeros.

Eerie.

Murphy spotted something that made the scene even more odd—someone had run his old number 13 jersey up the flagpole and it was flapping in the night breeze.

"Hello?" Murphy yelled, his voice disappearing into the parking lot.

What the hell is going on?

The school was empty, too.

"Hello!" he yelled louder to no one in particular.

He was halfway down Main Street when he started to panic. Fear clutched at Murphy's chest. Maybe he *was* dead.

The stop sign light was on, but everything was deserted. Even the firehouse. The doors were open, half-eaten plates of food and full coffee cups strewn on the big folding table, but all the rigs were gone.

The TV was blaring at Gino's Pizza, but the screen was static, the place deserted.

In the thirty-odd years Murphy had lived there, Coldwater had never been so devoid of life. It was as if aliens had come down and snatched them all.

There was not one car, one soul, anywhere in town—except Murphy, limping down Main Street, the only spirit left.

As Murphy got to the end of Main, he saw a faint glow through the trees to the west. It was as bright as the football stadium lights, but coming from the middle of nowhere.

Now he was sure of it. He was dead.

Murphy stepped into Jack Pritchard's cornfield and parted the stalks. The glow grew brighter, as if the moon had set just over the next hill.

Murphy pushed through the rows of corn toward it. He was heading for the light.

Chapter 72

MURPHY PUSHED OUT OF the far side of the cornfield. As the light washed over his face, he was overcome with emotion. Tears welled. He couldn't believe what he was seeing.

The glow he was chasing wasn't the afterlife—it was the combined headlights from every car, truck, tractor, van, bus, and bike in Coldwater. They'd parked around the perimeter of a soybean field. And inside the glow of their combined headlights was the entire town of Coldwater—every man, woman, and child—picking Murphy's soybeans by hand.

They carried hampers, baskets, bowls, pillowcases, every kind of container imaginable to collect the beans, and then bundled them up, bustling to and from his barn and farmhouse in the distance. The town was all here. Saving his crops.

Macy. She had known. She had always known.

A murmur rippled through the crowd as they spotted Murphy limping down the hill, trying to wipe away the wet evidence of emotion from his face with a muddy sleeve.

Murphy came upon Todd White kneeling in the field next to Sasha, of all people. The familiar scowl she greeted him with was a relief; he couldn't have changed things too much. But as Todd and Sasha picked together, Murphy could discern an easy familiarity between them. He even swore Todd's hands might have brushed over hers and she didn't punch his lights out.

It's just a coincidence. What happened to him was just a dream.

It had to be. There was no other reasonable explanation.

Murphy heard a whistle and saw Coach Hand yelling from atop a tractor as he pressed his team to put some hustle in their harvesting. "Come on, Bragdon. My grandmother can pick beans faster than that!"

Murphy smiled. The voice was a bit rougher, and the face had a lot more mileage on it, but the lines and the love behind the gruff voice were the same as they'd always been.

When Coach caught sight of Murphy, he wasn't about to let him off the hook. "What are you smiling about, Murphy? You're late. To your own damn party!"

"I know," Murphy said. Then added, with total sincerity, "Thank you."

Coach stared at him, a little taken aback. He could count the times "thank you" had come off Scott Murphy's lips in his direction over the past twenty years on one hand. Twice.

It didn't take Coach long to recover. "Yeah. Well, thanks nothing. A deal's a deal. So I'll see you on my field after school on Monday."

Murphy stared at him, taking a moment to connect the dots back to their fight at the fire about each of them staying out of the other's business. "Why don't you come coach my quarterbacks?" Coach had asked him. "Sure, as soon as you come help me work my back forty," Murphy had replied.

I guess it was a deal.

"Tell your quarterbacks to be dressed and ready at three o'clock. I work for a living and can't be waiting around."

"They'll be ready, unless they're too damn tired from picking all your beans!" Coach shot back as he drove off in the tractor, back to his comfortable gruff.

Despite the rough words, the two men shared a parting glance that spoke volumes. It was as close to an "I love you" as they would ever get, or would ever need to.

"Mr. Football!" rang out across the field and Murphy looked up to see Chris Hall and his wife, Jenny, picking beans as best they could in their designer clothes. Jenny smiled at him, and Murphy met her gaze with kindness for the first time since high school. Things between them had turned out exactly as they should have. She was with the right man. And he was with the right woman. *Life has a way of working out, just like mom always said.*

That thought lingered as he neared the edge of his field and passed the one car that didn't have its lights on—his mom's old Pinto, up on blocks, its body rusted. He ran his hand across the leaf-covered hood, admiring the lines of the old heap like another man might admire a new Ferrari. In that moment Murphy got as close to religion as he ever would. He realized then, without a doubt, that people who loved each other could be connected across time and space by something other than DNA. He knew his mom was there, in her Pinto, watching over him—had always been watching over him—and for the first time in his life, he knew she was proud of him.

Murphy walked toward his house, greeted by more familiar faces.

"Hey! Look who decided to show up!" Pierson said, hefting two heavy sacks of soybeans onto his shoulders to carry to the barn for sorting. Gig and Rodriguez were behind him, lugging their own loads.

"What the hell, Murphy? Ignoring a fire call? It was a code ten! Someone could've died!" Rodriguez said, chuckling.

"We were hoping you'd come driving out onto the football field, sirens blaring!" Gig chimed in.

"You missed it. This twig caught one lucky pass in the big game and still got a standing ovation twenty years later."

Murphy stared at Gig. "You caught a pass?"

They paused and looked at him like he was crazy.

Murphy scanned the field. Urgent. If Gig had caught a pass, that meant Murphy had changed at least one thing. And then there was Todd and Sasha…What if he'd changed something else? What if he wasn't married to Macy? What if he didn't have two daughters?

"My wife?" Murphy asked, an edge of panic in his voice.

"Where's Macy?"

"In the barn. She's been looking for you—"

Murphy lurched toward the barn, scanning for any sign of his family.

He heard a sweet shriek and saw his little Krista bobbing toward him through the beans, yelling. "Daddy, Daddy, Daddy, Daddy!" She jumped into his arms.

Jamie came right behind her, tackling his leg. He pulled her up, too.

Murphy kept scanning—overwhelmed, but his journey wasn't quite complete.

He finally found her.

Coming down the ramp from the barn, a basketful of shelled beans on her hip. Motherly care lines were worn into her face and she was a few pounds heavier than in high school, but her curly hair was still a tousled mess—the same as it was when he fell in love with her twenty years ago. She was, in that moment, hands down, the most beautiful woman he had ever seen.

"Macy!" he yelled, setting the girls down and hitching toward her.

"Hey!" She crinkled her nose in delight and gave him a look that spoke of hope, joy, and faith. "Can you believe this?" she said in reverence of the miracle of love and support happening in the field around them.

"Yeah," Murphy said, as tears rolled down his cheeks and he smiled the widest smile he'd ever worn.

It's because of you.

He embraced his wife with such passion that she dropped her bean basket. He kissed her for all he was worth and after her shock dissipated and he showed no signs of letting up, she threw her arms around his neck and gave it back as good as he was giving.

When it ended, he looked into her eyes. Reflected in them was the spark of someone she hadn't seen in a very, very long time. She cupped his face as she stared at him in recognition.

"You're back," she said simply.

Scott Murphy was home.

And that is how fairy tales are supposed to end.

Afterword

SCIENTISTS HAVE FOUND EVIDENCE that as you learn, you increase the folds in your brain. I believe that as you experience love and heartbreak in a profound way, you increase the folds in your soul.

Touchback has been a twenty-year journey for me, filled with many episodes of love, heartbreak and failure. This novel was born of that.

I always intended this book to be something that a man or woman could pick up from the airport book rack, or order on his Kindle and finish on a flight home—and hopefully hug the ones they love a little tighter on their return. It really is a story about appreciating what we have and how we are shaped by our failures. The things we hate and want to change are what form us, and so should perhaps be the things we most cherish. In other words, the thing that in the moment seems to be the worst thing that ever happened to us in retrospect can be the *best* thing that ever happened to us.

Touchback began as a screenplay many, many years ago. The idea grew from a combination of life experiences you may notice reflected in the story: blowing out my knee wrestling in high school, working on my uncle's dairy farm, learning from my college girlfriend and her family about a small town named Coldwater with a big football team. The first draft of the script was written after college, while I was a struggling actor-slash-screenwriter living in a rent-controlled apartment in Hollywood, broke and going through the demise of my first marriage. *Touchback* ended up being a breakthrough work for me, as things written in this state of heart usually are. That script got me a good agent, and was optioned by football great John Madden's company. Unfortunately, it never got off the ground, and the rights reverted to me. A few years later, Warner Brothers was interested in making it. They made *We Are Marshall* instead.

A few years after that, Morgan Creek optioned *Touchback* with legendary TV director David Nutter at the helm. That, too, fell apart.

After the dust had settled on the last failure, I was told *Touchback* was "dead." The movie would never get made.

The difficulty in getting the film produced, it seemed, was twofold:

First, American football movies don't play so well overseas.

Second, it was, at its core, a love story. Not a lot of those get produced in Hollywood anymore. The ones that do are based on books, and most of those books are written by Nicholas Sparks. It was this very train of thought late one night that led me to Nicholas Sparks' web site and blog.

The story behind *The Notebook* inspired me. I decided that to get *Touchback* the movie made, I would write the novel, get it published, and hope it became a bestseller. It seems ridiculous as I write this, but I was 70,000 words into the manuscript when I got the call from Freedom Films—they ended up financing the movie. Though the book had never been shared with anyone at that point, I believe the mere act of writing it helped will the movie into existence.

People have asked me about the difference between writing a novel and writing and directing a film. They are both challenging, magical, life-changing experiences, but the difference breaks down to this:

In making a movie, you are doing battle with reality: time, budget, personnel, and approvals. It's a monumental undertaking done by a massive amount of people and you are constantly forced to compromise.

For instance, if I want Bob Costas in my movie, I have to write him into the script, then get that through the gauntlet of the producers and financiers. Then, if I clear that hurdle, I have to talk to Bob Costas's agent. If I don't get Bob Costas, then I have to find someone different and rewrite the part. Not to mention what might happen if I do get Bob Costas and he shows up on set and doesn't like me.

If I want Bob Costas in my novel, it's as simple as typing his name.

(Note: I have never met Bob Costas, and he was never in the screenplay, nor was ever intended to be. He is, however, in the novel in a way that could never have happened in the film—it's a bit of a flight of fancy, but you can do that in books.)

I also have to say how much respect I have for prose writers. It's damn difficult. Despite twenty years of screenwriting experience, ten of that professionally, it is something I don't take lightly. It's an art form I enjoy immensely, but have yet to master.

All that being said, any work of cinema or prose is, at the very least, a tiny bit of your soul laid bare for people to praise, berate, or poke with sharp sticks. It's an odd feeling to have your first film and your first novel hitting the world at approximately the same point in time—and more than a little scary.

So poke away, but be gentle.

Sincerely,

Don Handfield

P.S. Please let me know what you thought of *Touchback*. You can email me at *don@donhandfieldink.com* or leave a comment on my blog at http://www.donhandfieldink.com

Acknowledgements

TOUCHBACK HAS BEEN AN incredible journey for me, one that has spanned almost twenty years. There are so many people to thank for their contributions, and I hope to remember them all.

My mother Joanne was a single parent for most of my youth and was tasked with raising two boys on her own. Her strength, wisdom, beauty, and tenacity infused the DNA of Thelma Murphy. She drove a green Pinto when I was a boy. She worked hard and sacrificed much to give my brother and me a better life. Her tireless support kept me afloat through the years and this novel and film would certainly not exist without her. She is my hero. Mom, I love you.

My wife, Tressa, is living proof that the second time is, indeed, the charm. Fifteen years ago, I wrote about a woman who supported her man no matter how rough things got, and then I found her. She is proof that dreams come true. If she didn't find *novelist* ten times sexier than *filmmaker*, I would have given up on the book idea a long time ago. Her tireless support, endless love, and incredible emotional intelligence make me a better human being. She has also blessed me with two beautiful children—Robinson Dawn, also known as 'The Bean" or 'The Rascally Zeets," and Deacon Bragdon, also known as "The Deke." I love my family with all my heart—they are my purpose and my light.

My older brother, Jay, is a personal hero of mine, and always has been. When my parents divorced, he grew up fast so I didn't have to. He was my protector, my mentor, and my favorite playmate. He is one of the kindest, most intelligent, hardest-working people I know. He is now a father to three kids of his own, and I must say, as a little brother, I prepared him for the worst. He's become, to no surprise of mine, one of the best dads in the world.

Thelma Murphy got her name and a bit of her spirit from my grandmother, who raised eight kids, the last few single-handedly after a divorce. She worked at a state hospital. She came home with bite marks. She was tough as nails with a guffaw you could hear down the block. She loved and laughed, like Thelma—at a very high volume. She beat cancer several times, and did so with dignity. She was possibly the toughest human being I have ever met. She passed on before she could watch the film or read this book, so it is meaningful to me that a piece of her spirit can live on inside them.

I saw my father, Jerry Handfield, every summer until my early teens, and then we lost touch. Twelve years ago, I had a hard breakup and found myself moving back to the states from Hawaii, with absolutely nothing but the clothes on my back. I'd lost it all in yet another unsuccessful relationship. I was working as a cable television producer at the time, and my plan was to go back to fourteen-hour days in Los Angeles. My dad was newly single himself and living alone on Puget Sound in Olympia, Washington. He invited me to stay with him and write a screenplay. I took him up on the offer, unsure if we would even get along. We got along famously. He's a great man, and someone I am happy to have in my life for good. That experience is something I am saving for another book!

All the characters in this work are fictional, except one, who was inspired by a real person. Coach Hand is both named for, and based on, my high-school wrestling coach, Bobby Hand. He was a father figure to me during a turbulent time in my life. I never played football in high school—I was too small—so I wrestled instead. If I weren't doing what I am now, I would happily be following in Coach Hand's footsteps, teaching high school and coaching wrestling. He was the rare coach who cared more about who his kids were as human beings than who they were as athletes. The most important lesson he taught me was that no matter how tired you are, or how badly you are getting beaten, always be the first man back to the middle of the circle to keep fighting. I draw on his wisdom every day.

Thanks to my other family members and friends who have shown me great support through this process or have inspired me: The Bragdons, Earl, Sarah, Susan, Lisa, Jeannie, George, and Ripple; Harry Seamen; Becky and Richard Chamblin; Kelby and Sandra Seamen; all of the Handfields—Nick, Marie, Jim, Krista, Brandon, Richard, Phil, Carol, John, Charlie; the Kasceks; the Valones; the Benders; Karen and Pat Kelly; Red and Pauline Robinson; Tina Trejo and the rest of the Trejo clan; Vinnie Di Figlia; Jennifer Greeson; Todd Smith; Cousin James Reed; the real Chris Hall; Zin Min; Dr. Hugh Donahue; Phil Flores; the McAllister family; Bill Rabkin; Jeremy Renner, my best friend and business partner; Josh Malkin, my sometime writing partner and full-time friend; Kevin Costner, for his insight and support; and everyone at The Ohio State University, including but not limited to Dr. E. Gordon Gee, Gene Smith, Diana Sabau, Rick Van Brimmer, Jerry Davis, and Beau Brown. And, of course, everyone involved in making *Touchback,* the movie.

Last, but certainly not least, gratitude to the team who helped to bring this book to life.

I particularly need to thank my editor, Alice Peck. You wouldn't be reading this book if I hadn't been lucky enough to connect with her. She took eighty-three-thousand words of gobbledygook and helped shape them into something readable. The task of finishing this book under a deadline while working fourteen hours a day on other endeavors and having two kids under four years old was monumental. There were times when I just wanted to quit. Alice's enthusiasm and encouragement kept me going. She convinced me there was something worthwhile buried in the mess, and rolled up her sleeves to help excavate it with me. I am, and will forever be, in her debt. Also many thanks to copy editor Ruth Mullen, cover designer Jeff Holmberg, Kimberly Konrade, Pavarti Tyler and the crew at novelpublicity.com, Arthur Goldwag, proofreader Jann Nyffeler, and illustrator Duane Stapp, who created what might be the first chapter header in history modeled after a Chevy pickup. Special thanks also to my formatting guru Steven Booth at Genius Book Services – you pulled my bacon from the fire. You guys are all amazing and I hope this is the first of many books we work on together.

Thank you all from the bottom of my heart.

Don Handfield

About the Author

DON HANDFIELD HAS WORKED as a farmhand and a construction worker, and studied journalism and theater at The Ohio State University. Now a full-time filmmaker and producer, he wrote and directed the feature film *Touchback,* starring Kurt Russell and Christine Lahti. He is currently writing and producing *Slingshot* for Paramount Pictures. Don lives in Los Angeles with his wife, Tressa, and their two children. *Touchback* is his first novel.